ASHES TO ASHES

ASHES TO ASHES

Margaret Duffy

This first world edition published 2015
in Great Britain and the USA by
SEVERN HOUSE PUBLISHERS LTD of
19 Cedar Road, Sutton, Surrey, England, SM2 5DA.
Trade paperback edition first published 2015 in Great
Britain and the USA by SEVERN HOUSE PUBLISHERS LTD.

Duffy, Margaret author.
  Ashes to ashes. – (A Patrick Gillard and Ingrid Langley
  mystery)
  1. Gillard, Patrick (Fictitious character)–Fiction.
  2. Langley, Ingrid (Fictitious character)–Fiction.
  3. Organized crime–Fiction. 4. Detective and mystery
  stories.
  I. Title II. Series
  823.9'14-dc23

ISBN-13: 978-0-7278-8482-4 (cased)
ISBN-13: 978-1-84751-586-5 (trade paper)
ISBN-13: 978-1-78010-635-9 (e-book)

Typeset by Palimpsest Book Production Ltd.,
Falkirk, Stirlingshire, Scotland.

ONE

The man; husband, father, retired lieutenant colonel, ex-operative of MI5, policeman, one-time cold-eyed killer, sat sprawled in an armchair, head back, his thoughts to anyone observing him a mystery. He – my husband Patrick – was taking a respite from the fifth of these past and present roles, having asked for six months unpaid leave from the National Crime Agency. The Serious Organized Crime Agency, for which he used to work, has now been absorbed into it. They had offered him three months; he had haggled stubbornly and got four, which was what he had wanted in the first place.

In my view, the break was vital as recent assignments had taken their toll on him. There was also a need to clear his head, take deep breaths and reassess his life. Should he carry on with such a hazardous occupation even though his role was officially, and merely, that of 'adviser'? There were the children to think of. Was this the time to find an equally well-paid but safer job? Or even to retire?

Patrick's first month at home had engendered a lighthearted holiday mood among all those in the household. The children had broken up from school for the summer and we took the two eldest, Matthew and Katie, whom we adopted after Patrick's brother Larry was killed, for a week to Scotland and then a few days in London. Carrie, our nannie, then went on leave and Patrick's parents, John and Elspeth – John is rector of the village of Hinton Littlemore in Somerset where we live – departed to stay with friends who had retired to Sark, their usual holiday destination.

This observer had rejoiced as Patrick put on weight and no longer appeared as though he had been recently ill. He was free to do those things that up until recently had been severely rationed: playing with the children, riding his horse, George, firing off emails to old comrades in arms and general loafing. He bought a ride-on lawn mower – I asked John to offer up a small prayer with regard to the maiden voyage of *that* – after attending to a greater part of the list of jobs that needed doing around the house and garden. The stress lines had disappeared from his face. He now looked younger by at least five years.

Now, though, at three weeks into his second month at home, there was a slight sense of ennui. Everything household-wise was tidy and mostly fixed. As far as the children went, Matthew had gone to spend a week with his friend Benedict, the son of Patrick's boss, Commander Michael Greenway; Katie and her Exmoor pony, Fudge, had been packed off to a pony club camp; and Justin, bizarrely, was on his best behaviour, probably because his father had him in his sights, and was spending a lot of time playing with his toy racing cars, which was right now his all-consuming passion. Vicky, bless her lovely little soul, likes nothing better than being in the company of baby brother Mark, who seems to idolize her plus, it must be said, her collection of dolls.

Was the man in my life bored?

'Shall have to go and have a shower,' Patrick yawned, starting to unbutton his shirt, an old check one he uses for gardening. Then: 'D'you fancy a meal out tonight?'

'Carrie's not back until tomorrow,' I reminded him.

'Can't we take the sprogs with us?'

Had I needed glasses to read I would have peered steadily at him over the top of them.

'No, s'pose not.' He got to his feet and sort of drifted from the room.

Yes, bored.

Although I am also employed by the NCA as a 'consultant', mostly to Patrick, I am a writer for most of the time. Nearing the end of a novel and, unusually for me, having a clear idea of exactly where it was going, I could not give too much attention to my other half's ennui. During the next few days I buried myself in the novel whenever possible, emerging only to attend to domestic matters, shop and cook, the latter of which I really enjoy, perhaps because it is also creative.

Patrick is not a man to sit around at a loose end and, having cut the grass in the churchyard with his new toy – the part as yet unused for graves, that is – he then discovered that the village green, which due to some ancient writ is the responsibility of the Parochial Church Council, was only partly shorn as the machine had broken down. He spent a whole morning attending to that. The next thing I knew, he had hired himself out to anyone in the village who needed his services, the money paying for fuel, any surplus 'beer tokens'.

This might run and run, I thought one morning, switching on the Mac, the two younger children in the room with me while Carrie went to the village shop for something and Justin was out in the hall with his cars, spittily making all the sound effects.

We now live in the rectory next to St Michael's Church in Hinton Littlemore, which is not far from Bath. The previous year, and while we were still leading a rather cramped existence in my cottage in Devon, the diocese had decided to sell the rectory and rehouse the rector and his wife in a small bungalow on a new estate at the bottom end of the village that has since been christened Micky Mouse Town by the locals. This having been the site of sidings at the one-time railway station and known to be liable to flooding, Patrick had declared he'd be hanged if his parents were going to end up *there* and promptly, after some hard bargaining – the rectory needed work doing to it, including a new roof – bought it. Building work had been completed, including an annexe for John and Elspeth created out of a stable, harness room and garage. There is a new floor above it consisting of two bedrooms and a bathroom connected to the first floor of the house. Finally, we had moved in.

The fact that other clergy in the benefice were sharing taking the services at St Michael's while John was away was the reason why, the following week, I wasn't too surprised to receive a call from the new curate at Wellow, the neighbouring village. He had forgotten when John and Elspeth were due back. I told him: in two days' time.

'Only I have a rather distressed lady who came to me with a problem I feel should be handled by someone far more senior than myself,' explained the young man, whose name I knew was Kenneth Watson. 'This isn't a spiritual matter, you understand,' he went on to add. 'In fact, she's wondering whether she ought to go to the police.'

I reasoned that this was for John to decide and promised to

ask him to phone her when he returned. Kenneth gave me her number, which I wrote down in John's 'work' diary, as I had been requested to do in connection with anything that might need his attention. I then promptly forgot all about it.

A few days later I finished the novel, printed it and took it into the village to post off to my agent. Then, and only then, I'm afraid, did I take proper notice of my husband.

'Hi,' he said. 'Welcome back.' Actually, he is used to this state of affairs.

I dropped into an armchair and muttered, 'Sorry.' I always feel a bit odd when I've finished a book; it's like a small bereavement. There was something now missing from my life.

'Dinner for two at the pub tonight, courtesy of my wages?' Patrick offered with a grin. 'Together with a bottle of something rather good?'

'You mean bangers and mash with a can of Diet Coke, don't you?' I enquired, grumpy and only half joking.

For answer, he took out his wallet, removed the wad of cash within and placed it triumphantly on the coffee table between us.

I think I gaped at him. '*That* much?'

'Woman, you've been off the planet for ages.' Then, 'Yes, that's well over a hundred quid. The folk at the grange next door have sacked their gardener after he was spotted loading some of their stainless-steel tools into his car. Apparently other stuff had gone missing before that but they don't want to get the police involved. There's over half an acre of lawns there and I said I'd fill in until they got someone. They wouldn't hear of me working for nothing. And then there was Miss Lawson, with another broken-down mower. She insisted on paying me too – "All those little kiddies to feed" – and new people have just moved into The Poplars; the place that's been empty for ages with grass like a hayfield. The bloke, Jim, and I had to tackle it with strimmers before the mower would look at it.'

With a pang I realized that this was the happiest I had seen him for ages. 'Patrick . . .' I began, but there was a light tap on the door and, after I had called 'Come in!', John put his head around it.

'Dad, you don't have to knock!' Patrick protested.

'Never know what you two might be up to,' he said with a

twinkle in his eyes. 'Can you spare a minute? You too, Ingrid, if you like. I know you're interested in what Patrick does.'

Although Elspeth is aware that I too work for the NCA, John appears not to. I say 'appears' as the man has a priest's discretion and, if he has guessed otherwise – there have been some fairly hefty hints in connection with various assignments over the years – he gives nothing away.

We followed him into the rear of the house, through the new conservatory – my very own Eden Project – and into the annexe, waving to Elspeth in her kitchen in passing. Their spare bedroom has been fitted out as John's study. The only item not now under his direct gaze is the safe where the church silver and parish records are kept, which remains where it was, far too heavy to move, in the older part of the house, and in the room where I now write. Other than that, his surroundings are exactly the same as before – the loaded book shelves, his pictures, even the colour of the walls, a sombre, pale grey.

'This is Mrs Anne Peters,' said John, introducing the pair of us. He added: 'I thought I'd ask Ingrid to come in so you don't feel too surrounded by men.'

For some reason known only to herself, the woman gave me a thin smile that told me she would far rather I had stayed right where I was. My skin is very thick – most authors are thus armoured. It comes from the early years of publishers' rejection slips.

'Please tell Patrick what you've just told me,' John said. And to him, added: 'I've mentioned to Mrs Peters that you're connected with the police as she's come to me for advice.'

I was prepared for anything: dodgy neighbours, unwanted advances from a member of the clergy, a ghastly scandal involving crime within her own family – anything. No, on second thoughts I reckoned I could cross out one of those on the grounds that any man making advances to this middle-aged lady either needed new glasses or had taken leave of his senses. To put it bluntly, and discounting the somewhat pointy nose and thin lips, she didn't look all that clean. Nor did the clothes she was wearing: an old navy-blue suit of a fashion that suggested it had belonged to her mother and an off-white blouse, the whole outfit incongruously topped with a feathered hat that looked as though a litter of kittens had tried to kill it for quite some time.

'My Archie died last month,' said Mrs Peters in nasal tones, looking at Patrick, not me, with her rather penetrating dark eyes.

He made suitable noises.

'Oh, it was all right really,' she went on, surprisingly even a little gaily. 'He'd been in a right old mess for years. Loads of things wrong with him. He was almost twenty years older than me, you see, in his seventies. And *complain*? He never stopped. Drove me mad, he did. Well, he had to go into hospital in the end and that was that. I have to say it was a real weight off my mind. The cremation was three weeks ago. No church service – he didn't hold with that. He was a horrible old pagan really.'

John hid a smile behind his hand.

Mrs Peters continued, 'But there's a problem – the cremation.'

'Something went wrong?' Patrick earnestly enquired.

'That's just it. I don't know what happened.' She took a deep breath. 'Before it happens they now ask you if you want any of the bits that are left over. You know, things that don't . . . well, burn, like hip replacements, or if there are any other metal pins or plates. Up until recently apparently things like that were buried all together on-site in a pit somewhere if relations didn't want them, but now they're being recycled – sold off to be made into road signs and things like that. I think it's terrible. How many people want bits of their relations ending up as Keep Left signs? Or even in one of those signs you get before farm entrances – a picture of a cow?'

I bit the tip of my tongue hard, a large giggle hatching. Had the late not-very-lamented Archie ever called her that? I wondered.

'So you told them you didn't want that to happen,' Patrick said, his face as long as a French fiddle.

'No.'

'No?'

'I said that he didn't have any replacement things. Everything else under the sun had been wrong with him, you name it: cancer, his heart, lungs, innards. But no problems with any of his joints. Probably because he'd never done anything strenuous – nothing wore out.' Shrilly, she added: 'It's the wives of men like that what get worn out, you know!'

John said, 'And then, a week later, after her husband's ashes had been placed in the Garden of Remembrance, Mrs Peters was given several . . . items.' He indicated a black fabric bag that I had not noticed before on his desk.

'According to my doctor, it's two hip replacements and a piece of metal that he said was probably a repair to someone's skull after they'd had terrible head injuries,' Mrs Peters elaborated, beginning to look a bit distressed.

'Shall I make some tea?' I asked John.

'No, please don't bother,' the widow said. 'I can't stay. I just don't know what to do now, that's all.'

Gently, John said, 'But as the curate at your church, Kenneth, said, don't you think this is just an administrative error?'

'I don't know what to think. The people at the crem are insisting it's absolutely right and everything's in order. I've been there several times and spoken to the manager or his secretary but they won't budge. Everything's labelled, they say. And double-checked. No mistakes possible. The coffin had my Archie's name on it; all the paperwork from the funeral directors was in order, full stop. And they also put the name on the door, or whatever, of the . . . oven . . . thing. Their attitude is that I must have forgotten what he'd had done and all I had to do was say whether I wanted them or not. How on earth can you forget things like that? They treated me as though I was suffering from dementia. That was when I got a bit angry, and when they offered to dispose of them for me I said no and that I was thinking of going to the police.'

I was sure that Patrick and his father are fully conversant with these practical details and had both come to the conclusion that this matter was no more than a terrible error on someone's part.

'What bothers me, as obviously there *has* been a mistake, is where's Archie now?' Mrs Peters continued, showing signs of getting upset again. 'I know he was a miserable old sod when he got old, but I still want to know what really happened to him.'

'Of course you do,' John murmured.

'And if these things had been his I'd have buried them in the garden somewhere. A bit more fitting, wouldn't you say? Not that he liked gardening – I did it all.'

I still couldn't understand, after what she'd said, why she wouldn't have wanted him to end up as a road sign. Still, she didn't seem to be very bright.

'I've really been thinking about this,' the woman went on. 'I mean, it could be some kind of crime, couldn't it? Getting rid of people like that, murdering them and, after swapping them over, chucking the right bodies off a cliff somewhere or just into a hole in the ground like so much rubbish.'

'I'll make some enquiries for you,' soothingly promised the one without much imagination, having observed his father looking at him desperately, willing him to do just that.

His wife, the one overburdened with such a characteristic, found herself going tingly all over.

'I think we must keep this conversation to ourselves,' John said after I had let Mrs Peters out.

'Tell Mum,' Patrick suggested. 'Otherwise it'll be awkward to talk about it *en famille.*'

John picked up the bag, which clinked, and held it out to his son. 'You're right; I'll mention it to her. And you can have this lot. I'm surrounded by plenty of old bones and relics as it is.'

'What did you make of that?' Patrick asked me a little later as we were getting ready to go out.

'I think that if you don't get any satisfactory answers we need to seriously consider if something illegal's going on.'

'It *could* be a scam.'

I handed over a silver pendant on a chain for him to do up for me. 'It could.'

'But not involving the crem.'

'I simply can't believe it was. It would be a good way for criminals to dispose of awkward corpses if they could get round the practicalities. Rival mobsters, kidnap victims whose families couldn't, or wouldn't, pay up, drunk pedestrians mown down on main roads at night . . .'

'But, come to think about it, why bother? Why not, as the woman said, just chuck the murder victim, or whoever, off a cliff or down a disused mine shaft?'

'Because if the substitute body, like Archie's, was ever found, there would be nothing, no evidence, to lead to the killers. Just a corpse, and possibly, if some years had elapsed, an unidentifiable one.'

'I can actually hear your imagination racing in overdrive,' he teased. 'Perhaps you ought to use it for the plot of your next novel.'

'You refer to me as your oracle,' I retorted. 'I've just oracled all over you. And I'm starving.'

He deliberately annoyed me then by kissing me smoochily, smudging my lipstick.

After breakfast the next morning, we stared soberly at the pile of metal pieces before us. Patrick had tipped them out on to a sheet of newspaper on my desk. Ash still adhered to the items.

'Things like any tooth fillings and the handles of the coffin would have been removed,' Patrick said, drawing back a little to avoid tiny pieces of bone and ash being blown away by his breath.

'Gold fillings and teeth?' I wondered.

'It would probably melt but still be recoverable. The thinking is that folk find that too distressing to be returned.'

'But valuable, though.'

'Too right,' he acknowledged with a wry expression, poking around under the three larger pieces of metal to reveal a couple of thin strips. 'These are probably plates from dentures. It's a bit more evidence, I suppose. I gather it's just about impossible to get DNA from cremated bones.' He glanced up. 'Are we making mountains out of molehills and getting involved in this because I've run out of things to do?'

'Pass,' I said. 'But, speaking personally, I'm very curious. For now, why not just call it giving your father a hand with parish matters?'

He glanced at his watch. 'Perhaps you can phone the crem and make an appointment to see the manager. I'm due to cut the lawn of another cottage by the green in twenty minutes. Mrs Jones's husband's in hospital. I won't let her pay.'

'Don't you have to have number plates, insurance and a crash helmet to take that thing on a public road?'

'All I have to do, as you well know, is *cross* the road and then ride it across the green.'

'But what about The Poplars? That's about a quarter of a mile away.'

'No problem. Jim has a Land Rover and a trailer with a ramp.'

OK, I'd mind my own business.

*   *   *

Bath has two crematoriums – one to the south of the city and this new one some miles to the north. It was set discreetly in a fold of hills, the outside resembling a very upmarket stable block and carriage house, complete with clock tower. Constructed of stone with a slate roof, the supporting woodwork of a covered way that led to the side entrance for mourners and the large canopy at the front were made of green oak. We followed the arrow signs to the office.

As one might have expected, the manager, Robin Williams, was softly spoken and charming. After Patrick had introduced us we were invited to seat ourselves in the comfortably furnished office: pale turquoise walls, pink and cream gently patterned chairs and matching curtains, the pictures those washed-out floral prints on the walls that were so fashionable a few years ago.

'I'm here partly on behalf of my father, the Reverend John Gillard,' Patrick began, no doubt gently reminding the man that keeping on good terms with the local clergy was a good idea. 'And partly because a lady who worships at St Julian's church in Wellow has been to see him with a problem she has concerning her husband's cremation. I'm sure you know who I mean – Mrs Anne Peters.'

Williams, wearing an expensive and suitable suit, visibly braced himself. He was very young, perhaps only in his mid-twenties, good looking and had a post-gradulate-but-failed-to-find-a-job-yet-in-his-particular-field look about him. 'She has been to see me twice,' he observed with a faintly injured air. 'We tried to set her mind at rest but I'm afraid I seem to have failed. Frankly, I don't see that there's anything else I can do.'

Patrick continued, 'The other reason I've come to see you is that the lady is determined to go to the police if there isn't a satisfactory outcome to the matter, and in that respect, and although obviously there's nothing official in my visit, I have connections with Bath CID.'

His was referring to his friendship with Detective Chief Inspector James Carrick, of course, with whom he has worked on several cases.

'Surely—' Williams began in horror, but Patrick was already making soothing hand movements.

'I'm merely explaining my involvement in this,' Patrick said.

'I'm on leave and my father is overburdened with work so I promised him, and Mrs Peters, that I'd make enquiries. It's nothing more than that.'

'I see,' said Williams, looking relieved but also baffled. 'I have to tell you that I've made my own enquiries into this and nothing appears to be amiss. The funeral directors are a local much-respected and long-established firm and—'

'Who?' Patrick interrupted.

'Stevens and Sons.'

'Thank you. Please go on.'

'And they're adamant that everything was absolutely above board.'

'Look,' Patrick said, 'Mrs Peters can't be accused of making a mistake when the items presented to her consisted of two hip replacements plus a plate that had, according to the doctor whom she showed all this to, been used to repair a serious injury to someone's head. There were also a couple of pieces of metal that I've confirmed with my dentist came from a set of dentures. I rang Mrs Peters about that and she said he may well have had some kind of dental treatment in the past – before they met – but hadn't been to the dentist in years and his teeth were awful. Sorry, but there *has* been some kind of mistake.'

'I simply don't know what to say,' Williams murmured. 'And I don't see how any mistakes on that dreadful scale could have taken place here. The funeral directors give us the relevant documents: a copy of the death certificate and the permission to cremate. The technicians here check those again and make sure that the name on the lid of the coffin exactly matches that on the paperwork. Anything remaining after cremation is also labelled with the same nameplate that is fixed to the window of the particular cremator used. Errors are impossible!'

'I take it no one asked to say a last farewell before the coffin lid was screwed down.'

'No. Very few British, or rather English people want to do that.'

'I must suggest to you that there was a certain cavalier attitude in giving these articles to Mrs Peters. Didn't anyone query it? Didn't anyone wonder about all these bits and pieces that she'd said, when asked beforehand, her husband hadn't had?'

'In hindsight, I agree. I'll change our procedures so more checks are done.'

'Did someone just go to her house and hand them over?'

'We'd hardly put something like that in the post,' replied Williams, aghast. 'And she was asked if she wanted them.'

'She feels that she was treated like someone with dementia who, frankly, had lost the plot.'

'If true, that's very regrettable. But all I can do now is offer my fullest cooperation. We have nothing to hide, Mr Gillard, and if this is found to be our fault I shall offer my sincere apologies. And even offer to resign,' he gallantly added.

'You must appreciate that Mrs Peters is mainly concerned, if somehow another body was cremated instead, with discovering where her husband's body is *now*,' Patrick said, not about to dish out any medals.

Williams went pale. 'Oh, God. I hadn't thought of that.'

'There might be nothing more sinister in this than a present or one-time employee with a grudge swapping the labels or name plates around to bring this establishment into disrepute.'

'But no one might find out for almost ever,' Williams pointed out.

'That's true, but some people, criminals especially, aren't very intelligent.'

The other shook his head. 'I have every faith in those who work in the cremator area. Any personal details concerning the deceased are kept here in the office and handled only by me and my secretary – who is out at the moment.'

'Has anyone been dismissed who might harbour a grudge?'

'Well – no. We've only been operating here for six months and have the same staff we opened with. Everyone seems to be very happy. Jobs are hard to come by, you know.'

'What about security?'

'No one – and by that I mean members of the public – can just walk in to this part of the building. Doors are locked with keys or have security devices on them. There is no access from the outside to those who shouldn't be here.'

'May I have a copy of the list of the other funeral services that were held on that day?' When Williams looked reluctant, Patrick added: 'It'll save me contacting all the local newspapers.'

This was done.

'Is there a foreman I could have a word with?' Patrick then went on to enquire.

'Indeed. But he's not here today as he's not well and I'm overseeing things. Which I shall have to do now, I'm afraid, as our next service is due.'

'First, please tell me how long metal from cremations has been recycled.'

'I'm not sure of the exact date it started, but it's not been going on for long. It's a pilot scheme in this area.'

Patrick rose to go. 'Thank you.'

'You will keep me informed, won't you?'

'Of course.'

We obtained the foreman's address and left, meeting a sad trail of people mostly wearing black coming from the direction of the car park.

TWO

I did not go with Patrick to speak to the foreman, who lived in Timsbury, as we had both become convinced that the trouble lay elsewhere and he was only ensuring that there were no grey areas left in his enquiries. As it was, the man in question was due to retire in about a year and had been taken on by the new facility because of his experience and, as Williams had emphasized as we were going out of his door, his references were impeccable. This caused Patrick merely to ask for the man's opinion on the matter and not give the impression that he was under any kind of suspicion. He learned nothing new – the crematorium's systems seemed infallible and the only advice he received was to double-check with the undertaker.

Over a period of three days, Patrick visited several undertakers, including Stevens and Sons, who had handled the Peters funeral, regarding cremations that had taken place at the same place on the same day. There had been only five more, none of which appeared to have possible links with our metal horde. They had been of a young couple who had been killed on holiday in Africa in an accident involving a light aircraft, a youth who had received fatal injuries when his motorbike had hit a bridge support – no other vehicles involved, a woman of forty who had never had hip replacements or suffered from serious injuries – someone asked her family, and lastly a child. All very tragic and upsetting but nothing that helped us at all.

'I can't do a lot more until someone makes this official,' Patrick commented, coming into the kitchen on the evening of the day he had obtained the last of this information. 'Obviously I can't ask questions waving my NCA ID as it isn't their business. So far I've had to rely on people's goodwill and by telling them that Dad needs a bit of help with the problem.'

'You've had to explain then.'

'Well, yes. There was much drawing in of breath through teeth but no real help or possible explanations. Suggestions from the oracle, please.'

'I *am* cooking dinner,' I told him.

'OK, I'll stir while you think.'

I handed over the cooking of the risotto – a large one, several hungry mouths to feed – poured us both a glass of wine, took a sip of mine and said, 'Phone James Carrick.'

'He'll have far too much on his plate already.'

'Just ask for his advice.'

'He'll say that Mrs Peters will have to make an official complaint before anything can be done.'

'Then persuade her to complain.'

There was silence for a few moments, then Patrick said, 'This is going a bit stodgy.'

I sloshed in some wine.

'All right, I'll give him a ring.' By the door, he paused. 'D'you always cook risottos like that? Just chuck stuff in?'

'No, I usually drink the wine.'

He laughed and went away. Two or three minutes later he reappeared to pick up his wine glass and say, 'We're invited over for a dram after dinner.'

Which had to be a result for him, of course, I thought, tipping in the rest of the ingredients: cooked chicken and mushrooms, plus a little cream. No, quite a lot of cream actually.

'I'm drowning in paperwork – directives, initiatives, schedules, outlines, proposals and a thousand other stupidities,' James Carrick said, 'only don't quote me.'

This hands-on policeman had to give far more attention to this kind of thing now Detective Inspector David Campbell had arrived after a long period during which Bath's CID department had had no permanent DI, just people on occasional loan from HQ in Portishead. After an extremely shaky start when the new boy had actually arrested his boss on suspicion of murder – a mobster had done a very good job of framing him – life had recently carried on a lot more smoothly. And dully. Bath is normally the kind of place where it makes newspaper headlines if someone falls off a bus.

'Something slightly crazy is bound to grab you then,' Patrick said, raising his whisky glass. 'Your health, and may all your lums for ever reek.'

'Reeking into the house actually,' said Joanna, his wife and one-time CID sergeant. 'We can't get a chimney sweep.'

I promised to give them the phone number of ours.

Patrick produced the bag of cremated metal bits and pieces and gave them the gist of the story.

'Now that's what I call a conversation stopper,' the Scotsman muttered, turning them over wonderingly. 'But aren't we talking about an awful mistake?'

'No other cremations that day were of people with surgical replacements,' I said.

'And if folk don't want them they're just chucked in a bin for recycling?'

'That's about it,' Patrick said.

'Someone's idea of a sick joke then?'

'Apparently all the staff are very happy, if that's the right way of putting it, and the place has only been up and running for a short time. No one's had the sack either.'

'It must be difficult to walk off the street into establishments like that and make mischief.'

'That's right and, as well as being out in the sticks, security's very tight. You can't have funerals being disrupted.'

'I've been to Scottish funerals where fights broke out among the mourners,' Carrick said reflectively. 'But they were pickled in whisky before they turned up.'

Joanna turned a wide-eyed stare on to him. 'You said that as though you miss that kind of thing!'

'Aye, once in a while there's nothing like a good shangie.'

'I'll fix something up for you,' Patrick promised with a smile.

'And, meanwhile, what do we do about this?' Joanna asked, tossing her long auburn hair away from her face with both hands. It was a very warm evening and we were sitting out in the garden of their restored farmhouse home.

'If anything?' Patrick wondered aloud.

'You promised Mrs Peters you'd look into it,' I reminded him.

'I have. And come up with absolutely nothing.'

'Then let's hit the missing persons' records and look for

someone with hip replacements who might also have been in a serious accident of some kind.'

'I suppose it's a start,' Joanna said sarcastically. Then: 'Sorry, that came out all wrong.'

Yes, this highly intelligent woman was miserable now her life revolved around domesticity and being alone with a small baby, Iona Flora, all day long in a semi-isolated rural environment.

'I really can't give this time until there's some kind of evidence that points to a crime having been committed,' her husband said slowly.

'Quoted straight out of a police procedural manual,' Joanna said, his words not having improved her mood.

'Oh, be fair!' he protested.

'*I'll* look into it,' she said defiantly.

'You can't. You don't have all the security codes for the websites. Nor the passwords.'

I was thinking that it had been rather kind of him not to tell her she didn't have the authority either.

He was presented with a *Mona Lisa* lookalike.

'You have?' he gasped. 'How, for God's sake?'

'I still have connections. I use someone else's passwords.'

'Who is it?' James demanded to know.

'And I have every intention of protecting my sources.'

'Jo . . .' he began warningly.

'Children, please,' Patrick murmured. And then, into the rather strained silence that followed, added: 'Me.'

'You!' Carrick exclaimed.

'Your other half is going to apply to rejoin the police. I think you already knew that. It doesn't hurt for her to be kept in the picture and in this case nothing is yet official. And, should you regard that as unwarranted interference on my part, I can either grovel an apology and leave or you can have your punch-up now. I quite fancy a good shangie too.'

'Isn't there a third option?' Carrick enquired with the hint of a smile.

'Yes; pour me another tot.'

'OK,' said Carrick after pausing only briefly. He then shoved all the metal bits back in the bag and plonked them in his wife's lap before grabbing the whisky bottle.

I don't think any of those present anticipated the thoroughness with which she would tackle her 'case'.

The fine weather broke, the two children came home, Fudge lame after having caught a hoof in a rabbit hole and thrown Katie who had landed safely, if scratchily, in a bush. The vet prescribed the pony be turned out to grass to rest, 'Tough as old boots these Exmoors,' and we went back to being a family with five children, the four elder ones having to be organized during the remainder of the school holidays.

Keeping fit can be a problem for Patrick, who lost the lower part of his right leg during covert army operations. It has been replaced by something which – although state of the art with a tiny in-built computer powered by lithium batteries, cost the same as a small family car, and no one who didn't know him would ever guess just seeing him moving about – does not lend itself to sustained running or jogging. Worried about losing fitness while being away from the gym he uses in London, and between grass-cutting sessions, Patrick started going to one locally and also swimming in Bath, taking Matthew, who was nervous, to the latter with him for lessons. Justin became unhappy about this – threw tantrums, that is, wanting to go as well but, at six years old, I thought him a bit too young, and he has a history of behaving badly in public. Patrick finally caved in and it was discovered that the boy not only behaved but took to the water like a seal, just as his father had.

The author, now between novels, devoted time to Vicky and baby Mark, Katie having gone off again, this time to a local friend's house for a few days, where, surprise, surprise, the parents bred show ponies. I'm not a very good mother in that small children soon exhaust my ability to amuse them, the two little ones humbly making it clear to me after a while that they preferred their own company, the baby content to watch Vicky playing at dolls' tea parties for *hours* and being allowed to hold, chew, wave around and throw the odd 'guest'.

'Is this baby downright strange, or what?' I asked Carrie at some stage.

'Different,' replied this forthright woman. 'He's not backward, mind,' she added hastily, 'if that's what you're thinking. No,

Mark watches and learns all the time. He'll start trying to talk soon.'

'But he's so good and quiet and loves all the pretty things.'

'So he's going to be like Laurence Llewelyn Bowen when he grows up. Gorgeous!'

I hadn't thought of it like that.

Some fitness aspects of the job cannot be dealt with locally and, ten days later, Patrick and I headed for London for firearms training. My husband is, and has to be, a fine shot. Due to his service in undercover units the Gillards are still on the hit lists of various terrorist organizations, not to mention those of aggrieved mobsters he has helped put behind bars. Most of them, thankfully, have no idea who he really is. But because of this he carries a Glock 17 in a shoulder harness and, even at home, when it is obviously out of sight, it is not far away, secured in a wall safe together with my Smith and Wesson, or in our car, a Range Rover which has a hidden safe in the cubby box between the front seats, fitted with electronic locks that can only be opened by us. Patrick also usually has in his possession his Italian throwing knife, and he is more dangerous with that than most men armed with a chainsaw. All of these weapons have saved our lives on more than one occasion.

I am quite a good shot and, having carried it around with me for quite a while, have recently, and at last, received official authorization to retain the short-barrelled Smith and Wesson with which Patrick was issued when he worked for D12, a department of MI5, but never quite got round to handing back. I do not want to be given anything else as I am used to it and that seems to find favour with those in charge, who have to bear in mind that retraining me with, say, a Glock, would take time and, due to drastic cuts in funding, cost too much money. I have used Patrick's Glock once, when a man was about to finish me off at close range with a rifle. There had been no risk of my missing him.

After the routine target practice, at which we both proved to be a little rusty, followed the second stage. This takes place at a training set-up run by the military set deep in the bowels of a Ministry of Defence building a short taxi ride away from the first venue. It is run by the army, and although police personnel do sometimes use the facility, Commander Greenway has no actual say in the fact that we do.

Scenarios of any kind can be put together there along the lines of stage or film sets using various and usually lightweight materials. That is just about the only concession to keeping participants in one piece. The basic arrangement is a series of tunnels, parts of which can collapse without warning, with crevices hiding targets which spring up and have to be dealt with in meaningful fashion otherwise one loses a 'life', of which a certain number, usually three, are issued at the start. The tunnels often lead into a large open space of some kind – where there are booby traps and more targets – that has to be crossed in order to reach, in convoluted fashion, a high point near the end; perhaps a tower.

All this has to be achieved within a time limit with the added distraction of young and very fit service people ordered to ambush participants in the tunnels. The occasional live electrical wire, low voltage but with a kick, waits for the unwary. Oh, and perhaps a soaking in water. And not to mention marksman perched high on a gantry taking careful but unnerving shots, also using live ammunition.

Patrick helped create this facility and wrote most of the early 'scripts', and it is for this reason, I think, that he has some kind of life membership. There is a tradition that they try to overpower him when he nears the end of the course, 'lives' lost or not, before he endeavours to demolish the entire set-up. People have been hurt, even ended up in hospital. Men of Patrick's ilk find this kind of thing vastly entertaining, if a challenge. I just somehow get through it and laugh afterwards and it goes without saying that, for most of the time, I rely very heavily on Patrick's assistance.

We were kitted out in the usual dark blue tracksuits and non-slip boots, the last another rare nod to staying out of A&E, and headed down the dimly lit approach corridor. As pre-arranged between us, Patrick had not drawn his Glock, but I had my weapon ready in my hand. This soon proved to be a good idea when a couple of men jumped on him from a hidden recess. He has a varied and effective choice of temporary disabling tactics, and these people were, frankly, naive and clumsy. One paid the price by being on the receiving end of a hefty box around the head; the other, breaking probably the only house safety rule by grabbing hold of Patrick around the neck, got an elbow, possibly accidental, smack on the nose, which gushed with blood as though someone had turned a tap on in it.

We moved on.

They usually try to split us up but I was determined that, this time, it would not happen. When someone lobbed a thunderflash at us from somewhere at the rear, however, I was momentarily deafened and blinded, and when the smoke cleared a little I was on my own. Too late, I remembered Patrick's words, uttered on more than one occasion: 'When they try to confuse and stop you, *move!*'

'You have two lives between you as your target practice was so lousy,' a voice boomed over a hidden speaker. 'And if we hear you talking to one another you've immediately failed.'

I already knew there were mikes all over the place and yelled, 'And if we talk to ourselves?'

There was no response.

Who made up these bloody rules?

I moved, ran down the rest of the corridor, through the swing doors at the end and in the 'lobby' I found myself in was confronted by a young woman dressed in combats. She didn't like the look of the gun at all but squared up to me with the brave intention of stopping me from going any further. I simply didn't want to have to hit her so shoved the gun in a pocket and carried out the manoeuvre Patrick does with those far weaker than himself. She wasn't weaker than me really but I still stuck out a leg, grabbed her, pulled and pushed in scientific fashion, got her off-balance and watched as she went over backwards. By the time she'd picked herself up I had barged through another pair of doors.

No tunnels, no Patrick, just a half-light moonscape of large boulders – polystyrene, probably – sand, pebbles, a slate scree and dead trees, actual branches stuck into the sand. And spiders. They were not real but very lifelike, hanging like oversized black grapes with long legs in the centre of lovingly fashioned webs strung between several of the trees and a tumbledown shed. There was an artificial breeze, which somehow made it worse, fanning through this nightmare, the creatures jigging up and down and from side to side in an unbelievably nasty dance.

If this was one of Patrick's ideas I would divorce him, again – we have been married twice – as soon as we got outside.

I am a complete and utter arachnophobe and was too slow to react when a target popped up – one of the usual cardboard replicas used indoors representing a leering gunman. But I got it in the guts, the crack of the shot very loud even though the walls of this extensive area are lined with bulletproof baffles. There was another shot, somewhere close by, off to my left – the Glock by the sound of it. Quickly, using a couple of the phoney rocks as cover, I went in that direction. But carefully – we didn't want to end up shooting each other.

Perhaps, I thought, the author of this had been hoping that I, in a panic, would waste my ammunition on the spiders. Congratulating myself that I had not fallen for this, I rounded a rock and came face-to-face with the eight eyes of a huge arachnid, at least three feet in height, that did not have a web but was on the ground and mobile, almost right upon me and moving in a way that can only be described as a metallic frenzy. Really, really wanting to run, shrieking, I picked up a largish rock that was real, tore around to one side of the thing, managed to kill another target on the way that appeared in a dark recess on the far side of the sandy space and smashed it down with all my strength. Reduced to half the height it had been, it tottered into a boulder then disintegrated, crunching into a twitching heap that still managed to look like a real spider in its death throes.

'Sammy's going to be really sad about that,' thundered the disembodied voice. 'It took him a long time to make that. It wouldn't have hurt you, duckie. We might have to send you the bill.'

I mentally told Sammy what he could do with his flattened spider.

Patrick appeared and towed me at speed through the trees. I collected only one of the spiders on my tracksuit top – why the hell hadn't Patrick? – and ripped it off. It burst, splashing me in some kind of black gunge. I hit freak-out level ten even though I knew they weren't real. In the next moment one of the smaller of the dead 'trees' keeled over as we went by, hitting Patrick on the shoulder, causing him to trip on the uneven ground and fall flat. I heaved it off him and ran on, leaving him to get to his feet.

The tumbledown shed did its thing – fell apart like a pack of cards shooting red dye everywhere. I had flung myself down and all of it missed me, squirting all over the spot lamps which provided what light there was, and everything became much dimmer.

We proceeded to systematically slaughter everything cardboard that they then threw at us as we crossed the rest of the open space. I let my partner, who had just one splash of red on his overalls, do most of the work, as he had started off with seventeen shots to my six. It took me a while to realize that he was on auto, bored and angry. When someone took a shot at us from the gantry that came just too close for comfort, he started on the lights serving that area, no doubt showering those up there with glass and other bits and pieces. I heard someone swear.

The tunnels, constructed of some kind of wooden panels that locked together, were on the far side and like a maze with several dead ends and false entrances. These had to be negotiated to reach the end but we worked as a team, not needing to speak, relying on hand signals and, seemingly, telepathy. We have done this many times before and I knew that the reason for Patrick's anger was that although they had given us less lives than normal, the entire set-up consisted of stale ideas padded out with gizmos. They were wasting our time.

Our tunnel world suddenly went almost completely dark so I guessed that someone else was angry too, and there was one bad moment when a man grabbed me, coming from nowhere. I yelled when he got me by the hair, somehow spun round and clouted him with my free hand. Then reinforcements took over and I'm not quite sure what happened next in the gloom. It sounded very much like someone being thrown several feet into an open wardrobe.

We were already in what seemed to be a promising route through the tunnels and continued at speed and little caution, although I was looking over my shoulder all the time. Very shortly afterwards we emerged into pitch darkness which seemed, if the deadened, muffled sound of our footsteps was to be believed, to be a small, enclosed space. I kept as close to Patrick as possible and, groping in the darkness, our hands encountered the rungs of a ladder. Looking up what appeared to be a tall shaft, I saw a faint circle of light overhead and, as I did so, a target-like shape was silhouetted against it. Patrick fired. There was a pause and then the light was blocked out as something heavy thundered down the ladder towards us. I flung myself to one side but was still clouted on the head by something hard and everything went fuzzy, odd ringing noises vibrating in my ears. But there was one clear thought in my mind: this thing down here with us was a body and we had killed someone.

'Are you all right?' breathed a voice in my ear.

'No,' I whispered.

'Good.'

I was hauled to my feet.

'It's a shop window dummy,' Patrick continued, stamping his feet to cover our conversation.

'A mannequin.'

'Is that what they're called? Yes.'

'You're getting time faults!' blared the loudspeaker.

'He lies because he knows he's a loser,' Patrick muttered under his breath, this a heavily censored version of what he actually said. Circumnavigating the dummy, he started up the ladder. This was not easy for someone with no sensation in his right foot, so I gave him plenty of room and then slowly followed, feeling dizzy and a bit sick.

I knew that war would be declared up there somewhere, this obvious to Patrick as he reholstered the Glock just before he reached the top. He went from my sight and I hurried as fast as I could, in my haste not putting my feet on the rungs properly and slipping off. I had to stop for a rest, hoping my world would stop revolving, and put the gun in my pocket to enable me to hold on with both hands.

Above me there were thumps, bangs and heavy breathing.

Taking an embarrassingly long time, I finally reached the top and emerged into the light only to make a complete mess of getting off the ladder, catching the toe of my boot on something and pitching full length. I rolled into what turned out to be the backs of someone's legs, causing him to overbalance and fall over. This someone not being Patrick, I wriggled around and quickly rolled him, protesting, off the edge of the large and slightly shaky platform we were on. There was a heart-stopping pause before a loud thud from somewhere below. I had no time to worry about this – another man came hurtling in my direction and I just had time to flatten myself before he followed his comrade over the edge.

Another two, one a woman, had pitched into Patrick, she, the bitch, punching him in the stomach while the other held him, my husband playing the gentleman, so far, by not kicking her away. She didn't see me coming, mostly because I was behind her, so I went with the trend, got her by her ginger ponytail and hauled her away. She rounded on me, thus lining herself up for me to clip her on the jaw. She staggered and I guided her into thin air with a kick to the backside.

Almost lovingly, Patrick carried the last man to the edge, planted a smacking kiss on his forehead and then dropped him over.

'It's OK,' he panted. 'There's a load of gym mats down there. No one's hurt. Are you?' he finished by bellowing below.

There were a few grunts.

'And, actually, it's *sir*!' Patrick went on to yell at them.

The remark that his target practice had been lousy and being punched in the stomach had obviously reached home.

'I'm getting old,' Patrick muttered to me when we had descended another ladder to reach floor level outside the tower. 'As in completely knackered. Are you OK now?'

'Sort of,' I replied.

I stood well back, very well back, when there was then a yanking out of the large metal pins with ring handles that held the platform together, followed by his putting his shoulder to it, a shout of 'Fore!' and the whole thing toppled over with a crash, taking quite a lot of other nearby stuff with it. There were shouts of alarm, followed by protests. I heard someone bleat that they were only doing their job, and the pair of us had got through without penalty, but it served them not. I went right away: when Patrick starts swearing I prefer not to be around.

'It was crap but I enjoyed that,' he said when he rejoined me.

As soon as he switched on his phone after we had showered, changed and been given back the last of our personal possessions, it rang.

'Oh, thank God,' I heard Joanna's voice say. 'James said you were going to London and I thought it would be better to contact you than dial 999. Can you help me? I'm in a spot of bother.'

'Where are you?' Patrick asked.

'Shut in a lock-up garage, possibly somewhere near Leytonstone.'

THREE

The signal was poor but we established – I eavesdropped – that she was standing on a wooden box by a small window, this being little more than an air vent. She was unhurt but, as she put it, 'A bit ruffled.' Patrick asked her if she could give him any other information about where she was but all she could tell us was that, following enquiries, she had gone to a housing estate not far from the railway station. The Leg o' Mutton public house, closed and boarded up, was on the corner of the road that led to it and there was another pub – she couldn't remember the name of it – close by. Not going into unnecessary details, she said she had, at some stage, been overwhelmed by sundry yobs, bundled into a car with someone's coat over her head, driven for some time and then dumped into the garage. Through the filthy glass of the tiny window she could see another row of at least twenty other garages opposite, the whole area being deserted and heavily vandalized. She had tried hammering on the door but no one had come.

Patrick promised to keep closely in touch with her as we headed to the area and flagged down a taxi after a quick pause to buy a couple of takeaway coffees and two doughnuts for instant energy.

'Deserted and heavily vandalized,' Patrick repeated, talking mostly to himself. 'That suggests somewhere due for demolition and redevelopment. Bloody hell, that could be just about anywhere in east London.'

'I don't suppose she has a tracking app on her phone.'

We asked and Joanna hadn't.

'Can't GCHQ roughly pinpoint mobiles?' I went on to ask.

'Probably, but let's utilize some of Hercule Poirot's little grey cells before we hit the panic button.' He flexed his shoulders, wincing.

'Is that where the tree landed on you?' I said.

He did not answer, lost in thought, and we travelled for a while in silence.

Joanna rang again. 'Sorry, my battery's going. I forgot to tell you that I can hear trains – quite close by.'

'Don't worry,' Patrick said to her. 'We're halfway there already.' Then to me, having ended the call, 'Did they forget to take her phone?' He stared at me more closely. 'You've a large, greenish bump on your forehead.'

'Someone dropped a body on me.'

We asked to be put down at the Leg o' Mutton pub and Patrick quizzed the taxi driver as to where redevelopment might be due to take place in the area. But although he knew the roads, he did not live in the locality. 'Better ask someone what lives here, Guv,' the man replied lugubriously. 'It changes every five minutes. Folk get lorst finding their way 'ome when they've just popped out to buy a paper.'

There was every chance that Joanna had merely been driven around in circles for a while so we found our way to the back of the housing estate, which consisted of several blocks of flats and a row of houses. It was all very drab and dreary, social housing of the old Soviet School of Architecture style. The only place for young children to play – of which there were a lot judging by the racket – were the walkways that acted as access. The open ground in the centre, once host to trees of which only the stumps remained, was obviously now the fiefdom of those older and used for playing football and riding bikes. We were subjected to hostile stares from a bunch of youths loafing around, smoking, and I was glad Patrick was with me. It bothered me a little that there had been no opportunity for us to change into different clothes – scruffy ones, that is – in order not to stand out as outsiders and possibly hazard Joanna's safety in some way if she were here. What she thought of as heavily vandalized and deserted might be normal for the place.

The rest of the people we came upon ignored us, and we followed a narrow roadway strewn with litter and broken glass which led around to the rear. We found two rows of garages facing one another. Every flat surface was loaded with graffiti, some garages with the doors ripped off or damaged. With just a few old cars in sight and more rubbish blowing about, this site could indeed be thought to be abandoned and awaiting demolition.

Patrick shouted Joanna's name in his parade ground voice, but there was no response, so we made sure by walking along both rows, banging on the doors where doors existed. Someone shouted obscenities at us from a fourth-floor window of the nearest block and a flock of pigeons took flight, but those were the only reactions.

'She's not here,' Patrick muttered and tried to phone her.

Nothing; her battery had gone.

'OK, we'll ask around.'

We made our way to the railway station and Patrick talked to the three taxi drivers parked outside, putting on an American accent and saying that he was a scout for an international property company. One in particular was keen to take us on a tour of the district, telling us that he was a local man and knew of two possibilities in nearby Leyton – semi-derelict areas which were once local authority housing and quite close to each other, now designated for redevelopment. He seemed to be quite excited about it.

At a frustratingly slow pace through heavy traffic and travelling west we had a whispered conversation, discussing what Joanna had said about the nearness of a railway line. We were assuming she meant surface trains and not the rumble of a Tube line somewhere beneath her. I learned from my working partner that due to rails being welded now, trains no longer clatter and bang, except over points, and very little rolling stock retains slam doors. This must mean that Joanna could mostly hear either the whine of electric motors or diesel engines somewhere between two stations.

'I can take you to the other place too,' said the taxi driver eagerly when we had arrived at the first.

'How far is it?' I asked.

'Around a quarter of a mile further along the road we came in on.'

'We'll walk, thank you.'

Here, it looked promising, the actual flats having already been demolished and that part of the site mostly cleared. Lock-up garages in an L-shaped formation remained on the far side, together with a few small piles of rubble, the usual dumped rubbish and a burned-out car. Plastic bags blew around in the light breeze and were draped in the scrubby vegetation that had sprung up, a sapling ash tree almost obscuring a notice board that detailed plans for the regeneration of the area with affordable housing, shops and children's play areas. I found myself wondering how local people could afford to buy even a cheap house when some of them looked as if they did not even have the money for a couple of days' groceries.

We hurried. It was almost four in the afternoon by now and it was imperative that we found Joanna soon. Having been up very early to set off for London, I personally was beginning to flag. I did not ask Patrick how he felt – I don't under these circumstances – but knew he was tired as he was limping slightly, a tell-tale sign. However, the more tired and stressed he is the more bloody-minded he becomes, so there would be no question of his giving up.

We repeated calling and knocking on all the garage doors.

Nothing, no answer.

A train rumbled by, nearby but out of sight.

'The other site might be just along the line if it's along the road,' Patrick observed, and set off.

We arrived and it was immediately obvious that this was different, the whole place still standing, concrete anarchy with over- and underpasses, most of the windows of the one-time homes smashed, curtains hanging down like so many rags on the outside walls. The fly-tipped rubbish here, which spread right out to the edge of the road, was on an industrial scale. Some had been set alight and still smouldered, including plastics melted into revolting heaps which now resembled suppurating flesh and gave off choking fumes. At some stage an attempt had been made by the local authorities to fence off the area with concrete posts and strong wire netting but what remained – the rest no doubt having been stolen – had been smashed down. There were several more burned-out cars here and another that had not yet suffered that fate, the ground around it glittering with broken glass and used hypodermic needles.

'For God's sake, look where you're putting your feet,' Patrick said, adding, 'I don't like the look of this place at all. Stick close to me. *Don't* go off on your own.' He gazed at me for a moment. 'I mean it.'

'I can see that,' I said.

We stepped over a section of the damaged fencing and, after a few yards, paused to look about us. The entrance road, almost blocked by rubbish, veered around to the right and disappeared into an underpass which might have been constructed to channel traffic away from what looked like the remains of a children's play area. Patrick gave it the thumbs down and headed across the overgrown grass, bearing left to skirt the buildings towards the rear. We were soon thwarted by a wall at least twenty feet in height that was at right angles to us, abutting the side of the nearest block at one end and some kind of utilities outbuilding at the other. It was impossible to go around it as the fencing was intact here.

It would have to be the traffic underpass after all.

The breeze was channelling quite strongly towards us through it and, although it was only around fifty yards in length and we could see daylight at the other end, the centre was very gloomy. It stank of rotting domestic rubbish and God alone knew what else, but I said nothing – there was no point in stating the obvious. No point in my saying anything at all.

We had not come to London kitted out for this kind of activity and had left the car, which carries things like torches and other useful bits and pieces, at SOCA's old HQ in Kensington, the building still in use. This meant that we had no means of lighting our way and had to rely on our eyes and ears alone. The latter soon told me that there were rats in the darkest part of the tunnel, a rustling, pattering sound. We carried on, rubbish not much impeding our progress now, as if the fly-tippers had not ventured this far. I glanced behind me to see if we were being followed just at the moment when Patrick paused and I cannoned into him, causing him to swear under his breath from taut nerves.

'You said to stick close,' I hissed.

He drew his Glock and carried on. We reached around halfway, walking in almost complete darkness, and I was sure that the rats were scuttling just in front of our feet. Then my foot touched one and it squeaked. Somehow I resisted the urge to kick out at it. The smell was ghastly. Had something died down here or was it just stagnant air?

'They taste good roasted,' Patrick murmured.

'You *haven't* eaten rat,' I gasped.

'Yup. When you're on a training exercise in the middle of nowhere and hungry, you eat anything.'

'I knew that you had to fend for yourselves and snared rabbits, but—'

'The group I was with once found a sheep caught in a barbed-wire fence. We killed and ate that. Did it a favour really.'

'What, ate *all* of it?'

'I seem to remember that we left the wool, skin, hooves, guts, bones and head. There were twenty of us, mind.'

'How on earth did you cook it?'

'In smallish biggish chunks on sticks over a hot fire. It was as tough as hell but better than nothing.' We had reached the end, stepped out into the light and he stopped and added: 'Be ready for anything.'

The access road spilt into three, one for each block, and during the next ten minutes or so of very cautious exploration we discovered that there were three rows of garages set apart towards the rear. In our sight, that is – there could be more. The whole place was like the set for a futuristic, soulless town in a sci-fi movie. And people had lived here?

Again, we repeated walking along the length of the first row, calling and banging on the doors. Only some of them were intact – around half had been kicked in. No Joanna. We went to the second group, a minute's walk away, and, when it was in view, saw two men ahead of us who dashed from our sight.

'Did you reload?' Patrick asked.

'Of course,' I replied.

'If anyone starts coming at us in a meaningful fashion, even if they're not armed, and you have to fire to protect yourself, aim high the first time and we'll try to scare them off. I just wish I knew what the hell was going on here.'

'You could involve the local police,' I suggested.

'Last resort. We don't want some young probationer getting hurt if they're daft enough to initially send just an area car.'

As he finished speaking a shot ricochetted off one of several abandoned large wheeled rubbish bins nearby.

'OK, we've done this already today, haven't we?' Patrick whispered when we had taken cover behind one of them. 'But our only aim is to find Joanna.' He grabbed my arm, listening. Then I heard what he had – footsteps.

As quietly as possible, we made our way along the rear of the bins. There were four of them; I went to the last and flattened myself against it as Patrick had a quick look around. He then caught my eye and raised a warning forefinger. Several very long seconds elapsed.

In a tone that he might have thought was a whisper but wasn't and, slurring his words, a man said, 'Dougie, you go that end, Will and I'll tackle this one. Don't kill them. We'll just show them that trespassers aren't wanted here.' Then, loudly, 'Yes, you two, you might have heard that. Come out now and we won't hurt you.'

Patrick leapt out and the Glock fired twice.

I followed, ready to shoot. Bugger aiming high.

The three were in a huddle like wagons encircled against a Sioux attack. While not bristling with arrows, one was grasping his right hand from which blood was slowly dripping, a damaged handgun on the ground, and another was staring at a hole in the tarmac at his feet, his trainers heaped with bits of road.

'Armed police,' Patrick murmured. 'Sorry I didn't have time to issue a warning. In exchange for plenty of information about what gives in this bloody hole I *might* not take you into custody. But first of all I want the location of the young woman who is locked up in a garage somewhere here.'

'He'll kill us if we get arrested,' said the man who had first spoken. From appearances – and I wasn't feeling particularly charitable right now – his IQ might have been a couple of notches higher than those of his chums – around the same as your average gerbil, that is. He did not look quite sober.

'OK,' said Patrick. 'I'll do you a deal. If you don't tell me everything I want to know I'll shoot bits off you that won't necessarily prove fatal. How's that?'

'You're not allowed to do things like that!' shouted the one with tarmac on his feet. It wasn't the first time this comment has been hurled at my working partner.

'My boss is quite a few miles from here,' Patrick responded nastily, not the first time he had replied thus either.

'She's down there,' revealed the one who had not been on the receiving end of anything, yet, jerking his head vaguely over to his left.

'More garages?'

'Yeah.'

'Show me,' Patrick ordered crisply. 'Do you have the key?'

'He has,' mumbled the man, pointing at the injured boss man.

'I'll kill you, Dougie,' that individual ground out, obviously in pain. He thought about it and then his left hand went towards his pocket.

'Slowly!' Patrick rapped out. 'Or I might get nervous.'

Very slowly, the key was handed over.

'Right, you two, Will and Dougie,' Patrick continued, 'get in a bin each and stay there. This lady here is a very good shot and if she even sees a finger over the top you'll lose it. Same goes for heads.'

Muttering, the two got into the bins. I rather got the impression that there was water in the bottom of them and Dougie was permitted to change his when he protested that people had been using it as a lavatory.

Having given him his handkerchief to bind around the damaged finger – it did not appear to be particularly serious – Patrick went off with the man in charge while I stationed myself at a reasonable distance from the bins, my back to a wall, in case one of them decided to jump out at me in jack-in-the-box fashion. The unhappy thought going through my mind was that the entire area might be heaving with most-wanteds and other undesirables, some of whom might be observing what was going on from high above me, and may even be in possession of long-range weapons.

I waited.

The wait began to stretch into a period of time during which I felt I could easily write a chapter of my new novel, an idea for which had just come into my head. It featured a condemned housing estate where criminals ruled and the police dared not go.

'No, bugger this!' Will's bin suddenly roared and he jumped up with every appearance of intending to try to escape.

My first shot whanged off the metal near where one of his hands was gripping the rim; the second went so close to his back-to-front baseball cap that he must have felt the draught as it went by. I went cold when I realized that had he moved . . . However, I knew that the man was still alive, he having disappeared from sight extremely rapidly, for the good reason that he was now hurling mind-blowingly obscene abuse at me, with Dougie joining in. Taking a deep breath, I thanked everything holy for the training earlier.

Shortly afterwards, another half-chapter perhaps, I heard hurrying footsteps and Patrick calling, 'It's us, Ingrid,' before they came into view. 'Do we need to book a hearse?'

'Not yet,' I replied.

He and Joanna, who looked as though she might have shed a tear or two, were without their guide, and I didn't bother to ask what Patrick had done with him because I knew – he had been locked up in Joanna's prison. We escorted the other two to the same destination, which was quite a walk, all went in and Patrick pulled down the up-and-over door, almost closing it but leaving enough of a gap so we could see.

There was a lot of junk piled within the gloomy interior: an untidy stack of cardboard boxes, some of which appeared to hold clothing, plus several old bikes and a row of rolls of carpet and other floor coverings standing on end, all soiled as though having been salvaged from fire or flood, that leaned, Pisa-style, as though they might topple over at any moment.

'Now then,' Patrick said. 'You with the illegally held handgun – what's your name?'

'Joe,' the man muttered.

'Joe what?'

'Hurley.'

He then asked for, and got, the surnames of Dougie and Will, Baker and Gibbs respectively, and I wrote them down. They refused to give their addresses and were not pushed on that – there were more important things we needed to know and they might be of no fixed address anyway. There was also the possibility that some, if not all, lived on the housing estate to which Joanna had originally gone. But obviously, we did not want to discuss her reasons for doing so in front of them.

'So is this some kind of rat hole for unemployables?' Patrick went on to ask.

Joe swore at him.

'Drugs for sale, heavies for hire, or are you ripping off illegal immigrants by renting them cupboards to sleep in? Talk!'

The man just shook his head.

Patrick took his knife from his pocket and flicked out the blade, observing as he did so, 'This is quieter. It's a throwing knife too, so if I got you from here it would probably go right through.'

Dougie burst out with, 'Nah, nuffin' like that, Guv. We just saw this bird and thought we'd have a bit of fun with 'er tonight. After a few beers, like.'

'A few more beers, you mean,' Joanna said heavily.

'Well, you gave us a load of lip!' shouted Joe. 'And we'd only asked you, nicely like, if you'd like to go to the pub with us.'

'Did they?' Patrick asked her.

She nodded. 'To begin with.'

'And you have a gun, and a car,' Patrick said to the men. 'Why?'

They exchanged glances.

'You work for a mobster, or even several,' Patrick suggested, 'and were kicking your heels, nothing to do, on a street corner. Does that tally with what happened?' he asked Joanna. 'Or were they actually at an address you were visiting?'

'It just about tallies,' she replied.

'OK, I want the names of the people you work for,' Patrick said.

'We never get to know their *names*,' Joe said, horrified. 'Just a geezer, a backup bod'll come and tell us what's up.'

'There's more than one mobster hiring then?'

'Only sometimes.'

'Why take a shot at anyone coming here?'

'We sort of keep an eye on the place and thought you was from a gang we don't want here,' said Joe.

'You're a liar!' Dougie bawled. 'You was drunk and wavin' the gun around, braggin' what a good shot you was and sayin' that no one was goin' to get the girl away from us.'

Patrick turned to Joanna and me. 'Shall I arrest them or blow their heads off on the grounds that it's a waste of public money to do anything else?'

We pretended to mull it over.

'One of them's sometimes just called JC,' Dougie then said very, very eagerly. 'I think he's—'

The door was flung up and I had a fleeting glimpse of several people outside before the shooting started. A man screamed hoarsely and, from my prone position on the floor, I saw someone, Joe perhaps, fall. Will and Dougie bolted. Deafened by the din, I rolled over towards the side of the garage too fast, thumping into the wall, found the Smith and Wesson and fired at a man taking aim over to my right, who, as I did so, was knocked aside by another man behind him who had tripped and almost fallen. He too had a handgun. Before I could do anything he fired at me but, still off-balance, missed. He then collided with several rolls of carpet as they keeled over and was felled utterly, pinned down and unable to move.

This had only taken seconds.

'Anyone else?' Patrick bellowed.

All I could hear was my own panting breathing and the footfalls of people pelting away.

Joanna struggled out from behind the pile of boxes, where, I discovered afterwards, Patrick had shoved her.

'Everyone all right?' he asked, still shouting, discounting the injured man and the one flattened by the rolls of carpet at his feet. Receiving our assurances that we were fine, he cautiously went over to the doorway and looked out. 'Bastards,' he muttered, reaching for his mobile.

FOUR

Patrick only slowly came off the boil and I thanked God that he had not gunned down those who had been fleeing – something he would have been perfectly capable of had he really lost his temper. His production of his NCA ID card helped things along somewhat, together with the fact that no one had been injured as a result of our actions. The man pinned down under the carpets, instantly recognized as a local 'trouble-maker' by the police personnel who attended, only had a bruised head where he had hit the floor. Patrick had not fired a shot within the garage and mine had gone wide due to the chaos. Joe Hurley – who had been taken to hospital – had been hit by what one must assume was friendly fire, while Will and Dougie had disappeared. As far as what had happened a little earlier was concerned, Patrick reported that he had initially shot a weapon from Joe's hand, the remains of which he duly handed over, adding that I had fired a couple of warning shots. For some reason we did not hear about those particular incidents again.

We would have to make statements the following morning about the rest of the affair, though and there would be more questions but now, after the formalities were over, we found a taxi to take the three of us to where we had left our overnight bags at the army training facility, and from there went to our favourite hotel in the West End. Joanna had come to London by train and had been travelling very light, everything she needed in an amazingly capacious handbag – even containing a change of clothing – which by some miracle was still in her possession. The men had stolen all her cash but not her credit cards and, as we already knew, had left her with her mobile phone.

'We must offer thanks to the patron saint of really stupid criminals for abandoning them,' Patrick commented over breakfast the next morning when we were discussing the previous day's events.

'Moronicus, wasn't it?' Joanna offered.

'That's the chap.'

'I feel very bad about this, although I don't think it happened because of anything I've been looking into,' Joanna continued. 'As I told the cops here, those three just tried to pick me up – they all seemed to be high on whatever – and I bawled them out, used rather awful language actually. It was bad judgement.'

She had already apologized for putting us in danger.

'I'm not convinced you haven't stirred up some criminal cesspit,' Patrick demurred. 'Where did you come upon them?'

'They were hanging around outside the other pub near the railway station, the one that's open, the Ram's Head.'

'Please tell us what you've been doing.'

'I decided to follow on with your enquiries into the crem. You'd hadn't investigated the manager and his secretary.'

Whoops, I thought.

'Robin Williams is, as you said, Patrick, an ideal man for the job. I found him cultured, charming and sympathetic, perfect for front of house in an establishment like that. He has degrees in English language and philosophy, and further recent qualifications in connection with organizing conferences and the leisure and holiday industries. I copied what you've sometimes done, Ingrid, and told him that I was freelance and writing articles about people with lesser-known jobs. He told me that he'd been born in Woking, Surrey, to middle-class parents, and regarded himself as very fortunate in getting the job when so many of his contemporaries were still out of work. But he didn't regard his present position as his future. I didn't have my laptop with me so asked James to do a criminal records check on him and he's absolutely clean – nothing. Not even traffic offences.'

'Good,' I said. 'I really liked him.'

'But he is involved with his secretary – all right, they're having it away – and—'

'Evidence, DS Carrick?' Patrick interrupted.

'I won't be able to go back as a DS and you know it. OK, at lunchtime, one till two, when the place closes right down, they both got in his car and drove to somewhere not too far away and, judging by the way the vehicle bounced around, had pretty lively sex.'

'You were hiding up a tree?' Patrick hazarded.

'Shut up,' Joanna told him with a big smile. 'No, I just waited around out of sight as I had an idea that something was going on, followed them for part of the way and then, guessing where they were heading – it's a well-known screwing spot – parked on a hill opposite with a very good pair of binoculars I happen to keep in my car. Oh, and she's married.'

'Did you talk to her?' I asked.

'I did. Her name's Sarah Dutton and she's in her thirties. She gave me the hint, not being sufficiently intelligent to know it's important to conceal things like that, that she found Williams attractive. It was difficult to stop her talking on account of her being so excited about a mention in a magazine article. She told me that she's always had secretarial and office jobs and this is the best one so far as the pay's very good. This may be the case as she was wearing some expensive jewellery, more expensive than one might have expected actually. Perhaps her husband's very generous. Anyway, she's not a native of the West Country either as she was born not far from here, in South Woodford. Her father was in finance but due to hard times the family moved from there to Leytonstone. I got his name from her by asking if it was a local one – Harold Fletcher, so could be from anywhere – and again, that afternoon, asked James to check up on him. There have been quite a few Harold Fletchers with criminal records over the years but there was one who lived in South Woodford when he was arrested for fraud and embezzlement. He got five years. That must have been the hard times she mentioned and the wife had to sell up and move to somewhere cheaper.'

'And Sarah Dutton?' I queried. 'Any form?'

'As a teenager when she was still living at home she was had for shoplifting on a fairly large scale with a gang of other girls and was fined and sentenced to a Youth Rehabilitation Order. There's a brother too – Guy Fletcher. He's inside for aggravated burglary – a pensioner whose house he smashed his way into had a heart attack and died – and it's thought he has gang connections.'

'What about this woman's husband?' Patrick wanted to know.

'Sorry, I haven't got that far yet – I was concentrating on her and her father.'

'So you were endeavouring to track down this family.'

'They're not living at the address listed in Records. Only one of the neighbours had a vague recollection of them so they must have moved away some time ago.'

'Where does Sarah live now?'

'I didn't like to ask that.'

'And you were coming away from the Leytonstone housing estate when those three accosted you outside the pub.'

'That's right.'

'More coffee?'

'Please.'

Patrick poured some for her and gave her the milk jug. 'What we have to work out is whether there's any connection between what happened yesterday and the pile of replacement medical bits and bobs back at home. But to be on the safe side, Joanna, I don't think you ought to investigate anywhere near Leytonstone again on your own.'

'I'm inclined to agree with you. If I was on the job I'd be with at least one other colleague.'

'What about the sprog?' Patrick murmured.

'I managed to get a nanny at very short notice. She's a lady of a mature age and was about to retire, has been with a family for years that I've got to know locally but they no longer need her services. I told her Iona was no bother at all and she took the job, initially for six months.'

'Did she believe you?' I asked.

'No. She laughed. I have to say I liked her straight away – and, more importantly, so does Iona, which is lovely as she has no grandmothers.'

Patrick pensively stirred his coffee. 'Will you be really mad with me if I suggest you go home?'

'I somehow knew you were going to say that.' Joanna sighed. There was a little silence.

'Yes, all right,' Joanna then said. 'I have to do my application to rejoin the police at home as I have all the details there. And I can talk to James about what's happened here and poke around at that end.' She smiled. 'Look for Archie's body, perhaps.'

'Please take care,' I said.

*   *   *

We all made our statements, which took most of the morning. Regular police are never happy with the fact that Patrick is armed, never mind his wife as well, and the relevant authorizations had to be checked. Over breakfast we had agreed that there was absolutely no point in bringing up the subject of possibly dodgy cremations. Joanna had explained her presence in the area by saying that she was trying to trace the whereabouts of someone's family for a friend, which was hardly a lie.

'You remember what Dougie said?' Patrick remarked on the way back from seeing Joanna into a taxi on her way to Paddington railway station. '"One of them's sometimes just called JC. I think he's—" Could he have been about to say Irish? I'm wondering if it's Jinty O'Connor. The Met never seem to be able to get their hands on that particular mobster.'

'Did you mention that to the good officers of the law?' I enquired.

'No, it's just guesswork on my part.'

'Besides which, you want first bite if it is him.'

'Absolutely. Besides which, again . . .'

'Yes?' I prompted when he stopped speaking.

'I owe him.'

'What?'

'A bullet.'

'How's that?'

'He shot and killed a chum of mine when we were both very young cops, probationers. There was a raid on a nightclub where the management was suspected of involvement with drugs and he got him from almost point-blank range. But he escaped, did a runner and spent rather a long time abroad before coming back to this country under a false identity. O'Connor is the name he's using now but his real name's Patrick O'Leary. It's probably arrogance on his part that makes him still prefer to be called by his old nickname of Jinty. He might just be JC to the hired thugs.'

I knew this would have been when Patrick joined the police virtually from school. He left after his probationary period – it wasn't exciting enough – to sign on with the Devon and Dorset Regiment, now part of The Rifles.

'What was your friend's name?' I asked.

'David Bowman.'

'Were you there when he was shot?'

'No, I was on another job.'

'You haven't mentioned this to me before.'

'You don't have to bother people with all your sorrows, do you?'

'And O'Connor was a criminal *then*.'

'He'd probably been a criminal at primary school. What really makes him stand out is the sheer originality of his crimes. He once staple-gunned a bloke, dead, to his own front door. Other mobsters hire him to take care of their rivals in crime. Cremating them, or his own enemies, dead or alive, would be right in his back yard.'

This time the one with more imagination did not tingle so much as shudder.

A couple of minutes later Patrick's mobile rang. It was his boss, Michael Greenway.

'Would we care to pop into the office as we're not far away?' Patrick duly reported with a wry smile when the call had ended. 'No doubt he's heard about the postscript to our target practice yesterday.'

Despite all the administrative upheaval of SOCA now being part of the National Crime Agency, Greenway had told Patrick that he was still, very temporarily, using the same office at SOCA's one-time HQ. He, and we, are now working within the Organized Crime Command sector of the NCA, over which Richard Daws, Patrick's old boss at MI5, is in overall charge, although I get the distinct impression that his influence is spread widely through the whole set-up.

When we arrived, Greenway gave every impression of having been pacing around his room restlessly just before we walked in. 'Having a good break?' he asked without smiling, seating himself in his leather swivel chair. He's a big man – tall and broad shouldered, that is – and, as usual, it creaked loudly in protest.

'Perfectly peaceful and rejuvenating until yesterday, thank you,' Patrick replied disarmingly.

'There's hot gossip that you rescued DCI Carrick's wife from a garage where she'd been imprisoned by yobs,' Greenway went on, but clearly not believing a word of it.

'We did, but I don't think they'd shut her in there because they fancied a little fun later on.'

'No?'

'She *may* have unwittingly stirred up a mobster sewer inhabited by someone along the lines of Jinty O'Connor.'

'I think you ought to explain.'

'Why? I'm on holiday, this isn't an official case and I happen to know that you're snowed under with work.'

'Patrick, when you get involved in shoot-outs with mobsters and it's become an official case with the Met I *need* to know about it,' Greenway virtually snarled.

'OK,' Patrick agreed. 'It all goes back to a woman complaining to my father that after her husband was cremated she was handed a whole lot of hip replacements and similar stuff that hadn't been his.'

There was a rather long silence.

'Are you *sure* you want to know about this?' Patrick broke it by saying.

The commander has a collection of brightly coloured paper clips with which he makes patterns on his desk when he's thinking and which otherwise reside in a small antique Chinese bowl. Now he swept up those that were scattered around in front of him and tipped them back into it.

'Yes,' he said. 'I do.'

Patrick gave him the story, concisely but with every important detail. He is very good at this – army officers have to be. When he had finished the commander sat still, giving it thought, staring into space.

'It wouldn't be the first time,' he then murmured.

'What, the wrong bodies being cremated?' I exclaimed.

'Well, not that we know of, but there have been wrong bodies buried and people's late nearest and dearest turning up in strange places.'

'Yes, but that was the Mafia, in Italy,' Patrick said. 'Plenty of handy catacombs there.'

'There were a couple of cases in Victorian London where coffins were hijacked during the night and the rightful occupants chucked into the Thames,' Greenway recalled. 'Does this manager and his secretary have anything to do with it, d'you reckon? With what happened to Joanna, I mean.'

Patrick said, 'She was asking questions in the neighbourhood where the secretary's parents used to live. And, having been a cop, she has a forthright manner that screams the law or, at the very least, a private investigator because she's been one of those as well. And, as I've just said, she was asking about a guy, the secretary's father, who has, or had, a criminal record. We don't know if he's still alive. She, Sarah Dutton, has a criminal record for shoplifting, and it goes without saying that these people might be dangerous. The only way to find out is to make more enquiries.'

'But it sounds like one of those estates where a large proportion of the population have form,' Greenway countered.

'That too,' Patrick concurred. 'And I have to say that the men who abducted her were a little drunk and hanging around outside a pub.'

'So really, all we can do now is wait and see if the Met turn up anything. What you do at your end of the woods is your affair but I can only advise, frankly, that you tell this lady your investigations have come to nothing and forget it.'

It seemed best not to tell him that the Met had not been given the full story.

We agreed to follow part of Greenway's advice: go home and wait. There was no point in staying in London with no real leads and I, for one, would far rather be around if Joanna was delving into the problem of possible missing late not-very-lamenteds. This might have been something to do with what my father had described as my 'cat's whiskers', a certain intuition I have that also told me that there was something strange about Anne Peters.

As it was, she was soon back and banging on the rector's door. Elspeth was not at all happy about that as, quite rightly, she values their privacy. Patrick was called in to John's study again and gave her an edited version of what he had done so far and how his enquiries had come to nothing. She was not pleased and, rather rudely, left abruptly, saying she would contact the police. All Patrick could do was forewarn James Carrick with a request to give Joanna the news. Obviously her involvement had not been mentioned to the widow.

'Methinks the lady protests too much,' Patrick muttered after telling me what had transpired.

'Yes, but *why*?' I said. I had heard the annexe front door slam as the woman herself had gone out. So had Mark, woken from sleep in his pram in the garden nearby. 'Why is she making such a fuss? Is she really thinking her Archie's in a ditch somewhere? She seemed quite glad he was dead, so what's going on?'

'You don't like her, do you?'

'No, she sets my teeth on edge.'

'So if you switch on your oracle . . .' Patrick had picked up Vicky and was waltzing around the room with her, much to the child's delight.

'Oh, I shall go right over the top. You don't want to hear it.'

'Yes, I do.'

'All right. We really must answer the question of why she protests so much. She's angry. There's a lot of resentment there. I also get the impression she's frightened. It might be nothing to do with her husband but she seems bent on making trouble. She's that kind of woman and I'm convinced she really will go to the police. *If* there's a criminal angle to all this then she's probably part of it, or has been.'

'That's creative, Ingrid.'

'I know, right off the wall. But she might enjoy the prospect of the police tinkering at the edges of whatever scam it is, if it exists – get people really nervous.'

He seated himself and the pair cuddled Vicky's teddy bear. Then he said, 'How much money would you put on this theory?'

'Not much. I'm also wondering if she's acting.'

'Acting!'

'Yes, you know, one of those attention seekers and it's all hogwash. Either that or trying to cover herself, having been part of whatever it is.'

'I wonder if the woman has any form.'

There was no listing of anyone called Anne Peters who fitted the woman's age and description in Criminal Records.

A couple of evenings later, James Carrick called at the rectory on his way home from work. It is not on his direct route but only involves making a detour of a couple of miles. His visit was unusual insofar as if he wants a chat he usually suggests we meet at the local pub, the Ring o' Bells, this being more convenient for one very obvious reason.

'A dram?' Patrick asked, endeavouring to repair the damage.

'Thank you, but my conscience tells me to have half a dram,' the DCI replied. 'We have a big crackdown on drinking and driving right now and your drams are very generous.'

We were sitting in the conservatory, where the younger children are allowed to play only if supervised, Justin in particular not respecting his mother's collection of tender and semi-hardy plants. Having to research which of them might be poisonous if munched on by unknowing and curious youngsters has been a nightmare and I had ended up by having to give away a few that were iffy in that direction.

'Joanna's really getting into this Mrs Peters thing,' Carrick then said, sinking into one of the cane chairs. 'She's not saying much but I've a nasty feeling that she's poking around God knows where looking for the corpse.'

'But with what evidence?' I asked.

'No idea. As I said, she's not being forthcoming. I was wondering if – well, you'd have more success in finding out exactly what she's doing. To be honest, I'm getting really worried, especially after what happened last time.'

'She's probably worried that you're going to ask her to stop investigating if she tells you too much,' I pointed out.

'That had occurred to me.'

'And the Peters woman still hasn't made an official complaint?' Patrick put in.

'No.'

'But, on reflection, she must be realistic enough to know that her bag of bits and pieces isn't actually evidence that points towards a crime having been committed,' I said. 'And she can't know what happened to Joanna.'

Or, on the other hand . . . a little inner voice seemed to say.

Carrick was looking at us rather searchingly, which was probably the reason for Patrick saying, 'Suppose Ingrid asks her over for coffee one morning and just happens to mention it?'

'No,' I immediately objected. 'Joanna knows full well that I don't normally have people here for coffee as I don't have the time, and we do our socializing in the evenings. It would look odd. Why don't you both come to dinner on Saturday and we'll introduce the subject?'

'Well?' Joanna said when we were relaxing over coffee. And when everyone just looked at her, added: 'Isn't this all about finding out what I've been up to?'

'And of course for the pleasure of your company,' Patrick responded with a big smile but avoided my eye. I had told him that I was sure she would suspect there was a hidden agenda.

'When James just *pops in* to see you on the way home from work and comes back with an invitation, having been pestering me for days about what I'm doing . . .' She beamed at us all and then laughed out loud.

Patrick handed over a box of chocolates as a peace offering. 'As far as I'm concerned please don't feel obliged to say anything if you don't want to.'

'Oh, but it's interesting and I didn't find out one of the best bits until this afternoon.' She took a chocolate and bit into it, giving him a little wave by way of thanks.

'I really hope you haven't been trawling around in lonely places,' fretted her husband.

'No. Today I was in the public library actually.'

'Public records?' I guessed.

'Sort of – back numbers of the local paper. But to start at the beginning, I thought I'd find out where Anne Peters lives. I drove to Wellow – as you know it's all of ten minutes from where we live – and asked at the pub. The girl behind the bar was a foreign student and didn't know but then I was lucky and spotted a man delivering gas bottles. He told me that she lives at a hamlet about a quarter of a mile down the road at what used to be a small market garden. He delivers both coal and gas bottles there. He said that the land had been sold off quite recently and built on, and local people had been furious about it as several fine protected trees had been cut down.'

'Was that the Peterses?' James asked.

'Well, him anyway. I was just going to tell you about that.'

'Sorry. Do go on.'

'They were fined and she's still pretty unpopular apparently.

But you know what village life is like – people still winge on about things that happened generations ago.'

'There be nuthin' loike a good sloice of ferret pie,' Patrick said in a broad Somerset accent.

'Oh, please don't start on that,' I begged, laughing, remembering all too well him transfixing the public bar of a village pub with his 'recipe' for this non-existent rural delicacy.

'Anyway,' Joanna continued loudly, displaying a hint of her one-time DS mailed-fist manner, 'it turned out to be a run-down bungalow almost surrounded by the newish, much more attractive ones. Rather handily, one was for sale, so I pretended to write down the agent's details and it gave me the excuse to have a look around. A man was clipping the hedge in the front garden of another house so I wandered over and asked him what it was like living there. He said it was very quiet. He sounded like a local so I then asked him if he remembered the market garden and he told me that his father had worked there and, as a boy, he'd spent a lot of time there in the school holidays. So coming back evoked old memories and he was carrying on growing the chrysanthemums his father had excelled at. The place was owned by people called Robertson in those days, who he said grew wonderful produce, and it was sold to a couple he couldn't remember the name of when Mr Robertson had to give up due to arthritis. They sold it to Mr Peters. He went on to say that he thought the man had only bought it with a view to selling the land off for housing – it had been turned into paddocks for horses – and he was glad he couldn't see *her* house from his.'

'She wasn't too popular with him either then,' Carrick mused.

'Neither of them were, although – and this is a bit odd but there must be a perfectly simple explanation – no one can remember seeing the woman when Mr Peters first moved in. Archie, as you say she refers to him as, was downright nasty. But my confidant did hasten to say that people made excuses for him on account of his being very ill. I gathered, though, that there was relief all round when he died. According to people who live in the village itself, it was a very quiet funeral, hardly anyone there. Then he hesitated a bit before saying that he hoped I didn't think the people round there were a nosy and gossiping lot but the woman who lived in the bungalow that was for sale had said that she thought how strange it was, seeing that no one appeared to have stayed with Mrs Peters the night before the funeral and hardly anyone turned up, that the coffin had been placed in the house overnight.' Joanna surveyed our faces. 'I thought you'd like that.'

'I take it then that the place for sale has good views of Mrs Peters's place,' Patrick said as we soaked up the implications and possibilities of this.

'Yes, it's next door on the Wellow side. And there's something else. Quite shortly after the funeral last month – and obviously, there might be absolutely no connection – one of the partners of the firm of undertakers was killed in a road accident.'

Both upholders of the law looked at one another and Carrick said, 'I remember now. It happened in a lane that joins the A36 in the Bradford on Avon area, which, as you know, is just over the border in Wiltshire. That meant that our Wiltshire colleagues investigated. I seem to remember that his car left the road and went into a tree. No other vehicles were involved. It burst into flames and he was only formally identified from dental records.'

'No one was else in the vehicle with him?' Patrick wondered.

'No. Was it mentioned when you made enquiries at the firm?'

'No.'

'But there's no reason why they should have done, really. Very sad but these things happen.'

'I agree, but it's a neat way of getting rid of someone.'

Joanna said, 'If Mrs Peters was complicit in anything illegal that took place – and surely she must know what went on in her own home – then why has she brought it to your father's attention, Patrick?'

'Perhaps she didn't get paid,' I said.

FIVE

A ll this was mere conjecture, and Joanna agreed that she could not proceed further with that particular line of enquiry as she had no mandate to do so. Probably as a consolation and acutely worried that his other half might now hurtle off and search old barns, derelict silage and slurry pits in the middle of nowhere for Archie's corpse, Carrick promised her that he would contact someone he knew at Wiltshire Police's HQ in Devizes to discover a few facts about the death of the funeral director.

'No crime has been committed,' Patrick muttered to himself later that night when our guests had departed, we had cleared up and were getting ready for bed. 'No one's made a formal complaint. There's not the merest hint that serious crime's involved. I shall just have to set up a grass-cutting empire instead.'

'You usually make things happen,' I told him, remembering his determination to catch up with Jinty O'Connor.

'Such as?'

'Question Mrs Peters about the night before the funeral. She started all this off and is demanding results. Turn the tables on her and get a look inside the house.'

'I might just do that.'

I gazed at him, my man with his rangy frame, dark wavy hair going a little grey, those wonderful eyes – a sort of slightly taller Paul McGann – and said, 'Meanwhile, you could make red hot love to me.'

He subsided into bed. 'Tell me why you always get really randy when I've been splitting logs all day.'

I snuggled up and gently massaged his chest, working downwards. 'It's seeing your muscles rippling and the way the axe slices through the wood. It's dead sexy.'

He snorted with derisive laughter and commenced to kiss me silly.

* * *

'It's a family tradition to have the coffin in the house the previous night,' said Anne Peters, obviously very put out by our visit. 'Goes back a long way. Besides, what business is it of yours?'

Patrick stared at the woman in amazement. 'I would like to remind you that you have made it my business. You have also been rather rudely banging on my parents' front door and demanding answers. Or is this some kind of stupid hoax because you enjoy making trouble?'

'Of course not!'

'Well, I'm trying to find those answers for you. There only appears to be one lapse in security in the series of events surrounding your husband's funeral and that is the fact that the coffin was here, in this house, overnight.'

'How do you know that?'

'Investigating things involves asking questions. Who else was here besides you?'

'Er . . . no one.'

It was a little after ten the following morning and we had called without making an appointment, a certain bloody-mindedness having set in. I had been determined to go along as I was finding the whole affair fascinating, material for novels notwithstanding. As I had expected from both its owner and the outside appearance of the bungalow – which was almost hidden from the road by a wildly out-of-control hedge – the interior was fusty and in dire need of redecoration. The airless living room into which we had been shown was furnished with a brown Dralon three-piece suite that matched the carpet, a coffee table with a Formica top and a couple of other items: a bookcase and bureau that could have been utility pieces and were so old they might have belonged to her grandparents during the last war. The 'ornaments' on the mantelpiece of the fireplace surrounding a drab gas fire consisted of a small pair of brass candlesticks, tarnished, a plastic frame holding a black-and-white photo of a couple on their wedding day, the fashions suggesting the 1940s – the said grandparents perhaps – and a group of three pottery dogs of different sizes painted a bilious shade of green.

'Just you and the coffin,' Patrick was saying. 'Where, in here?'

'No, in the dining room, always the dining room,' Mrs Peters replied, sounding shocked.

'Show me.'

Flustered, she led the way down to the end of the short hallway into which we had first stepped and into a room slightly smaller than where we had come from. The table and four chairs were more utility-type furniture, and to one side of the room was an unbelievably old brown leather sofa with the horsehair bottom dropping out, and a bent standard lamp with a fringed shade lowering over it like a vulture in a tree waiting for something on the ground underneath it to die.

'All this got moved to the sides of the room,' Mrs Peters explained, gesturing impatiently towards the table and chairs.

Patrick went over to examine the catches on the aluminium windows and returned with an impatient shake of his head. 'Anyone could have got in here. Did you notice if any of these windows had been left open the next morning?'

'No, but I'd opened one of the top ones as it was rather warm in here.'

'It was even easier then, as someone could have reached in and opened one of the others. Were there any signs of disturbance?'

'No.'

'Why didn't you mention before that the coffin was in here overnight?'

'Why should I mention it? It's a perfectly normal thing to do.'

'Surely it must have occurred to you afterwards that if anyone tampered with the coffin that was the perfect opportunity.'

'I've never thought of anything like that. It happened somewhere else or I'd have heard noises during the night, wouldn't I? As I said, some kind of fiddle's going on.'

Patrick turned away from her dismissively to open one of the large lower windows and looked out, examining the ground below it. 'The plants in the border here are flattened as though they've been trodden on,' he said over his shoulder.

'Oh dear. I hadn't noticed that. You mean someone could have . . .' She floundered to a halt.

I found myself wondering whether this woman was monumentally stupid, as mad as a spanner or actually quite clever and we were being presented with a stinking red herring.

'I don't think I personally can help you any more with this,'

Patrick told her, closing the window. 'But there might be grounds for you to take your concerns to the local police.'

'I was under the impression that you *were* a policeman,' Mrs Peters protested.

'I am. But I normally work in London trying to catch serious criminals.' He flicked a little smile in my direction; I took the hint and we left.

'We really wrong-footed her,' I commented when we were back in the car. 'Her default position seems to be damned rude.'

'We'll come back – tonight. I want to have a look in those sheds in the garden.'

To call the open space to the rear of the house a garden was paying it a huge compliment as it consisted of little more than rough grass, overgrown and weed-filled borders and a couple of ancient apple trees, the whole area enclosed by brick walls in a poor state of repair. Patrick had noted, as he looked out of the dining-room window, that there were two sheds: one quite large, around fifteen feet by ten, and an older, smaller one at right angles to it; the former near the house facing the garden, the other at the far end facing the house, both on the right-hand side. The one near the house appeared to be nearly new, the other much older.

There was no good reason for me to tag along but Patrick made no objection to my doing so even though I have the unfortunate habit of succumbing to the giggles when creeping around in the dark on surveillance and search missions. I can only blame my imagination.

'It's really important that she doesn't hear us,' Patrick muttered in my ear as we got out of the car parked in a lay-by several hundred yards away on the Wellow side from our target, perhaps speaking with my weakness in mind.

It was just before one a.m. and fully dark – there were no street lights here – the sky partly clouded over, just a few stars visible, no moon. We were dressed in our navy-blue tracksuits that hopefully made us almost invisible, and carried matching balaclavas. Going down a little track that led through the trees at the side of the road which Patrick had noted earlier, we stood silently for a couple of minutes to allow our eyes to grow accustomed to the darkness. All we would have was Patrick's little 'burglar's torch' to pick out any obstacles. A couple of cars

whooshed passed on the road but we were out of the range of
the headlights.

'If you remember, there's a short distance to be covered where
there's no choice but to walk along the road,' Patrick informed
me. 'If you hear a car coming, lie face down on the verge.'

'Dog poo,' I moaned.

'Can't be helped.' He then chuckled. 'Sorry, I'm joking. Just
don't let anyone see your face.'

'I shall run anyway.'

'Please yourself. Stop when you get to the postbox.'

'How far is it?'

'About as far as you can run flat out without having to slow
down.'

Having run a hell of a long way in the past when pursued by
mobsters, I staunchly made no comment and, as soon as we
emerged and I had listened carefully for several moments, I tore
off. Sure enough, just as I was getting seriously out of breath,
no cars, I made out the post box a few feet in front of me set in
a stone wall, which just goes to show what adrenaline can do
for you. Patrick strolled up not twenty seconds later, still no cars.

'You jogged down there somewhere,' I panted.

He chuckled again and gently cuffed my shoulder.

Patrick had carried out a reconnoitre on the return journey that
morning while I waited in the car, and now turned sharp right
into a narrow lane between houses, or rather between the walls
bordering the wooded grounds of two large houses. It was very
dark here but I could just see him outlined against something
lighter ahead. This turned out to be a side gate painted white
where the lane turned left. We left the walls behind and walked
between fields. I started when a horse grazing near the fence to
our right snorted in alarm and galloped off. We stopped, listening,
but nothing happened so we walked on.

I already knew that the small estate of bungalows, covering
what was once the market garden, jutted into one of these fields,
suggesting that a far larger area of land had belonged to the
previous owners. Perhaps their descendants still owned it. I
thought that the fact these properties virtually surrounded the
house owned by Mrs Peters would be a problem for us, as was
the possibility of there being dogs.

My arm was taken and I was guided round to the left towards what proved to be a gate. We climbed over it and went down a gentle slope, emerging on what had to be the same road. Twin searchlights approached as a vehicle came towards us around a bend, and we both flung ourselves into an overgrown hedge.

Our guardian angels must be smiling on us tonight: no thorns.

A single street light half hidden by the foliage of trees hardly illuminated a crossroads some fifty yards away and affected us not at all, although one of the bungalows nearest to the road, which turned out to be the one for sale, had an exterior lamp switched on by the front door. By the light from it we found the entrance into Mrs Peters's front garden. As we had discovered that morning, the gate was either missing or buried somewhere in the all-pervading hedge. There were no lights at the front of the house.

Patrick switched on his tiny pencil-beamed torch again to illuminate anything we might trip over and we made our way down the side of the house. My trained-to-burgle companion, I knew, had made a mental map of the layout indoors on his previous visit, and I too had noticed, through doors that were open, signs of present use within, and that her bedroom was at the back. Emerging into the open space at the rear, we saw that there were no lights on here either.

I almost fell over then, having to grab hold of Patrick's shoulder, when a cat, black and even more invisible than we were, came from nowhere and commenced to rub around my legs, purring. I spent a few moments stroking it, hoping that it would then be satisfied and go away. Otherwise, I had an idea I would be falling over it for the duration of our stay.

We moved on, the cat happily chasing Patrick's tiny torch beam along a path of sorts, forcing us to walk very slowly. We went the full length of the garden, quite a long way, to the smaller of the two sheds, which proved to be more dilapidated than it had looked from a distance. The door was padlocked but the wood into which the hinged hasp had been fixed was rotten. It was comparatively easy for Patrick to prise out the screws with a little tool on the ring with his set of skeleton keys. These are fine for old-fashioned locks but not most modern ones.

I was only partly aware of this going on as I had my back to him, keeping watch. Then, nudged, I moved aside as he opened the door. It juddered on its hinges as though it might fall off them at any moment and then there were a few seconds silence as he gazed within.

'Well?' I hissed.

'Nothing, rusty garden tools, an ancient push mower, two deckchairs, an old bike, a rotary washing line, stuff on shelves – the usual junk sheds are filled with.'

'For heaven's sake, don't let the cat go in there.'

'It's already tried. You shut the door.'

This I did, and then realized that it was in his arms, still purring. He put it down and made as good a job of re-securing the door as possible.

We went back to the first shed which we already knew was in much better condition. Not only that, it was only a matter of yards from Mrs Peters's bedroom window, which, luckily, was closed. But the shed had stable-style doors with padlocked bolts top and bottom.

'No,' Patrick whispered and investigated the side nearest the garden, forcing his way into a shrub of some kind that was growing up against it. I fretted – no, sweated – at the slight sounds he was making, then jumped out of my skin when there was the snarling and shrieking mother of all cat fights somewhere behind us, flinging myself into the bush Patrick had already disappeared in.

Seconds later, a window was flung open and a woman's voice shouted, 'Bloody cats! Sod off!' There was the sound of something heavy crashing into the plants and this was followed by a wildly aimed rain of objects, one of which landed on the shed roof, tumbled down and hit me. Perhaps a shoe with a sharp heel, I thought inconsequentially, rubbing my head and hoping the old cow would go back to bed. Patrick must have grabbed the shoe, for when the next missile landed he broke a window that I could not see, timing tapping out some more glass as there was one last short barrage of the contents of the room before the window was slammed shut.

'Surely she was *drunk*!' I whispered into the leaves.

'You'll never guess what's in here.'

'What?'

'Coffins.'

*   *   *

'*Coffins?*' James Carrick said incredulously. 'D'you reckon there was anything in them?'

'Or anyone?' Patrick said, pulling a face. 'Probably not as they were standing on end, not laid flat.'

'How many were there?'

'Seven or eight – they looked brand new too. But not polished, just plain wood – pine, probably.'

'Bloody hell,' the DCI muttered. 'But it isn't illegal to have that kind of thing at home.'

'No, of course not. But it's odd in the circumstances.'

'She might just be storing them for the local undertaker.'

'Oh, get real! When did funeral directors farm out that kind of thing to people's garden sheds?'

'You must know that I still can't do anything.'

'I don't want anyone to do anything – I'm just providing a little interesting info over a friendly pint.'

They held their tankards aloft in silent acknowledgement of this.

Joanna joined us – it was the following evening and, for a change, we were at their local pub. Her husband went to the bar to fetch her a drink.

'You've bruised your forehead,' she said to me sympathetically.

I explained what had happened, then finished by saying, 'But at least Patrick was able to use the shoe to break the window. I can't imagine them being hers unless she's kept them from her teenage years.'

'As ammo for the local cats?' Patrick suggested.

'Has James told you that he checked up on Sarah Dutton's husband?' Joanna enquired in an undertone.

'The manager's secretary at the crem?' I said. 'No.'

'He's a Londoner, name of Paul Dutton, and from the same area where she lived when she was younger – Woodford. He's not squeaky clean – was had up for dangerous driving some years ago after the driver of another car was forced off the road and through a hedge. Fortunately the other man wasn't injured but his car was a write-off. There was also another charge of driving while not insured.'

'Doesn't add up to serious crime,' Carrick said, returning with a glass of white wine.

'Giant oaks from little acorns . . .' I murmured.

'Anyone in the car with Dutton?' Patrick went on to ask Joanna.

'Records didn't say.'

'Any theories about where the late Archie's remains might have ended up?'

'No, not yet. I've been trying to track down missing people, or criminals, who had survived car crashes or similar but suffered serious head injuries. It's a waste of time bothering with the hip replacement side of things as quite a large percentage of the population over sixty has them. Also, as you know, one only has knowledge of people who have gone missing if someone tells the police.'

'Quite,' Patrick agreed. 'And as far as mobsters go that's the last people to inform if they've been tidied away somehow. Any luck?'

'I've a list of three possibles on the missing person's register and have written down the names. Two are female. One was in her seventies and in a nursing home due to dementia brought on, it was thought, by her having survived a plane crash in which she was badly injured. She walked out one night from the home in Weston-super-Mare, and despite searches being made was never found. Who knows? She could have just walked into the sea. I don't think she's of interest to us.

'The other woman, who lived in London, had been shot in the head during an attack by terrorists while on holiday in Egypt. She subsequently underwent surgery and had largely recovered although, according to a neighbour, she suffered from bouts of depression and was sometimes suicidal. Perhaps that was the reason for her disappearance – she went out one day and didn't come back. She's interesting insofar as she had a criminal record – for trafficking young women from Poland and Romania for prostitution. That appears to have come to a stop after her holiday disaster.'

'That *is* interesting,' James said. 'And the man?'

'He's an army officer who was invalided out of the Royal Engineers after being severely injured in a road accident when the Land Rover he was travelling in rolled off a track and ended up upside down in a gully during a training exercise. It happened quite a while ago. The driver was only slightly injured but the major had multiple fractures and serious head injuries from which he almost died. He recovered, after a fashion but, according to his family, his character changed completely and, after a while, he suffered from arthritis and had hip replacements. Not long after this his mental health went and he became a virtual dropout. He ended up living rough and consorting with what his family described as 'undesirables' and they, of course, were at their wits' end by this time. Finally, after several months had gone by, they gave up trying to track him down themselves and he just disappeared. That ticks quite a few boxes.'

I could completely understand this anxiety, living as I do with an ex-army officer who sometimes lives rough, very, and consorts with undesirables in the course of his job.

'I think I might have heard about that,' Patrick said thoughtfully. 'Where was he living rough?'

'London, plus round and about. They lived in Staines. Which, as I don't think the woman who was shot in Egypt is a possible even though trafficking is a serious crime and she might have been the target of a mobster, leaves criminals,' Joanna continued. 'I asked James to check up on that.' This last remark with a broad smile in his direction.

'And I haven't had time.' Her husband sighed.

'I'll do it, if you like,' Patrick offered. 'Through the NCA's files.'

I said, 'We haven't really thought about kidnap victims where the ransom hadn't been paid or someone off their head but with no criminal record starting up this racket targeting people with no criminal records who they just don't happen to like. If there even *is* a racket.'

'It's endless when you think about it,' Joanna concluded dismally.

A fire engine howled passed on the main road nearby and then the pub windows rattled as an explosion followed not all that far away.

Patrick, who, it goes without saying, is inured to things that go bang, muttered, 'Those bloody coffins have gone up,' and we all laughed until we practically cried.

They had.

More correctly, the site of the explosion had been the bungalow, the resulting blaze spreading to the shed nearest to it and threatening neighbouring properties, some of which had been slightly damaged by the blast. By the time the fire brigade had arrived, the crew by a miracle escaping serious injury, the whole place was an inferno. They had been called out by the woman whose home was for sale – now with two broken windows and some missing roof tiles – she having spotted smoke coming from an open window before the explosion occurred.

The fire took over twenty-four hours to cool sufficiently in order to allow investigating fire officers to ascertain the cause and discover if anyone had been in the house at the time. At first there was no sign of the owner, and enquiries nearby did not result in any clue as to her whereabouts that night as she spoke to hardly anyone and never, to people's knowledge, entertained. It was only on the following day when it was possible to rake and sift through the ash and wreckage that fragments of human bones and what were described as 'small body parts' were found in several areas beneath the timbers and the remaining slates of the roof, which had collapsed. Work continuing the next day and a blackened skull was found in the general area of the kitchen. It had two bullet holes in the forehead, most of the back of the cranium blasted away.

'Murder,' James Carrick had said over the phone to Patrick, having given him this information the morning after the find. 'Do you happen to know if she had any children? Officially identifying the remains will be hellish difficult if we don't have a DNA sample to compare them with.'

'No, sorry,' Patrick had said. 'No idea.'

'It looks as though she finally made an official complaint,' the DCI had then remarked with typical Scottish pragmatism. 'I'm away to the scene of the crime if you're interested in meeting me there.'

'Why did the killer advertise it as murder?' I said to Patrick once he had told me the news. 'Why shoot the woman when all they had to do was strangle or smother her before setting the house on fire?'

'And was the explosion caused by the gas bottles we know she used or something a bit more meaningful?' Patrick responded. 'Coming?'

SIX

I found myself gaping at the devastation, the twin chimney stack, three outer and a couple of interior walls the only things left standing. The road was closed while investigations continued, police incident tape everywhere. It would have had to be closed to traffic anyway as it was covered with torn-off branches and vegetation, together with the slates, bricks and other masonry that were not piled up on the tattered remnants of the front hedge, which appeared to have taken the full force of the blast. I fervently hoped that the black cat did not belong to Mrs Peters and had been safely somewhere else at the time. Somehow I thought it had another home – it was too well fed, its fur too silky to be hers. Anyway, she hated cats, didn't she? I agonized a bit over this.

Carrick, whose presence signified the seriousness with which the crime was being regarded, was with a couple of members of the fire brigade investigation team, standing just outside what had been the front door. Having introduced us to the others he went on to say that, following a change of mind due to the state of the building, no one was permitted to re-enter the blackened ruin until a structural surveyor had examined it. He apologized for calling us out for nothing.

'It looks OK but there's nothing supporting that wall over there,' Carrick finished by saying, pointing. Then, to Patrick in particular, 'First impressions?'

'Explosives,' was his instant verdict. 'Probably plastic, like Semtex.'

'There'll be not a crumb of evidence,' Carrick said, shaking his head.

DI David Campbell came down the path at the side of the house, followed by DS Lynn Outhwaite, Carrick's assistant. The latter gave us a big smile, while Campbell merely nodded in our direction. He's like that.

'Nothing to see,' Campbell reported with a shrug. 'Just a shed with a broken window at the far end of the garden. The poor woman and her house were blasted from the face of the earth and I guess the only possible way she can be identified is from her dental records.'

'I'll try and find out who her dentist was,' Lynn offered, and, as no response came from Campbell, Carrick thanked her and asked her to make a start.

There seemed to be no point in commenting that as Mrs Peters's husband had not bothered with dental treatment she might not have done so either. Also, I had an idea Campbell didn't know the tale of the dodgy cremation, and it was not my business to enlighten him.

'And there are some flattened plants under a window at the back,' Campbell went on to say. 'As though someone tried to get in that way.'

'I'll take a look in a minute,' Carrick promised.

Patrick asked if we could have a look round at the rear of the house.

'Go ahead,' the DCI said. 'Just don't lean on that wall.'

The shed near the house was a just a pile of wood ash, the air flowing down the narrow path blowing it on to the overgrown, now scorched and littered with detritus, grass that had once been a lawn. A window catch was visible in the still-smouldering heap, together with one of the hinges from the door.

'Our cop friends are right,' Patrick said quietly. 'There'll be precious little evidence left on this bombsite. The answers will lie elsewhere.'

'What about those damaged plants?' I queried. 'You noticed those on our first visit.'

We went over and had a look.

'It's not firing me up,' Patrick concluded as we stared at some squashed greenery, mostly weeds. 'I don't think anyone got in this way as there weren't any marks on the window ledge or frame here and none inside. No muddy marks on the carpet either. Surely, if there had been she would have left them there as evidence.'

'But she's insisting it all happened somewhere else,' I pointed out.

'Why though?' He straightened. 'This whole place gives me the creeps.'

Our shoes crunching on broken glass, we made our way down the path past a hedge that separated the wreck of what had obviously been a vegetable garden from the area nearer the house. As Campbell had observed, one of the windows of the shed was broken but the flames had not reached this far.

'Were you wearing gloves the other night when we came here?' I asked in a whisper.

Patrick turned. 'Of course.'

'Only it would be a bit embarrassing if your fingerprints were found here.'

'I'm not sure that scenes of crime people have got this far yet.' He donned a pair of evidence protection gloves – we always carry them – and opened the door the same way that he had previously, saying, 'I'm wondering why only one window's broken, and only part of the pane at that. Perhaps something small and heavy like a stone or piece of slate came over the hedge. But it's quite a way from the house.' He bent down. 'On the other hand . . .'

'This only happens on TV detective shows!' I exclaimed when I leaned over and saw what he was now looking at.

'When the ex-MI5 hero outwits all the cops and finds the murder weapon,' Patrick said with a chuckle. 'God, they'll hate me. Shall I shut the door again and say nothing?'

'No!'

'I'm not serious.' He smiled reflectively. 'No, this is a once in a lifetime thing and I'm going to enjoy it.'

We returned to the others, Lynn having left, the other four still talking.

Patrick said, 'Gentlemen, you might like to consider as evidence the Beretta M9 lying on rubbish on the floor of the shed at the far end of the garden. As you must know, they're issued to US forces, so it's most probably stolen.'

They wouldn't know.

Keeping our faces straight and leaving at least two gaping mouths in our wake, we said goodbye and went in the direction of our car. As we passed the bungalow that was for sale a woman called to us from the front door.

'Excuse me, are you the police?'

'Sort of,' Patrick responded.

'May I have a word with you?'

We made our way around there.

'I'm very worried about the damage to my house,' she continued as we walked up the front path. 'I shall have to take photographs to send to my insurance company but how do I prove anything?'

Patrick said, 'The police will give you an incident number – the number the case will be known by, and also the name of the investigating officer. You quote those on your claim. That's all you need to do when you fill in the form and send it with the photos.'

'Do I have to talk to someone else at the police station – phone up?'

'No. I'll make sure you receive the relevant information.'

'Thank you, you're really kind. I was very lucky as the broken windows are in the utility room and spare bedroom. There was glass everywhere in there.'

'Those are the windows on the side of your house.'

'That's right.'

'You called the fire brigade, didn't you?'

'Yes, I did. There was black smoke coming from a window over there. I saw the smoke first rising over the hedge and had to walk round to see where it was actually coming from.'

'So which window was it?'

'The one to the left of the front door. The top window, you understand, not a bigger lower one.'

'Were there any lights on indoors?'

'Not that I could see at the front and I didn't go round the back. It was only just starting to get dark so she might not have needed one, although I have to say the house always looked very dim and gloomy. Does anyone know if Mrs Peters was there at the time?'

'Not officially. But human remains have been found.'

The woman, in her fifties perhaps, plump and kindly looking, clapped both hands to her face. 'Oh, dear, how terrible.' She went on: 'I know it's a daft thing to say but I had a horrible feeling about that smoke. I ran back here to the phone and Henry dashed in and hid under my bed just before the explosion. He spends a lot of time in that garden as it's like a jungle over there.'

'Your cat?' I queried.

'Yes. He's black so it must have brought him luck. He could have been killed!'

'Had you seen or heard any cars there prior to all this happening?' Patrick asked.

'I didn't notice any. But I'd heard voices about half an hour before. Oh, and a couple of bangs, but there was often banging going on over there. Fred, next door, said he reckoned she threw things in a temper. Someone told me – not idle gossip mind – that she used to throw things at Archie.'

'These voices . . . were they men's? Did you hear anything that was said?'

'Yes, men's. A bit of shouting but I couldn't make out anything and it could have been the TV for all I knew. I was bringing a blanket off the washing line, you see, and anyway, I don't try to overhear what the neighbours are saying.'

'No, of course not. Did Mrs Peters have a car?'

'They had one when Archie was alive but she must have sold it as I haven't seen it lately. Perhaps she couldn't drive. The bus service isn't that good so, personally, I'd hate to have to rely on it.'

'I take it that you didn't really know this lady.'

'I didn't, for the very good reason that she kept herself to herself and made it perfectly plain she had no time for anyone.'

'Did she have *any* friends?'

'Not that I know of. You could ask Kenneth, the new curate at the church. He might be able to help you with that.'

We thanked her and left.

'Result,' I murmured. 'We found what is probably the murder weapon and Henry's all right.'

'Why chuck it in the shed, though? It was bound to be discovered.'

'Not a clue.'

We decided to leave questioning anyone else locally to the investigating officers.

'It's reasonable to assume that Mrs Peters is dead,' Patrick said when we had called in back home for some lunch. 'It's also fairly safe to think that she endeavoured to blow the whistle on someone and they've shut her up. As the only people she spoke to about it, as far as we know, are the curate, Dad and us, how did whoever it was know she'd blabbed?'

'She could have told them she was going public,' I hazarded. 'But started in a very small way.'

'Which means, if you're right – and I have to say you're very consistent on this – that she was part of some scam or other and was threatening to tell all for some reason or other. You've already suggested it was about money and, let's face it, crime nearly always has money in there somewhere. What else should we factor in?'

'The fact that we and Kenneth might be next on the death list, for a start. Not to mention your father.'

After a short pause while he thought about it, Patrick said, 'I'm of the view that she didn't tell them exactly *who* she was going to inform, or had told. If she'd said she was going to the local church about it they would have laughed in her face. If she'd mentioned the police they'd have just got very angry. They did.'

I had to admit that there was some logic in this. And right now, Patrick's excellent grasp of the criminal mind – male, that is – was all I had by way of reassurance. It would have to suffice. But, nevertheless, the woman had told someone *respectable*, a handy detail to have in the bag in the event of having to appear in a court of law.

As it stood right now, nothing really made sense.

To keep him in the picture, Patrick emailed Commander Greenway with the latest developments, without comment, and we went back to living everyday life. The explosion at a quiet hamlet in the West Country made the national media, provoking a dialogue on the safety of using gas bottles. Avon and Somerset Police, meanwhile, and for the time being, did not provide the general public with details about the finding of any weapons, or the fact that the investigation was now a murder inquiry, keeping their thoughts to themselves.

Until, that is . . .

'It's not her,' said James Carrick's voice one evening several days later when I answered Patrick's mobile in our bedroom, he being in the shower.

'Not Mrs Peters!' I exclaimed.

'No. Lynn managed to track down her dentist and he was sent photos of the upper and lower jaws of the skull found in the kitchen area. It's definitely not her. Not only that, it's the skull of a male. I won't bother you with all the scientific stuff about measurements and ratios. But it's that of a bloke, elderly, with very poor teeth. He had suffered from abcesses in them that had eaten right into the bone.'

'Yuck,' I muttered.

Carrick continued, 'Having finally been able to get into the shell of the building, forensics have come up with something interesting too. Some bod on the team, ex-military, reckons that the explosives were actually placed on the deceased either before or after he was shot, and detonated there. Although there were fragments of scorched human remains everywhere in what had been the living room, the fact that the head was on its own in the kitchen area bears him out, as when suicide bombers who have explosives attached to their bodies blow themselves up the head can end up as much as forty yards away.'

I was beginning to wish Patrick had taken the call.

'Are you still there?' the DCI asked anxiously.

I told him I was.

'This is beginning to sound like one of your plots,' the DCI went on. 'And David's gone off on a week's course to HQ. As you were involved with this first, would you and Patrick be interested in giving me your thoughts on it tomorrow morning at the nick, or have you something else planned?'

'One moment,' I said, observing Patrick just emerging from the shower, a bathrobe not quite wrapped around himself. The state-of-the-art replacement for the lower part of his right leg is not designed to get really wet so he was, of necessity, hopping on the other and steadying himself by holding on to things. I relayed the suggestion and he readily agreed.

'I simply can't believe he's actually asking for our opinion when the case isn't officially anything to do with us,' Patrick said with a laugh when the call had ended. 'It's a first. I shall have a tot to toast all proud Caledonian cops.'

I gave him the rest of the information.

'So who the hell was in the bungalow?' he responded, staggered, which was unusual for him.

'An old man with bad teeth?' I said. 'It could have been Archie.'

'Oh, for God's sake, Ingrid!'

*   *   *

'This bangs quite a few theories on the head – if you'll forgive my choice of words,' said James Carrick. 'There appears to be only one set of human remains in the house, something that initial DNA findings have confirmed. The skull is that of an elderly male, identity unknown and, I've a nasty feeling, likely to remain that way. We can ask for a reconstruction to be done but as you know it's very expensive and I think that should only be done as a last resort.'

He had provided coffee in his office on the top floor and we now shifted our chairs slightly to make room for Lynn Outhwaite, who had just arrived.

'The Beretta M9 handgun found in the shed had no fingerprints on it,' she said to Patrick. 'And as you may have noticed, there was no magazine – it was empty.'

'Yes, I did,' he replied. 'Have any ejected cartridge cases been found inside the ruins of the house? On second thoughts, it's unlikely they'd have survived as they would have probably melted in the heat.'

'Not yet. It'll take a while to sift through all the debris – there's tons of it because of the roof slates. They had to wait until a contractor erected scaffolding so that a builder could stabilize that dangerous outer wall.'

Patrick said, 'How a weapon issued to US Armed Forces ended up there is baffling and one can only assume that, originally, it was stolen. The manufacturer might have no bearing on the case at all and it's simply a gun purchased from an illegal supplier.'

'How easy is that around here?' Carrick asked him.

'No idea, and I think you're fishing in case I know more than you do,' Patrick answered with a smile. 'I can only speak with regard to London, where it's very easy indeed.'

'This was research you were carrying out?' Lynn enquired, all innocence. It is important to point out here that Lynn, in her late-twenties, dark haired and petite, is very clever. Carrick is pushing for her promotion; partly, I know, because he wants to get rid of Campbell as, in this instance, two Scots a bannock didn't bake.

Patrick wagged a finger at her. 'Actually, no.'

She did not ask any more questions, which was perhaps just as well.

'Any ideas, Ingrid?' Carrick asked.

'Well, it doesn't appear that, ding, dong, the witch is dead,' I replied. 'Unless the man who was blown up was her boyfriend, she'd just popped out for something and they shot her with the remainder of the fifteen shots in the magazine when she got back, planted the explosives on the boyfriend, having shot him too, and left, taking her blooded-boltered corpse with them.'

Three pairs of eyes stared at me.

Carrick laughed softly and Patrick said, 'Look, I know you love being flippant sometimes but—'

I butted in with, 'I can distinctly remember you saying, "Oh for God's sake, Ingrid!" when I offered you a theory earlier. So, right now, flippant it shall have to be.'

'You were *serious*?' His voice had risen a whole octave.

'Of course.'

'You really think the remains were of Archie, her husband? What, as a substitute body to make it look as though she was dead?'

'It's perfectly possible. Hence the explosives, to try to ensure that whatever was left would be unidentifiable.'

'But why?'

'I think she's a criminal. Only criminals have access to things like that. For some reason or other, she needed to disappear.'

'But she raised the matter of what she regarded as his dodgy cremation in the first place,' the DCI argued.

'Perhaps to make it look as though she's just a batty old woman,' I said. 'Something might have happened to make her feel insecure, perhaps a police investigation into one of those she's involved with. She may well have been of the opinion that the local police would be unable to do anything, not realizing that she would be rattling the bars of the cage of the NCA. And, you must appreciate, this is only a theory of mine.'

'There's still the possibility that she may be a victim of crime and has merely been taken away by those responsible,' Carrick countered.

'Absolutely,' I said. 'There may well be a scam involving getting rid of inconvenient people by substituting them for those due to be cremated and she is, as you say, a victim. But I'm much happier with the notion that she's moved out, for now, and if everything quietens down in several months' time will turn up, express horror at what happened to her place while she was away on a last-minute holiday, claim the insurance and move somewhere else.'

'Those coffins in the shed . . .' Lynn mused. 'Archie could have been in one of them.'

'God, he'd have been a bit high by then,' Carrick muttered. 'Mrs Peters doing a runner could have been triggered by your visit, Patrick. You do have a way of unsettling people.'

'For which, in MI5 days, I used to get paid a hell of a lot more,' said my husband grimly. 'I suggest we try to find her, low key.'

Carrick shook his head. 'I can't work like that. I have a murder inquiry involving an unknown male on which I have to concentrate until further evidence comes to hand.'

Joanna was right: he did sometimes talk like a police procedures manual.

'I know,' Patrick said. 'I'll do it. Any feedback will come straight to you. Do you have any useful info about the death of that funeral director?'

'I did ask and there was nothing suspicious about it. He, Hereward Stevens, had been to a party here in Bath and left late-ish to drive home to Bradford on Avon at around eleven thirty. Sometime later, on a country lane that he'd turned on to at Limpley Stoke, his car left the road, having seemingly failed to take a bend, hit a tree and burst into flames. There wasn't a lot left by the time the fire brigade arrived – it's a very quiet road, apparently, with little passing traffic. As I said before, his remains were identified from dental records.'

'And he was on his own?'

'Yes, divorced, and no girlfriend that any of the other party guests knew about.'

'Car well-maintained?'

'A practically brand-new BMW.'

'Road conditions?

'Dry; a clear night.'

'Do we know anything about his health?'

'Only that he played squash and went running, so unless he had an underlying heart problem one can only conclude that he was a fit man.'

'Drink? Drugs?' I queried.

'My contact said that it was a birthday celebration. Nearly all of those present were in their forties and fifties and said when questioned that there had been moderate drinking but definitely no drugs. It was assumed that he'd been over the limit but not excessively so. Reputed to be a very good and careful driver, normally.'

'I think we'll go and have a look at the place where he died before we do anything else,' Patrick decided.

The site of the accident was not difficult to find in the wooded lane because the foliage of the oak tree the vehicle had hit, the ground beneath it and other vegetation nearby was withered and scorched. The tree's trunk was blackened, a large wound in the bark. It would probably die. Even now there was evidence of emergency vehicles, tyre marks and churned-up grass, although green shoots were already emerging through the mud. Broken windscreen and window glass was everywhere, but also clearly visible on the surrounding forest floor were small pieces of clear, red and orange plastic from the car's lights that had been hurled clear as they were smashed on impact. We both, without a word being said, started searching for anything that might provide clues as to what had happened here.

Almost immediately, Patrick found what was left of one of the tyres; all the outer layers gone, just coils of thin wire left together with bits of metal from the wheel hub and larger pieces lying nearby, possibly from the vehicle's suspension system. Then I came across a small pile of oddments that appeared to have been kicked or raked aside, perhaps by the police who had investigated the crash. I crouched down and began to sort through it but there was there was nothing recognizable, not by me anyway, just the tiny blackened remains of a wrecked car. Patrick, meanwhile, had walked back to the roadside and then went from my sight.

I rose and gazed around me. A man had died here, a man who had reputedly been a good driver and had been at the wheel of an almost new car. The weather had been fine, the road dry. Had he had a heart attack? Had he dozed off? Had he consumed rather more alcohol than his friends thought or had admitted at the time, not wanting to blacken his character?

Or he could have been murdered.

I covered an area of around twenty yards radius from the crash site, this difficult in places due to hidden hollows, tree roots and fallen branches. There were also several large thickets of brambles which were completely impenetrable – only badgers would be able to get inside them, and probably did. I found nothing except wild flowers, a wasps' nest in a tree, which I left severely alone, and a few items of litter that must have blown in from the road.

I suddenly realized that Patrick was standing right in front of me a short distance away, startling me. 'I do wish you wouldn't creep up like that,' I scolded.

'Sorry, but you do know I have a PhD in creeping about,' he said.

OK, that was training for Special Forces.

He held out a plastic specimen bag and I went over to see what he had found.

Two cartridge cases.

'I reckon someone took out the windscreen – or perhaps a tyre, or tyres. I'm not sure of the weapon type.'

'Where did you find them?'

He waved an arm. 'Back there. At the optimum spot where drivers have to slow down a little at the bend.'

'There may be more of them in the undergrowth.'

'Quite likely, and there ought to be a proper police search. I'll have to take them to Wiltshire Police and stir them up to do it. The situation's far from ideal as Carrick's not involved with this angle, yet, and the NCA isn't involved at all, so looking for the Peters woman has to be put on hold. Which, as far as we're concerned, is a bloody nuisance.'

'You could always do something about that.'

'I don't see what. All we have is a load of wacky theories – and let's face it, what happened to Joanna might not have been anything to do with it – plus a blown-up bungalow with a body in it. As Carrick said, he's heading a murder inquiry.'

What I didn't understand is why, if body swapping went on at the Peterses' bungalow the night before the funeral, the funeral director had to die.

SEVEN

'My brother Hereward and I are, or in his case were, the sons,' Oliver Stevens explained, Patrick having introduced the pair of us. 'Our father, Derek, set up the business in the late-sixties and I think we're maintaining the high standards that he insisted on.'

We were sitting in his tasteful and mostly different shades of green office. I supposed the man to be in his mid-forties. He had fair, thinning hair, the kind of complexion that would burn readily in the sun and pale blue eyes. A trifle overweight, he was nevertheless good looking, although right now a frown was creasing his forehead and he was slightly on the defensive.

Patrick said, 'When I visited this establishment before I spoke to your assistant, Miss Fraser, as I understood you were out on business.'

'That's right. Our usual business – a funeral.'

'I explained to her that someone had approached my father, who is the rector of St Michael's Church in Hinton Littlemore, as she was concerned about the circumstances surrounding her husband's cremation.'

'Yes, Jill told me about it. The funeral of Mr Peters.'

'I thought it unnecessary to mention at the time that, although I was making enquiries to assist my father with parish matters, I work for the National Crime Agency.'

Stevens merely nodded.

Patrick continued, 'But, as last time, I'm here – and I really must stress this – in an unofficial capacity. I should like to ask you a few questions but you're under no obligation to answer and, if you wish, we'll leave.'

As it was unofficial I had been introduced properly, as Patrick's wife.

'May I ask the reason for this second visit?' Stevens wanted to know.

'I can only tell you that circumstances have changed.'

Stevens shrugged. 'Ask away. I've absolutely nothing to hide.'

For the first time, Patrick smiled. 'You're not under any kind of suspicion. I understand that your brother was in charge of that particular funeral.'

'That's right.'

'Everything went off smoothly?'

'It did, although I understand it was a very quiet affair, with just a handful of mourners.'

'Do you know who they were?'

'No, I'm afraid not. Hereward mentioned to me that no notices were to be put in the local paper so a list of those attending wasn't required. So no, sorry. The widow plus a couple of friends, perhaps.'

'You have no idea then if there were any issue of the marriage.'

'No.'

'It would appear that the coffin was at the house the night before.'

'I believe it was. That's unusual these days.'

'Especially as hardly anyone turned up.'

'You'd be amazed at the things people want at funerals.'

'I'm sorry to bring back unpleasant memories but do you have any theories about your brother's death?'

The man grimaced. 'He hadn't had the car long and it was a more powerful motor than he was used to. A drop too much wine? Driving a bit too fast? Horrible, but it happens all the time. I miss him dreadfully.'

'I must ask you this: did he have any enemies?'

'Hereward? No! I know it sounds corny but he was loved by everyone.'

'Even his ex-wife?'

'Sandra. Yes, even her – now, that is. She left him for someone else – an old flame apparently, but realized after a couple of years when that relationship had gone sour that she'd made a bad mistake. Too late, as the divorce had gone through by then. I believe she'd got in touch again, though.'

'I'm sure you were told the details behind the reason for my original visit.'

'Yes. Amazing! The widow was presented with a couple of hip replacements that she didn't know about. I never met the lady. Is she a little, shall I say, vague?'

Patrick shook his head. 'No. Her concerns seem perfectly genuine. There were also some metal pieces from dentures – her husband hadn't had false teeth, plus a plate that had repaired a skull following serious head injury. You'd have to be very vague indeed to be unaware of that with regard to your spouse.'

'A ghastly error at the crem then. That's what Hereward thought.'

'It would appear not.'

'Then I can offer you no explanation.'

I said, 'Did your brother accompany the coffin to Mrs Peters's house the evening before the funeral?'

'Yes, indeed. That would be the correct formal procedure – not just have it brought by delivery boys, as it were. I remember now him being annoyed as he had to go back later – he'd left his mobile phone behind.'

'What time was this?' Patrick asked.

'Sorry, I've no idea. He told me the next morning when I saw him and was still a bit cross as he had missed a match he wanted to see on TV and had forgotten to record it.'

'Did he mention seeing anyone at the house?'

'I believe he said there were people there.'

'Any descriptions?'

'No, he'd have thought nothing of it.'

'Or even if they were the same folk who turned up at the funeral?'

'Sorry, again, no idea.'

'You've been extremely helpful.'

'He went back, saw certain people and they must have killed him to prevent any possible identification,' I insisted, dumping down my bag on the hall table. This remark followed a lively discussion as we had driven the few miles home.

'You can't jump to conclusions like that without a shred of evidence,' Patrick said, again.

'Fine, it was the rest of the witches' coven doing their oil of toad thing then,' I retorted, and went away to find something for lunch, distinctly hearing a deep sigh behind me. This drove me to call back, 'And don't forget, she told us that no one had been in the house that night but her. She lied.'

Wiltshire Police were now in possession of the cartridge cases
and the DI to whom we had spoken – it having proved necessary
for Patrick to produce his NCA ID in order to see her – had
promised to contact James Carrick.

There was not a lot else we could do while our employer was
not involved.

'No, to hell with this!' Patrick exclaimed just after lunch. 'I
shall go to London, find Jinty O'Connor and threaten to wring
his neck, then perhaps we'll get somewhere.'

'Talk to Mike Greenway first,' I urged.

'Permission to go off piste, sir,' Patrick requested crisply.

The commander gave him a tiny smile, the business of 'sir'
having been dropped a good while ago on the grounds that, 'You
used to be a lieutenant colonel, for God's sake.'

'You're on leave,' Greenway pointed out.

'And when I return to duty this won't be a case I'll be working
on.'

'Is it a case?'

'No, not really, but it has all the makings of being one.'

'The affair of the iffy cremation, the explosion out in the sticks
and a skull with two bullet holes in it?'

'That's right.'

A big smile this time. 'Patrick, why don't you just go home
and carry on having a rest?'

'Because my father expects me to do something about it.'

I looked at him in surprise.

'Plus, I have an idea Jinty O'Connor's involved.'

Greenway pointed an accusing forefinger. 'You want O'Connor,
preferably in a fridge in a mortuary. I know you do, someone
told me.'

'Yes, I do.'

'The NCA isn't a hit-squad.'

'I'm on leave,' Patrick responded, annoyingly.

There was quite a long silence, during which Greenway's blood
pressure probably went up several notches, and then he said, 'Go
and see Richard Daws. I'm not sure I ought to make the
decision.'

'Is he here today?'

'Room thirteen on the top floor. I think he chose that one on purpose as he says superstition's rubbish.'

This was our first visit to the new HQ in central London, the whole place like an ant heap right now, giving the impression that most people were either unpacking or completely lost. I hate plodding around in a maze of corridors, all looking exactly the same, but we had found Greenway's new office easily enough – I thought it very much on the small side – and room thirteen promised to be a push-over.

Not so; on the top floor there were codes to remember and key in before one could proceed through doorways, pads to be pressed against with the tips of fingers for the examination of prints deposited thereon, and cameras to be looked into for iris recognition. At last, we reached room thirteen.

The door was open.

'You made it through the security then,' said a voice from inside that I recognized.

Colonel Richard Daws, 14th Earl of Hartwood, was Patrick's boss when we worked for D12, a department of MI5, from which he retired to grow roses and write letters to *The Times*. He was persuaded to leave his castle in Sussex on a part-time basis and is now officially acting as adviser to, actually running, this section of the new agency. We had discovered that he'd recommended Patrick for the job when it was the Serious Organized Crime Agency.

It was like entering the office he had had in Whitehall years previously – although we have met several times in the interim I had not visited him at the SOCA HQ in Kensington. His long-case clock with a particularly sonorous tick was here, as were the Chinese rugs, watercolours and pair of glass-fronted cabinets holding his jade collection.

'Don't worry, you'll get your electronic passes when you officially return from leave and just be able to walk in,' he told us. 'Do sit down.'

Daws hadn't changed either. Tall and aristocratic-looking, he was elegant in a traditional pinstripe suit, no doubt from a tailor in Savile Row. For now, this was the charming side of the man who enjoyed playing the old duffer when socializing. Beneath this is an utterly ruthless organizer in possession of a keen intellect. It is a side of him that I don't like very much because, in the past and in the name of testing his staff's efficiency, he has made Patrick really suffer.

'Mike just called to say you were here,' he said genially, sweeping his fair, greying hair from his forehead, a lifetime's gesture, all the while fixing Patrick with his steely blue-grey gaze. 'He told me that you wanted to go after some mobster or other.'

Over the years Patrick has learned patience and honed his natural cunning. He said, 'I should like the authority to raise a case of my own, sir, and follow it through, involving whichever police forces I think necessary.'

'Ah, that's better – but it's a promotion,' Daws remarked quietly. 'I'm sure you must know that.'

'Then that's my request.'

Daws appeared to think about it. Then he said, 'The NCA was set up with the view to give its operatives more power and flexibility to catch serious criminals. But you hadn't been working for SOCA all that long.'

'Perhaps not, but I worked for you for quite a few years before that.'

'You're a loose cannon.'

'I get better results that way.'

'And one day, I have a notion, you may well end up behind bars. There would be no support from me, you know, if you got into serious trouble.'

'Like the time when a cop thought I'd killed a man you gave me an alibi by saying that I'd met you for lunch half an hour earlier than I actually did?'

It had made no difference as Patrick had been on time for his appointment with him at his club.

Momentarily back in duffer mode, Daws made harrumphing noises. Then he said, 'Did you?'

'Yes.'

There was no shock, horror reaction to this, Daws merely murmuring, 'Jethro Hulton, wasn't it? Murdering bastard was like a rabid hyena.'

As well as attacking me when I had come upon him in an empty house during an investigation. Men – criminals, that is – who assault Patrick Gillard's wife don't usually live for very long afterwards.

'That's right,' Patrick answered tautly.

'Which rather demonstrates that you need to be kept on a tight rein.'

Patrick made no further comment.

Then Daws rose and held out his hand. 'Congratulations. But you'll still have to report to Greenway.' He added, as we were leaving: 'By the way, I want O'Connor alive. *Don't* go after him until you have a gold-plated case against him.'

'Does John really expect you to sort this out?' I asked when we were in a lift going down to the ground floor. I had already given Patrick a congratulatory kiss.

'He's getting old,' he replied, 'and worries about not being to do things as well as he used to. I promised him I'd get the Peters woman off his and Mum's back. So, yes, in that respect, he's relying on me.'

It transpired that nothing more could be done in London. No real work could start until the following Monday, as Greenway was having the rest of the week off and there would be formalities to go through in connection with Patrick being given more authority.

We went back to Somerset.

I was feeling a little depressed by all this. Events had escalated during the day, which, I supposed, I ought to have expected. It would have been wonderful to have had Patrick at home for longer, but I realized that it was not fair of me to try to tie him to life at home now he gave every sign of feeling fully recovered. Wrong, too, of me to look forward to the day when he retired.

Was it though? Really?

Involving whichever police forces Patrick thought necessary was acted upon without delay and we met the Carricks for a drink in the Ring o' Bells that same evening.

'You know, this is much better,' Carrick began by saying to Patrick. 'The fact that you'll be getting under my feet officially from now on is a great improvement on your just poking around in my cases and showing me up by finding murder weapons right under my nose. No doubt the boys in Wiltshire will feel the same.' He laughed loudly, not something this particular DCI goes in for an awful lot.

Patrick had already reported our conversation with Oliver Stevens and now asked Carrick if Wiltshire Police had been in contact in connection with the cartridge cases he had found.

'Y-e-s,' he replied slowly. 'They have nothing, of course, in the way of evidence to point to this death having been murder. The remains of the car have been crushed. The official attitude is – and I can't say I blame them – that if Avon and Somerset and/or the NCA manage to find evidence, perhaps in connection with another case, then they will be delighted to help. Meanwhile, the coroner has been informed with a view to getting the inquest postponed. I think, Patrick, that with regard to that, the ball is in your court.

'I have a small item of news for you about the weapon you found,' he went on. 'The Beretta, which, as you said, is an unusual one to be found at a crime scene. Someone at Manvers Street who really knows about guns phoned a few contacts – one in Bristol, another two in London – and asked questions. One of these characters, and it doesn't do to enquire too deeply about them, mentioned a small, "consignment", as he put it, of weapons from the States that were brought, smuggled into this country by sea, last year. God knows how. The source of this information hadn't handled the stuff himself, it was just on the grapevine and he couldn't tell us anything else about them.'

'Not even serial numbers?' Patrick asked.

'No. It's not a lead but explains how the weapon might have got into the illegal pipeline in this country.'

'Any leads on the skull?'

'Until I have some DNA to compare it to, no.'

'And the wife's off the map so we can't ask her if she has anything of his that might have a few strands of hair on it.'

'I reckon she binned all his possessions before he was cold, don't you?'

'Quite likely,' Patrick agreed.

The men brooded gloomily into their beer.

Joanna, who had been quiet up until now, relaxing, said, 'How about in that shed that survived the explosion and fire? There might be an old coat in there or something like that.'

'Is your application to rejoin the police likely to go through soon?' I asked her and the pair of us had a good cackle at our husbands' expense.

'Scenes of Crime *have* taken everything like that away,' James said a little sheepishly. 'Tomorrow morning I'll check if David Campbell asked them to look for clothing and personal possessions in connection with formally identifying what remained of the body before he went on his course. At first, as you know, everyone assumed it was the woman who had died in the fire.'

Campbell had not.

Patrick spent most of the next day questioning people in Wellow about Anne Peters, endeavouring to discover whether she had friends, or at least acquaintances, who might know where she could have gone. He also tried to discover what had happened to the couple's car, but with no success. It was impossible for him to do any of this without using his NCA ID, but as the case was up and running, if only in his mind and barring the formalities, in his view it mattered little. Anyway, what Richard Daws says is as good as already in the history books.

'Let's look at this from a different angle,' Patrick said that evening. 'The body that was cremated – who the hell was it? Why did he, or she, have to be got rid of in that fashion? Joanna came up with some names of missing people but none of them lit any fires with me.'

'Bound to have been a bloke,' I said. 'Someone dodgy or a mobster and, from the evidence we have, quite old and having been in a serious accident. It shouldn't be *that* difficult to discover his identity. If O'Connor's involved we might be talking about a rival, another crime baron. Anyway, why can't the Met lay their hands on him?'

'No idea.'

'Daws wants him, no doubt to prove that the NCA's getting results,' I added, definitely not wagging a warning finger. 'And alive, he said. A corpse full of bullet holes will be no good to him at all.'

Patrick merely grunted.

*   *   *

Attempting to discover the identity of the late owner of the medical hardware had to wait, for as soon as Patrick arrived at the NCA HQ the following Monday morning he was required to attend courses – as he put it, 'brain washing', that would take up the next two days. I stayed at home – the children were back at school – the distaff side of the partnership not required at this stage. In truth, I wondered if his promotion would result in a job that was less hands on, though this was not necessarily what he had been after. I was also a little concerned that his patience to remain polite while coping with being 'lectured' for hours on end, no doubt about health and safety matters, might run out quite early in the proceedings.

'How did you get on?' I enquired when he rang me late afternoon on the Wednesday.

'It was OK.'

'Not boring?'

'Not at all. The courses were for new entrants and when those in charge read their info and discovered I'd worked for both MI5 and SOCA I was roped in to give a couple of talks. Tomorrow I start work for real. Do you want to come up?'

'No courses?'

'I'll give you my notes on anything you need to know about.'

Right now I really wanted to get on with my latest novel. And the garden was looking lovely, baby Mark with me in the warm sunshine on a blanket on the lawn under a parasol, trying to crawl over to where one of the kittens, Pirate, named after her predecessor, was washing herself close by on the grass . . .

'I value your company,' Patrick wheedled.

'As in, in bed?' I asked.

'That too. But mostly because when you're not around I miss the constant twittering noise by my side when I'm on a job.'

I drove up to London the next morning.

He had his own office, small like Greenway's, but perfectly formed, containing the regulation desk and chair – but not a leather one like the commander's – plus necessities such as another couple of chairs for visitors, a computer, a set of shelves and a metal cupboard. Other essentials to civilized living, such as a coffee-making machine, a small refrigerator and a microwave cooker, he had gone out and bought himself. Oh, and an orchid plant on the window ledge.

'They don't like full sun,' I told him, taking it off and placing it on the shelf next to the coffee maker.

'I thought they liked it hot,' Patrick said.

'They live in jungles so need warm, shady and humid conditions.'

'I'll breathe on it sometimes.'

'Is there anything to do today?' I went on to enquire, seating myself.

'I might have found out who the hip replacements belonged to.'

'Really! How?'

'It involved nothing more complicated yesterday afternoon after the courses had finished than going round introducing myself – there are a lot of bods here, both sexes, whom I've never met before – and asking if anyone knew of a clapped-out mobster who's gone off the radar lately. One name came up twice – Frederick Judd, known as Freddie the Bent on account of his appearance after being involved in a hang-gliding accident when he was in his forties and subsequently being seriously afflicted with arthritis. Criminal grapevines say that he's dead, quite recently.'

'Was O'Connor's name mentioned in connection with him?'

'No.'

'If mobsters want to get rid of a rival they usually do something like shooting them and dropping them in a weighted sack into a canal or river,' I pointed out. 'Or just leave them where they fall. Why go to more bother with him?'

'Perhaps they wanted him to really disappear – no chance of ever finding the corpse. Or he could have been made an example of along the lines of get off my manor or burn . . . perhaps alive.'

'That would fit in with what you've already said about O'Connor.'

'Yes, quite.'

EIGHT

The last known address for Judd was in Feltham, Middlesex. The house where he had lived – or still might live if the rumours of his death were incorrect – was one of hundreds of semi-detached homes on a sprawling estate not far from Feltham Young Offenders Institution. The tops of the high fences crowned with razor wire were within our sight as we walked, through light drizzle, down the slightly sloping road towards the house number we wanted. The Range Rover had been left several streets away – you avoid allowing potentially criminal people to glimpse your vehicle.

Before leaving HQ, we had researched our target and discovered quite a lot from various computer files. Wealthy quite early in life – he had lived here during that time – it was assumed from the proceeds of crime carried out by him and his extended family, Judd had set himself up as a restaurateur in the High Street of the town, put in a manager, his brother-in-law, and turned the place into the headquarters of a money-laundering operation. Other local businesses had been bought: a nightclub above which he opened a brothel in rooms on the first floor, the girls trafficked from central Europe, and a hairdressers that was turned into what one local police officer had described as 'a supermarket for Class A and Class B drugs'.

All these enterprises had finally been closed down quite a while ago. Judd and other family members had been arrested and he had gone to prison for ten years, the charges including car theft and grievous bodily harm – an attack on another drugs dealer. When released, Judd had scorned family connections and set himself up on his own, hiring help, or heavies, when he needed it. Burning resentment of being imprisoned was now manifested as he became prone to extreme violence against anyone who crossed him. Outwardly respectable, he got married, bought a house in Harrow and lived the life of a successful businessman. During this time he probably drew on funds he had salted away as well as masterminding several serious robberies of works of art and antiques in the Home Counties. No one had ever been arrested, nor the stolen property recovered following these crimes, and the only evidence to connect him with them was extremely flimsy. It was round about then that he had the hang-gliding accident, which had almost killed him.

At which time, according to reliable sources, he went more than a little mad. Turning into what one informer described as 'a monster' both physically and mentally, his wife soon left him, as did all members of the house staff. He was forced to sell up, went 'home' and bought the property in Feltham where he no doubt hoped to disappear below the police radar but was thought to have continued organizing crime, re-employing his 'boys' – those who were not behind bars, that is – one of whom was reputed to cook and clean for him. Several years went by and, according to police informers, Judd became seriously rich.

'This man was being monitored, low key, in an effort to nab him, catch him red-handed, as the saying goes,' Patrick had said once we'd finished reading. 'They weren't getting anywhere. Then – this was around a couple of months ago – the place went quiet, overnight, apparently. This was a relief to those living nearby, who said when questioned that he had given them the horrors by his behaviour, including the way he had sworn at their children. Someone said he had heard shouting in the early hours one morning, he wasn't sure exactly when, but it was nothing new as those living there and others who appeared to wander in and out drank heavily and, he suspected, took drugs. Bottles and other rubbish were often thrown over into neighbouring gardens.'

'Has anyone been inside the house?' I now asked.

'From the law? Not so far as I know, and he might be abroad. You can't just break in without good reason. I intend to, though.'

'He might be lying dead on the floor, his "boys" having got fed up with him and spitted him with the bread knife.'

'That's perfectly possible.'

'Is Greenway really OK with your carrying on investigating this?'

'I did raise the matter with him and he said he'd not get any sense out of me until I'd got it out of my system and anyway, as he put it, it would be a good thing for me to cut my teeth on.'

I thought the remark a bit rich considering what Patrick has achieved in the past.

'Daws wants O'Connor too,' I reminded him. 'Like you, he might be of the opinion that he's part of this package.'

'You think he might have had a word with Mike?'

'Umm.'

The house was like the others in the immediate vicinity, a thirties semi, but was shabbier by some margin: filthy windows, peeling paintwork, black bags of rubbish dumped on the long grass in the front garden. An old car with a flat tyre was parked outside, a wheel up on the kerb.

We went up the front path and Patrick rang the doorbell or, at least, pressed the bell push but with no audible result. The plastic front door possessed no knocker so he then battered on it with a fist, making the cheap structure bounce in its frame. There was continued silence within. Not one to wait for very long, if at all, my husband then set off down a sideway and I followed, always giving him plenty of space in such situations. The last thing he needs if suddenly ambushed is to find me in the way.

Around half of the small back garden looked like some kind of open-air bottle bank, most of the bottles smashed as they had been thrown at a tailor's dummy propped up against a shed, a traffic cone jammed on top of it by way of a head. The seats of the plastic chairs remaining upright were filled with rain water and rotting leaves and were scattered about, more bottles and dozens of beer cans arrayed around them. Another heap of black bags filled with rubbish were piled up by a boundary fence.

'He could even be in one of those,' Patrick muttered, nodding in that direction before trying the handle of the back door. The door opened.

There was no need for me to urge caution.

'In view of the fact that this is unlocked I can't believe that someone from the local police hasn't had a look round,' Patrick whispered. 'I'll phone and find out before we do anything else.'

We returned to the front where, after a couple of calls – they said they did not want to discuss cases with someone they'd never heard of, which, I thought, was reasonable – we ended up driving to Feltham police station. I waited in the car while Patrick went in, and, probably, vented his impatience. But when he returned he was smiling.

'No one's been inside the place,' he reported. 'It was securely locked up when someone last checked and there were no grounds to issue a search warrant. That was around a month ago so someone's obviously been in since. If we want to have a look round that's up to us and they'll be interested to know if we find anything interesting.'

'As in booby traps, corpses and stuff like that? That's real cooperation,' I grumbled.

'Perhaps you need some lunch.'

'Yes, I do. I had a very early start.'

'Diddums. Needless to say, they're hoping he was the one who ended up at the crem. I asked about getting his medical records as that's the clincher, but the DI I spoke to said that as Judd had lived in Harrow when he had his prang and to her knowledge there are no hills big enough around there to hang glide off – she might be wrong, of course – only the good Lord knows where he was treated for his injuries.'

'But the hip replacements might have been done locally, to here, I mean.'

'Yes, but this man has, or had, several aliases. I suppose we could email all the doctors in the area. Not *now*, though.'

My mention of the possible presence of hidden dangerous devices had been deliberate, as even though we hadn't the slightest proof that he was involved I was haunted by my working partner's descriptions of O'Connor's methods. A door was open where previously it had been locked . . .

Patrick pushed the back door open as far as it would go and we stood well clear. Gazing within a few moments later, all there was to be seen was just a dated and grubby-looking kitchen, the number of footprints on the worn and once-white tile-effect vinyl flooring suggesting that it had not been washed for months, if ever. The worktops within our sight were cluttered with yet more bottles and beer tins and the remains of take-away meals. The smell of rotting food wafted out.

'I hadn't expected there would be a bucket of water on top of the door,' Patrick murmured to himself as he crossed the threshold.

Then he stopped, moving this way and that, seemingly looking at something about a foot from the floor roughly his own height in front of him. Then I saw it, a tiny flash as something caught the light streaming in behind us.

'Fine gauge fishing line,' Patrick said, still mostly to himself. 'I have no intention of cutting it to see what happens; I'll just try to see what it is.' He glanced back at me. 'Please go right away, around the corner of the house, and don't move until I say so.'

Around a quarter of a minute later, there was a bang like a small firework going off.

'Are you all right?' I yelled from my place of safety.

'Fine,' he called back. 'Just nudged the only full can of lager off the worktop.'

Moments later, Patrick appeared. 'I don't feel like being blown up today so I shall call out the experts. That thing's a trip device designed to set off something that's in one of the lower kitchen units. Should the whole place be stashed out with explosives half the district'll go up with it.'

It was, plus the body of a man we knew as Dougie Baker, one of those who had abducted Joanna.

In addition to the device in the kitchen, the corpse, in a bedroom with the door shut, had been wired with explosives similar to the method used by suicide bombers, and arranged so that they would detonate when the door to the room was opened. Members of the Bomb Squad who attended – they had to cope with the fact that large numbers of floorboards had been ripped up right through the house – were familiar with similar traps for the unwary and first of all carried out an examination of the room courtesy of a tiny camera inserted through the gap beneath the door. Entry was then gained via the window. The explosion, had it taken place, possibly setting off other devices that were found in the house, if they hadn't exploded already, that is, would have done dreadful damage to the houses nearby, causing injuries and possible fatalities.

The whole road was evacuated before any investigations could begin, and it was not until quite late the following afternoon, when householders and their families had been permitted to return, that Patrick was invited by the DI to whom he had originally spoken to view the body, which was still in situ, but, of necessity, minus the explosives. This gesture by the local constabulary, together with heartfelt thanks, paid off for them when he immediately identified the deceased. This author stayed away, decomposing human beings not being my strong point and, besides, my presence wasn't necessary. There was also the question mark over the ripped up floorboards. Obviously those responsible had been looking for something.

'Whoever organized that probably went off feeling very pleased with themselves,' Patrick commented when we met up again at just after seven that evening. 'But, in fact, it's provided links, admittedly some a little tenuous, between just about everything we know so far.' He counted off on his fingers. 'Joanna was checking up on the crematorium manager's secretary's background when she was accosted by Joe, Will and Dougie. Later, Dougie told us that he knew that the man who issued orders was referred to sometimes as JC, possibly Jinty O'Connor, known for his imaginative ways of getting rid of the opposition. Dougie's now dead – did someone hear what he said just before they flung up the door to that lock-up garage we were in? We've found Dougie's body – he'd been shot once through the head, incidentally – in the home of a man who could possibly fit the bill regarding the bits and pieces left over from what should have been Archie Peters funeral. Archie Peters's body appears to have been blown up with his own home. There are a lot of links here. But where's the woman, his wife, and what's her connection with all this?'

He flung himself into an armchair in our hotel room.

'Perhaps she's related to O'Connor,' I suggested.

'What, and content to be stuck down in Wellow married to an old misery who's slowly falling apart?'

'Perhaps he was loaded and she didn't want there to anything obviously iffy about his demise so she could have the money no bother.'

'Then told people that she had suspicions about the cremation to cover herself should the real story subsequently emerge when the dosh was safely in the bank. That hangs together.'

'I take it we're assuming that the bullet holes in the skull were done afterwards to Archie's corpse, to make it look as though it was his wife who had died.'

'Yes, but in my view, that was unnecessary. A bit desperate.'

'But this is about money – more than he had, surely,' I said. 'Money, money, money.'

After a little pause, Patrick said, 'A man after midnight?'

'Wrong song. OK, but only after you've wined and dined me and generally told me how wonderful I am.'

'Shower,' he suddenly decided, getting up and starting to throw off his clothes. Then: 'If I do the last thing now can we postpone the others and . . .' He gave me a big hopeful smile.

I shook my head. 'Nice try.'

There was progress the following morning when the news came through that DNA from the skull and other human remains found at the Peterses' bungalow matched that on an old and greasy cap found on a top shelf in the shed at the bottom of their garden. While not cast-iron proof that the remains were those of Archie Peters, James Carrick thought that was as good as it was likely to get.

'The Peters woman must have been closely involved in the body swap,' Patrick said quietly, thinking aloud after the call. 'All that stuff about, "Where's my Archie now?" too. And as you said, she was probably paid. But why the Peterses? Why them? You're also probably right about there being every chance that there's some connection between her and the perpetrators. If we could only discover what that is and prove that Judd was the one cremated it would be extremely helpful. But why did whoever it was do it? What was so important about him that he had to disappear without trace?'

'And it looks as though Hereward Stevens was murdered because he went back to the Peterses' house for his phone,' I observed. 'I wonder if he spoke to anyone about it that night.'

'Such as his ex-wife, Sandra? Oliver Stevens said they'd got back in touch so it's worth a try.'

We were in Patrick's office at HQ and while he rang Oliver, the deceased funeral director's brother, hoping to get Sandra's phone number, I got to grips with the new coffee machine. It appeared to require a degree in electrical engineering to make it work but I finally succeeded in producing two full, steaming mugs after searching for a few minutes around the corridors for a source of water to refill it.

'Tomorrow's Friday, when we can go home,' Patrick announced in the manner of someone who had just discovered an amazing truth. 'Sandra Stevens now lives in Bath and I've arranged to talk to her on Saturday morning at ten thirty.'

'This is good coffee.'

'It should be; that thing cost a small fortune.'

'No one else from the police has wanted to interview me,' said Hereward Stevens's ex-wife.

'I'm sure there was no real need to at the time,' Patrick replied.

We had been invited to seat ourselves in the sunny and large living room of the city centre second-floor apartment, the room overlooking a square with a plane tree in the middle. This meant that, leaning back where I was seated on a black leather sofa for two, all I could see through the window was blue sky, foliage and the top of one of the spires on the tower of the abbey. When I'm old, I thought, something like this will do me very nicely.

'And there's need now?' asked Sandra.

She looked like a model: tall, slim, fair and wearing the kind of clothes, cream-coloured linen skirt, matching jacket, rose-pink silk blouse, that this parent of five children can only countenance when without them on holiday. She also seemed nervous – nothing to do with our presence, I hoped, as my husband was all charm and smiles. He had no reason to be otherwise.

'There's fairly strong evidence that's emerged now that might point to it having not been an accident,' Patrick told her.

Wiltshire Police, when pushed for news, had come up with the information that although enquiries were ongoing, they had fully investigated the area that Patrick had surmised was where a gunman had waited and discovered a couple more cartridge cases together with a cigarette butt. There was nothing to connect any of these findings with the death of Hereward Stevens, although it was hoped that the remains of the cigarette would yield some DNA despite several weeks having passed.

'Not an accident!' the woman gasped. 'But what then?'

'Were you in contact with him?' Patrick went on to ask but giving her another smile instead of answering the question.

'Well – yes. We rang each other sometimes, when we felt like a chat.' She coloured. 'A newspaper reporter asked me that, although I don't see what it has to do with anyone.'

'You were interviewed by someone from the local paper?'

'No. Someone knocked on the door and started asking questions. I refused to speak to her. But something was printed anyway, which made me absolutely furious.'

'I'm not after any private life details,' Patrick assured her. 'I'm not here to dig out things like that. I just need to know if, shortly before he died, he rang you, possibly one evening, and mentioned that he'd had to go back to an address near Wellow after taking a coffin there as he'd left his mobile phone behind.'

'I don't think so,' Sandra replied, frowning.

'Apparently he was doubly annoyed as he'd missed a football match on TV and had forgotten to record it.'

'Oh! Yes! The match, the semi-final of something. Heaven knows what, I loathe football. Rugby's much more of a man's game, don't you think?'

'I might agree with you there. Can you remember exactly what he said?'

'No, not really.'

'Please try; it's very important.'

She sat back in her chair, a swivel one that matched the two sofas, and crossed her legs, somehow contriving to show him rather a lot of them. Ye gods, she was flirting with him now. And, to be fair, I had been introduced, as was the norm in this kind of situation, as just the assistant.

'That might have been the time when he said everything was a bit strange,' Sandra said after about half a minute's silence while she thought about it. 'The deceased was an old man and his widow rather unpleasant.' She pulled herself up in some alarm. 'This is all strictly confidential, you must understand.'

'Nothing of what you say will come out unless what I'm working on ends up in a court of law,' Patrick smoothly promised, possibly thinking the same as I, that it hadn't been that confidential if the man had shared details with his ex-wife.

'I remember now,' the woman continued. 'He was asked to

take the coffin to the house the night before. That's uncommon now, although I understand does happen more in the Highlands and Islands of Scotland. And, as you said, he had to go back for his mobile. Very cross about that, he was, but of course he couldn't do without it as he was on standby that night.'

'Did he tell you anything else about it – about people at the house when he returned, for example?'

'No, I don't think so. Only that the woman was annoyed when she saw who it was at the door.'

'Had he left his phone in the room with the coffin?'

'I really don't know.'

'Did the widow fetch it for him or did he do that himself?'

'Sorry, he didn't say.'

'Did she ask him in?'

'No, she didn't – she left him standing in the rain. Oh, she must have fetched it for him then.'

'Is there anything else at all that he said about it?'

'Only that there was a van and another couple of cars parked outside the place and he had to walk from some distance away, which made him even crosser as it was really pouring.'

'What sort of van?'

'Hereward didn't say. He probably wouldn't have noticed in that weather.'

'Did he notice if anyone was sitting in it, or in the other cars?'

Sandra stared into space for a few moments. 'He said something . . .' she began slowly. Then shook her head. 'No, sorry. I simply can't remember.'

Not one ever to give up easily, Patrick leaned forward in his seat and said, 'Let's try to picture what happened. It was raining heavily but presumably not dark.'

'That's right,' she agreed. 'It would have been around seven thirty by then as he rang me at a little after eight fifteen when he got back home. I only noticed because the ads were on in the middle of a TV programme I was watching.'

'And he would have hurried because of the rain so perhaps wouldn't have glanced at the vehicles as he went by. But on the return journey, mission accomplished, he might possibly have noticed someone and—'

Several things happened very quickly and without warning.

The front door of the flat was battered in, there were pounding footsteps and I got a fleeting impression of men in the room before I was flung down on the carpet and several shots were fired, a couple seemingly only a matter of inches from my head. There was the crash of breaking glass. Someone – Sandra? – screamed as I headed, on all fours, behind the cover of the sofa I had been sitting on, grabbed my bag from the floor where it had fallen and dug out the Smith and Wesson.

'I don't normally shoot to kill before the introductions have been made so you're safe – for now,' Patrick said a little shakily. 'But as I have a good idea who you are it doesn't really matter. You're under arrest.'

A man with a deep voice laughed and then murmured, 'A cop! It's easy, shooting a blind cop. I might do it, in a little while, when you've wriggled a bit.'

Sometimes you have to make decisions. I jumped out from behind my chair, fired at a man holding a gun standing over by the door and then at another, also armed, his weapon aimed at Patrick, whose right arm was hanging uselessly by his side. Amazingly, my shot blasted the gun from the man's hand and the weapon fell to the floor. Mouthing hatred, this individual – big, with long, matted black hair and unshaven – ran at me so fast that my next shot missed. I threw myself to one side as he blundered by.

'Out!' he boomed and he and his henchman, clutching his shoulder, almost collided in their rush to get away, dragging another man I hadn't noticed on the floor by the collar of his shirt.

NINE

Patrick was trying to wipe the blood from his eyes, his face a sheet of red. I had no idea how badly he was hurt and steered him, on reflection not all that gently, backwards into a chair, then found and tossed in his direction a towel from the bathroom. I then dialled 999 on Sandra's landline phone. She was slumped forwards in the swivel chair in which she had been seated, but with no visible sign of injury. I thought it best not to move her and had a horrible feeling that she had taken a bullet in the chest and was dead. But when I checked there was a faint pulse. I still didn't feel I ought to move her.

'Like a bloody blind coming down,' Patrick was muttering, accurately as it happened, when I went back to him. Then, 'Are you and Sandra all right?'

'Sandra isn't,' I replied. 'I've called the police and an ambulance.'

'Have they gone?'

'It would appear so.'

'Is the top of my head still there?'

'Yes.'

'Good.'

I got another towel, wetting it this time, and endeavoured to clean him up. The long gash on his forehead was still welling blood – head wounds always bleed a lot – but it was possible to hold one end of the towel firmly to it while cleaning his face. There was broken glass everywhere, including dagger-like shards, one of which was probably the cause of Patrick's wound, the source of it what had once belonged to a large, and very expensive, light fitting hanging from the ceiling.

Finally able to open his eyes properly as I cleaned off his eyelashes, Patrick took the towel from me and got to his feet, swearing under his breath as he tried to move his right arm. He went over to Sandra.

I had already picked up his Glock from the floor and wondered if the arm was broken, picturing the vicious downward blow, probably with the man's handgun, when Patrick had been rendered unable to see.

'There were three of them,' I told him, not sure how much he had seen. 'You must have shot one of them because they dragged him away. I got the one by the door in the shoulder and by an amazing fluke shot the weapon from the other bloke's hand. You think you know him, you said.'

'That bastard O'Connor,' Patrick raged, finally allowing his fury to surface. 'I'm sure it was him. He had a deep voice like that. God, I simply daren't move this woman to see how badly she's hurt. Where the hell's the ambulance got to?'

It arrived shortly afterwards, together with an area car. Patrick had the choice of making a statement there and then if he wished, or being taken to A&E to get his cut, which was still bleeding, seen to, which was mine. I won and stayed behind to talk to DS Lynn Outhwaite, who turned up as Sandra Stevens was being placed in another ambulance. Quite a crowd seemed to have gathered outside.

'No, you go,' she said after I had given her the bare bones of the story. 'You'll need to collect Patrick from the hospital, by which time he'll have calmed down a bit. We can do the official bits at the nick later and I'll persuade the boss – who's in a bit of a mood today – to have a proper de-briefing at the pub you all go to – the Ring o' Bells? – this evening as both blokes will be in a better frame of mind by then. Meanwhile, I'll start the hunt for these mobsters. How does that grab you?'

'You know my husband almost as well as I do,' I said jokingly. 'Seven thirty?'

Haunted by how Sandra had looked I did not feel remotely like joking, and only realized that Lynn had recognized that I was suffering from mild shock when I had pushed through the gawpers, walked to the car and found that my hands were shaking so much that I had to sit in the driving seat for five minutes before I could trust myself to drive away. Praying to the patron saint of Land Rovers that I wouldn't do anything stupid in Bath's nightmare traffic, I made my way to the Royal United Hospital.

Probably on account of the gore all down the front of his shirt – the man had looked like something out of a vampire movie

– Patrick had been seen immediately. I sat and waited. And waited. And then, on enquiring, was told that he had gone to have an X-ray on his arm. Finally, around another hour later, when it was getting on for two in the afternoon, he appeared, very pale and with a neat row of hemming, six stitches, across his forehead. Another couple of inches or so away and he would probably have been blinded for life.

'I'm supposed to rest,' he said laconically, collapsing beside me on the bench seat and closing his eyes. 'Lost blood. Feel like crap.'

'And your arm?' I asked.

'Not bust. That feels like crap too.'

There was nothing for it but to deliver him to his mother and then go back to Bath to the Manvers Street nick to give whoever was there the full details. This also involved my creating a photofit image of the gunman Patrick thought was O'Connor and comparing it with a couple of mugshots of him on record. These had been taken some years previously when he had been con-siderably less hirsute, but there was a marked resemblance. Patrick would need to look at them as well, perhaps the next day, but I emailed the photofit image to his iPhone. I had no memory of the faces of the other two.

'No, this is on me,' said James Carrick, giving Patrick a whisky double. 'There's nothing like it as a remedy for bother.'

'I thought it was just about the best thing to drink if you fancy rather a lot of bother,' Patrick replied, then thanked him and tasted it appreciatively, left-handed, his right arm in a makeshift sling made from one of my silk scarves to rest it and already showing signs of being heavily bruised.

'That only applies to Scotland,' he was soothingly assured.

Elspeth's remedy had been more practical, a little brandy, for medicinal purposes only, of course, before a large helping of reheated chicken pie, homemade and leftover from her and John's midday meal, followed by strawberries and cream. Patrick admitted later that he could not remember sitting down and falling asleep in one of his parents' armchairs afterwards but that was where he awoke, about three hours later, feeling a lot better. A quick shower and he decided he could face the pub, easily.

Despite the good humour between the two men, we were all in a subdued frame of mind – Joanna had also come along because, in a way, she was part of the 'team' and, as this meeting had been her idea, Lynn was here too. I was agonizing over the thought that Patrick and I had somehow been responsible for an innocent woman having been shot because we had been followed. Sandra Stevens was in intensive care and under police guard following an operation to remove a bullet from her chest. The medics were cautiously hopeful as, miraculously, it had missed all vital organs. The next forty-eight hours would be critical.

Patrick, I knew, was also acutely worried that someone was watching and tailing us despite the precautions that he takes when we visit witnesses, potential and otherwise. What had happened, he had told me, was a reflection on him and, like me, he was feeling responsible for it.

'There was blood everywhere so there'll be five lots of DNA,' Carrick was saying encouragingly. 'Patrick's, to eliminate him from the inquiry, of course, Sandra's, the man he shot who they took with them, the one you hit over by the door, Ingrid, and the other one holding a weapon on Patrick who had it shot from his grasp, the guy you reckon was O'Connor.'

'I'm convinced it was but that's not proof,' Patrick asserted. 'I could recognize him from that photofit created from Ingrid's description alone, even though he's a lot older. His face was slightly lopsided even years ago, almost as though he'd had a slight stroke.'

'His hand might not have bled,' I pointed out.

'It takes just one drop to have fallen on the carpet,' Carrick said. 'Although I'm not sure if we have his DNA on record. But we have the remains of the gun as well so there may be fingerprints on it.'

I had an idea he had been he wearing gloves but said nothing as I could not really remember.

'Did those mobsters seem surprised that they met with an armed response?' the DCI asked.

'I didn't have time to see the expression on their faces,' Patrick said with a hint of impatience. 'But they weren't wearing balaclavas, which might suggest they only expected to find Sandra in the apartment and, besides which, they intended to kill her.'

'At least we now have proof that there *is* a case,' Joanna said. 'I wonder if Sandra told anyone that the NCA was going to pay her a visit this morning.'

'Canny, aren't you, hen?' her husband said to her. 'That's far more plausible than them having tailed Patrick and Ingrid to the flat.'

'How about Sarah Dutton, the secretary of the crematorium's manager?' I suggested. 'She's possibly a suspect and Sandra, as the ex-wife of a funeral director, might have got to know crem staff. Did she at one time work for her husband and his brother in the office?'

'I'll ask him,' Patrick decided, finding his mobile.

The answer was that she had but after the divorce had made funeral arrangements, handled announcements and booked hotels and restaurants from home.

Full details of the shooting had been kept out of the media, who knew only that a woman had been injured following the attack and that the police had several good leads. A little spin is always a good idea.

'O'Connor was probably bringing up the rear as they entered,' Patrick said. 'I'm only saying that from what I know about him and the fact that I shot the bloke in front, causing him to fire high as he fell, taking out the light fitting. Although I never shoot to wound under those circumstances and I reckon he's dead by now, the other bloke might still be alive. Has anyone with gunshot injuries been taken to hospital in the past twenty-four hours?'

We were half an hour into an early morning brainstorming session in Carrick's office the following Monday, just the three of us present. DI Campbell was still on his course and Lynn was coordinating most of the rest of the CID team in house-to-house enquiries in the immediate vicinity of the crime scene.

James Carrick shook his head. 'Not in Bristol, Somerset, Devon, Wiltshire, or Gloucestershire. We're still asking – all the way to London. I just wish to God I knew what all this was *about* other than that someone's trying to destroy evidence and, one way or another, there has to be an awful lot of money involved.'

I said, 'Whether we were followed or not – and I don't see

how we could have been – it's getting really serious if people we interview are targeted.'

Patrick said, 'I'm all in favour of putting a very low-key watch on Sarah Dutton.'

Carrick stretched and then got to his feet. 'That's not a bad idea. How are the head and arm today?'

'Both would much rather be somewhere else, thank you,' was the immediate reply.

'OK, coffee then with a couple of painkillers for you that I know Lynn has in a desk drawer, and then when she gets back we'll have an in-depth briefing with everyone in the main office.'

'It's his nick,' I said quietly to Patrick after Carrick had gone on ahead, saying, 'I'll make sure we don't get it in those damned polystyrene things.'

'Within these four walls he's king,' Patrick agreed. '*We'll* watch the Dutton woman.'

The tablets were for period pains but Patrick took two anyway.

After the briefing, during which the entire case was presented to the team, going right back to when Anne Peters had complained to Patrick's father, Carrick announced that he wanted to visit the scene of the previous day's shooting – he had been tied up with a meeting at HQ at the time. But it turned out that forensic personnel were still on site and would probably not be finished until the following morning. I persuaded Patrick, whose right arm was painful and because of this was taking a couple of days' sick leave as he was worried about not being 'firearms fit', that the best thing for him would be to go home and rest it, and he reluctantly agreed. This did not mean that I could not carry on with a little investigating. Later.

At a little before five that afternoon, having made sure that she did not need it, I borrowed Carrie's car and went out to the crematorium involved in the case. Driving in, I circled around the car park as though I had made a wrong turning and then exited. There were no vehicles in this public area so business must have finished for the day, as I'd thought, but around the side of the complex three cars were visible – I could only assume that they belonged to the staff. Joanna had said that Robin Williams had a silver-grey VW Golf, and I had glimpsed a car of that colour but had been too far away to make a proper identification.

Back in the main road I turned the car and parked in a lay-by a short distance away, where I pretended to make a phone call. Remembering our working rules, I then *did* make a phone call, to Patrick, to tell him what I was doing. He appeared to have vanished from the house when I left and I had not been in the mood for a full-scale manhunt. Perhaps he had been in the annexe talking to his parents. It was engaged so I left a message.

Another car, one I recognized, drew up behind me and I got out and waved.

'No boring remarks from me along the lines of great minds thinking alike,' Joanna said as she joined me in the car. 'Besides which, Patrick suggested it. I take it you are going to follow Sarah Dutton.'

I nodded, and then said, 'But only to find out where she lives.'

'Same here. I have some news. The latest on Sandra Stevens is that she'll probably pull through.'

'I'm so glad to hear that,' I replied.

'And I received a letter this morning with a date and time for my interview at HQ.'

'Brilliant!'

'And a woman, or women, answering Mrs Peters's description have been seen in Hammersmith, Oxford Circus and Fulham.'

'I hadn't realized her details had been circulated that widely.'

'James got on to the Met. He thinks she's in London on account of Fred Judd operating, or having operated, there, O'Connor being a mobster there, Dougie I've-forgotten-his-surname having been a henchman there and yours truly being set upon there when I was trying to trace Sarah Dutton's family. It's got a lot going for it but the sightings might be a no-no. What the hell are they doing in there, having another session?' This last remark had been with a nod of her head in the direction of the building almost opposite us.

'There are three cars parked at the side,' I pointed out.

'Having sex in a crem would have a certain edge to it,' Joanna commented thoughtfully.

We then agreed that when and if Sarah Dutton appeared we would tail her in the car I was driving and I would bring Joanna back afterwards. We had just arranged this when we heard a car, or cars, coming out. I grabbed a road map I had noticed on the

back seat – Carrie can't be bothered with satnavs – and we
pretended to be looking at it, lowering our faces.

'The manager, Williams, first, Sarah Dutton second in a black
hatchback,' Joanna said. She has the advantage of having long
hair she can peer through. 'There's another vehicle some distance
behind them.'

'Probably the foreman,' I told her, waiting until the first two
had gone a short distance in the same direction, towards Bath,
before starting the car. 'He's OK.'

'I take it we just need to get this woman's address and have
a general sniff round,' Joanna said when we had travelled around
half a mile.

'I think that's best, don't you?'

After a couple more miles Robin Williams turned into a slip
road that served a small row of shops. Sarah Dutton carried
straight on. I have been well tutored in the art of covert shad-
owing so was careful not to drive too close to her. The real
hazard in built-up areas is traffic lights where you get a red
when your quarry has gone through them on green. There was
one very close call on the outskirts of the city when I sneaked
through an amber, but otherwise I was lucky. Finally, as we
were entering the district of Larkhall, the black car two vehicles
in front of me indicated left into a side road. I followed and
then went right on past the drive of the modern semi-detached
house it had turned into.

'Number twenty-three,' Joanna reported when I had parked a
little further along the street. 'We can't really snoop any closer,
though, can we? She knows what we look like.'

I got out, opened the boot and delved inside. Among an amazing
collection of things that might come in handy – Carrie is actually
very organized – I discovered an old anorak with a hood and put
it on. Signing to Joanna what I was going to do, I walked back.
As I approached the house another car, one of those flat-as-a-
pancake sports cars with what Patrick calls a 'picnic shelf' on
the back, drew into the drive and, either accidentally or on
purpose, the driver tooted the horn. A man got out: early middle-
aged, dark-haired, of medium height, grabbed a briefcase from
the back seat, slammed both doors and went in the house. This
had to be Sarah Dutton's husband, Paul.

I carried on and took the next turning left, wondering if there was a back way to the properties. There was not and I retraced my footsteps. Nothing else could be achieved now and if a 'general sniff round' was wanted it would have to be at another time, when nobody was in.

'I think we ought to go and talk to the woman,' Patrick said when I got home and told him the story. 'Now.'

'Young mouths to feed,' I reminded him. 'I'm late with starting dinner already.'

'That's OK, I'll go on my own.'

'You can't drive with your arm like that.'

'You're probably right,' he agreed after a few moments. 'Feed the kids then and we'll have something in the pub later.'

I prepared vegetables, threw together a massive shepherds' pie with the remains of Sunday's joint that I had already dismembered and chopped, put it in the oven and begged Carrie to serve it and oversee the meal when it was cooked. They could have ice cream afterwards.

'It's late and I'd prefer it if you make an appointment and come back tomorrow,' Paul Dutton said angrily after we had identified ourselves and established who he was.

'Preference doesn't come into it when a woman has been shot and very seriously injured,' Patrick retorted. 'I would like to talk to your wife. Or, if you *prefer*, we can carry on this conversation at Manvers Street police station.'

The man flounced off to fetch her. He was not my idea of the perfect catch, having small, too close together eyes, a weak mouth and not much in the way of a chin. I wondered if he'd removed his pinny before answering the door.

Sarah appeared. Joanna had not really described her to us but I had built up a mental picture from what she had said of a rather fluffy, good-time girl whose abilities would go little further than the type of job she now had. But in reality this brunette with brown eyes, a slim figure and a tight smile that she switched on in slightly unnerving fashion when she saw us was as hard as nails.

'Rather an unsocial time to call on people, isn't it?' she said,

achieving speaking with the smile intact and teeth just about
closed.

'Is there somewhere we can talk in private?' Patrick enquired,
giving a look to her husband, hovering by her shoulder, that
caused him to step back several paces.

'We can go in the study,' she said, turning on her heel and
leading the way into a room towards the rear.

On entering, I immediately surmised that this was the original
dining room and they now ate in the kitchen. There was a swivel
chair by a reproduction desk with a computer on it, a bookcase
containing mostly magazines, DVDs and videos, and that was
about all if one discounted the cardboard boxes of various sizes,
the contents of which, an assortment of possessions, had spilled
out on to the floor.

'We haven't been here very long,' said Sarah Dutton when she
saw where I was looking.

'Is Sandra Stevens a friend of yours?' Patrick began by asking.

The woman seated herself by the desk and, because there were
no other chairs in the room, we remained standing. Swinging
herself gently from side to side, she gazed up at Patrick and said,
'No, but I know who you mean. It was in the paper. She was
attacked in her flat. Terrible.'

'You did business with her when she helped Stevens and Sons
– the funeral directors firm.'

'Yes, but Sandra and Hereward were already divorced by the
time the crematorium opened. We spoke on the phone a few
times. But it was just . . . business.'

'You never met socially.'

'No, but she called in at the crematorium a few times in
connection with work.'

'Has she phoned you lately?'

'No.'

'Are you sure? It's very important.'

'I can't see how. Two women, just having a chat sometimes?'

Patrick said nothing, just gazed fixedly back.

'Well, er, she might have done a couple of times. But I do
speak to hundreds of people on the phone every week.'

'Perhaps she was a bit lonely and needed a little female
conversation.'

'That might have been the reason.'

'Did she phone you at any time between Thursday and Saturday morning last week?'

'No.'

'Are you quite sure about that?'

'Yes.'

If she thought she had put herself in a superior position by sitting where she had, as though she was interviewing us, Patrick now blew this ruse out of the water by perching on a corner of the desk, facing her.

'Do you know a man by the name of Fred Judd?' he asked.

'No, should I?'

'He's referred to as Freddie the Bent.'

'I've never heard of him,' the woman declared.

'How long have you been having an affair with Robin Williams? Please don't deny it – you've been watched.'

Sarah Dutton's jaw dropped. 'Watched?' she whispered. Then added: 'For God's sake, keep your voice down.'

'Doesn't your husband know? I think he might.'

'What the hell has it to do with you anyway? With the police? Or are you one of those men who gets a kick out of digging dirt?'

This wasn't the kind of stuff that makes Patrick lose his temper. 'The question bothers you. Which means that you are.'

'You're a bastard, aren't you?' she flung back at him.

'When I worked for MI5 they used to let me loose on people that, in those days, were referred to as traitors. Mrs Dutton, I haven't even started yet.'

This had been kindly said and no, he hadn't.

'What has it to do with the police?' she again demanded to know.

'How about murder, serious crime and one of the most wanted mobsters in London?'

'I'm not involved with things like that.'

'So your little lunchtime sorties out to the beauty spot with Williams are because you've married a weed and for no other reason.'

She set her jaw furiously but said nothing.

'*Does* your husband know about it?'

Silence.

'Is that why he buys you expensive jewellery? To try to win you back? The bangle and diamond earrings you're wearing must be worth a couple of thousand pounds, at least.'

'My husband can't afford that kind of thing,' she answered without thinking.

'Thought not. Who then?'

Sarah Dutton shot to her feet. 'I'm going. And you can't stop me!'

'Of course not. I shall just arrest you.'

'Look, I save the money to buy myself things I like from my wages,' she said desperately, clinging on to the back of the swivel chair.

'You're lying. And you're afraid. Sandra Stevens told you that we were going to see her on Saturday morning and you told someone else. Who?'

'You're making a completely innocent remark into a *crime*.' She dashed away a few tears. 'All right. I lied – but you're trying to connect me with someone shooting Sandra.'

'Who did you *tell*?'

After a short pause, she replied, 'Only Robin. I think he quite fancied her at one time but doesn't now. We both felt sorry for her when her ex-husband was killed. Hereward was really nice.'

'Does Williams buy you the jewellery?'

She shook her head. 'No.'

'Look, we've just discovered that Sandra Stevens's husband was murdered.'

This shocked her and she moaned, 'Oh, God! But it's got nothing to do with *me*!'

'Your brother,' I murmured, having had a flash of inspiration. 'Is he still in prison?'

'Guy? Yes, unfortunately he is.'

There had been a certain wariness in the reply.

'Aggravated burglary, wasn't it?'

She actually shrugged. 'That's what they called it.'

'That tends to be the charge when a man smashes his way into someone else's home and that someone ends up dying.'

'I understand the old lady had a weak heart.'

'That makes it all right then.'

'No, of course it—'

I carved her up with, 'Is it her jewellery you're wearing? No, on reflection that's more modern than an elderly lady would probably have owned. Someone else's then – the booty from other burglaries?'

'I'm not saying any more,' Sarah Dutton said.

Patrick got off the desk with a gesture of weariness and said, 'Go and get it. All of it. All the stolen property he's given you.'

'I paid him for it,' the woman argued stubbornly.

'Go and get it!' Patrick yelled in her face.

She went, and I went with her.

TEN

Almost a week went by. We were both of a mind that, despite her hostility in answering questions, Sarah Dutton was not involved with what we were working on. Nevertheless, everything had to be investigated properly. She was charged with receiving stolen property – at least fifteen items of gold jewellery – and released on police bail, the case referred to the Met as her brother's crimes had been committed in London. Patrick went to interview Robin Williams again, who confirmed that Mrs Dutton had indeed given him the news that Sandra Stevens had told her that people from the National Crime Agency were going to speak to her. They had pondered what the reason for this might be. He denied utterly that he had spoken to anyone else about it, insisting that he knew no one who would be remotely interested. Patrick was inclined to believe him.

James Carrick had visited the scene of the shooting – everyone still waiting for DNA test results to come through – and Patrick 'walked' him through what had happened. There wasn't a lot to see. The day before he had gone to have the stitches out of his forehead at the hospital. Hopefully the scar would fade with time. His arm, black and blue, was at least less painful and he could now drive, which was a relief to me as I had plenty of other things to do.

The next morning we went back to London and, as a courtesy, I called in to see Michael Greenway.

'I simply can't believe that you were in the same room as this man,' he said. It might have crossed his mind to add, 'And didn't manage to arrest him,' but to his credit, he didn't. He did ask where Patrick was, though.

'Weapons training,' I told him. 'Just shooting at targets – his arm was seriously bruised and he's worried about it. We started off very early this morning so he should be here soon.'

'All the man said was that mobsters burst in and shot the woman you were interviewing.' He consulted a notepad before

him. 'A Mrs Sandra Stevens, and then did a runner, although
you, Ingrid, got a good look at one of them. He's since been
identified as O'Connor and a warrant's out for his arrest. The
latest in a series of warrants, that is – he just seems to disappear
into thin air.'

'Patrick didn't mention the bit about a light fitting being shot
out and a large splinter of glass slicing across his forehead so
he couldn't see for blood?'

'God, no.'

'He must have phoned you from somewhere in the hospital
when he went to have an X-ray on his arm. O'Connor slammed
a handgun down on it to make him drop the Glock. I expect
someone called him in just then and he couldn't go into any
more details.'

'So that's why he wanted a couple of days off. It does pay to
keep me completely in the picture, you know.'

'Sorry, but I didn't think you were that interested,' I countered.
'This job was just something for Patrick to cut his teeth on.'

Greenway went a little pink, studying his notepad again, then
cleared his throat and said, 'I *have* been following this – out of
interest, you understand. Patrick must know that it's vital to
discover the reason behind all these happenings. Several questions need answering. Has Frederick Judd been murdered, and
if so, was the body cremated his? If it was, why did they go to
all that trouble to get rid of him? How is the Peters woman
involved and where is she now? There's more we need to know,
but that'll do to start with.'

'Judd was reputed to be off his head,' I recollected.

'Mad, bad and dangerous,' Greenway mused. 'Yes, and perhaps
making a real nuisance of himself in certain criminal circles.'

'Well, he certainly was to his neighbours. It would be worth
talking to them if the Met haven't done so already.'

The commander wrote 'neighbours' on his pad, got up and
left the room to ask his secretary to fix us some coffee. He is
not a man to shout and expect people to come running.

'Would he have been a rival to O'Connor, I wonder?' he said
on his return.

'Pass,' I said. 'The Met are working on it and we've heard
nothing since his house was made safe from the explosives.'

'Which were intended to kill and maim police, of course, never mind any kids who might have decided to have a look round.'

Patrick's arrival coincided with our coffee arriving but he declined, saying that he had had some already. He didn't look very happy.

'The shooting practice?' Greenway enquired.

'Not good. Even picking up the weapon makes my hand shake.'

'To be expected, surely,' said the commander. 'It's not long since it happened.'

'It's possible to lose accuracy permanently.'

'In that case, I think you ought to consider having treatment at one of those specialist clinics.'

Patrick shook his head. 'I've had enough time off already. I'll ask Dad to say a few words over it.'

Greenway did not laugh, or even smile, saying instead, 'Please yourself.'

'Just to keep you abreast of what I'm doing, I'm going to speak to Fred Judd's immediate neighbours.'

The commander turned around his notepad and held it up for Patrick to see what he had written.

I supposed I had to let him take the credit for it.

I drove to give Patrick's arm a rest, convinced that he should have more treatment. I really examined my motives, wondering whether it was because I was selfishly worrying about my own safety when there was a question mark over his ability to protect us should a dangerous situation arise, or it was just wifely concern. Ashamed, I could not decide, so settled for both. Nevertheless, I felt somehow naked and had to put it into words. 'Frankly, I'm not too happy wandering around here after what happened at Judd's house.'

'Ingrid, I might be a bit under the weather but I can still put a few holes in a barn door,' he retorted.

'Sorry. But I didn't really mean it like that,' I lied. 'It might jeopardize the case if someone sees us, that's all.'

He leaned over and put his head on my shoulder for a few moments. 'Sorry.'

'Does your head hurt?'

'A bit.'

I had an idea that his head, and his arm, were giving him hell. We had reached a residential road near where we had left the car on our first visit, and I pulled in and parked just in time before bursting into tears.

Patrick put his arm around my shoulders. 'What's up?'

'I don't want to do this anymore,' I sobbed. I had really lied to him for the first time, ever. 'And you're always getting hurt.'

'Then let's go home,' Patrick said quietly.

'But—'

'Where we'll have a think about whether we carry on or if I get a less hazardous job. It's probably about time I did, anyway – it doesn't mean that much to me, not now. Honestly.'

'We can't just walk away,' I said, gazing at him with blurred eyes.

'We can.'

'You want O'Connor.'

'I have the rest of my life to find him.'

'And you promised your father you'd sort it out.'

'He'll understand that this has developed into something I have no choice but to hand over to others.'

I simply had to tell him. 'I lied to you just now. I'm so scared.' I wept afresh, just managing to get out, 'And so sorry if it offends you.'

When I became aware that he had got out of the car, I thought my admission had been too much for him, but he came round to the driver's side, opened the door, helped me out and then ensconced me in the passenger seat. We drove away. Not very far, though. Patrick parked in a vacant space reserved for the superintendent at the local police station, muttered something about 'his lordship's probably playing golf' and went inside. Around twenty minutes later, when I had got myself back together and was feeling very small, he reappeared.

'*They* are going to talk to Judd's neighbours and those living nearby,' he announced. 'The DI I spoke to before agrees that the pair of us have too high a profile – finding the explosives in Judd's house – to, as you put it, go wandering around that area. We've also recently come face-to-face with O'Connor. If he, or some of the cronies he was with in Bath, are somewhere here – according to her the neighbourhood where Judd lived is stiff with ex-cons and those helping with enquiries – house-to-house enquiries might find them. Obviously, there's a full murder investigation taking place on account of Dougie's body having been found in the building and they've carried out some local questioning already, but she's prepared, in view of what I said, to divert a few more people to it.'

I looked at him and he smiled, then said, 'Actually your freak-out made me remember what my promotion means – being able to involve other police forces. Lunch?'

Even I did not recognize at the time that nerves, evolving into something approaching a panic attack, had rather a lot to do with intuition, my 'cats' whiskers' crashing in with a red alert. Rightly, as it turned out.

'That *is* interesting,' Patrick murmured.

During a quiet discussion – now postponed until the weekend – about my reservations I had received a call from Joanna, who, still working with terrier-like tenacity, had been to see the curate at Wellow, Kenneth Watson. With no mandate to investigate officially she had told him the truth: that she knew the Reverend and Mrs Gillard and was helping to get to the bottom of the puzzle of the whereabouts of Mrs Peters. Mentioning in passing that her husband was DCI in Bath had provided all the credentials she needed.

Recognizing that what the woman had told him could hardly be described as 'confessional' confidences, Watson had been delighted to talk to her, this of course having nothing to do with the fact that Joanna is a strikingly beautiful woman. He had recollected Mrs Peters's concerns about her husband's funeral and how upset she had been. He then spoke of experiences of his own as he had visited the couple in their home when he had first moved to the village to take up his post, a task that was part of his job. The couple, he recollected, had been daggers drawn and, seemingly, in the middle of an argument, a description he immediately amended to a 'blazing row' as he had heard them shouting at one another as he approached the front door. Things had simmered down a little on his arrival and, the woman disappearing, grudgingly, into the kitchen to make tea, Archie had bawled after her, 'Silly old bat, you'll have me in tears next. Perhaps you oughta have gone on the stage for real!' Whereupon his wife had poked her head around the door to say, or perhaps, he thought, hiss, 'I'll have you know that the drama society relied on me at one time for female leads!'

'Did he know what they were arguing about?' I had asked Joanna.

'Money. The old man muttered something about her always wanting more housekeeping money.'

'Did Kenneth know where they had lived previously?'

'I gather he hadn't liked to ask.'

'OK,' Patrick said. 'This does tend to fit in with your theory that she told tales about what happened, perhaps having threatened whoever worked the scam that she'd go to the police. As you said, she might not have been paid. We've just discovered that she can act. As I said, it's interesting and useful, but that's all. We've still no clue as to the connection between her and the mobsters who appear to be involved. *Why* didn't they kill her? I can see that it was useful to get rid of evidence, that is, Archie's corpse, by blowing up the bungalow, but why not dispose of her at the same time?' He took a bite from his beef sandwich and chewed gloomily. 'Come on, put that bloody wonderful imagination of yours to work.'

'Look, we're cops, or rather, you are. We're not writing a crime novel here.'

'So if you *were* writing a crime novel, what would the answer be?'

'If I told you you'd have to verify loads of info, look up records, try to prove masses of things and it would probably come to absolutely nothing.'

Patrick slapped his lunch back on the plate and stared at me. 'You've already worked it out!'

'Only thought up the plot for a novel.'

'When?' he demanded to know.

'Just now. When you asked why hadn't they killed her.'

'For God's sake, put me out of my misery. *Why* didn't they?'

'Because they're working for her.'

'*What?*'

'In the book I probably won't write she was Judd's wife, her first marriage.'

It isn't often that my husband is rendered speechless.

'He went round the bend,' I continued, 'perhaps due to some

inherited mental problem and chucked her out, or she bailed out, at around the same time as all the staff left. There was loads of money stashed away somewhere, the proceeds of crime, but she had no access to it. As she was involved with his criminal activities, big time, she had to go into hiding because she no longer had protection. She changed her identity to that of ordinary housewife, moved to Somerset and hitched up with Archie Peters – do we know if they were ever actually married? – who was old, ill and loaded, and needed someone to look after him. It suited her to disappear into the countryside just then as she had no money of her own which she needed to get her own back on Judd, plus a share of his money. In other words, she needed the wherewithal to hire hitmen. She probably knew exactly who she needed: O'Connor.'

'It might have been his idea to cremate Judd's remains.'

'Well, you said yourself that he was different.'

'Which means the theory that she came to see Dad because she hadn't been paid for services rendered is wrong.'

'Yes, it is, but we've already had an alternative idea: she was covering herself if it all went pear-shaped. She'd go back to being poor little Mrs Peters in the sticks, leaving her mobsters to save themselves as well as they could. Who would a court believe if the whole thing crashed around their ears?'

'She might even have hastened old Archie's demise with a little weed killer in his cocoa. From what the curate said she was struggling to get the shopping.'

'And Archie's money could have been hidden in his mattress. *And* they might have tortured Judd to make him reveal where his was located before they murdered him. Patrick, please remember that this *is* only a bit of make-believe on my part.'

'No harm in checking to try to discover her actual status and working carefully to see if there's any truth in it.' Patrick remembered his sandwich. 'She might not be safe, though. Not if she's now sitting on two piles of cash and possibly stolen property courtesy of her one-time husband. O'Connor's going to want that.'

I wouldn't lose any sleep over that possibility. Was any of it true or just a product of my imagination? The description circulated of Mrs Peters had been as she had appeared to us that day at the rectory: middle-aged, of medium height, straggly grey-brown hair, dark brown eyes and shabbily dressed, details that would fit thousands of women in London alone.

Uninvolved with house-to-house enquiries and not 'wandering around' that area did not mean that we could not engage in a little low-key investigating in the High Street. We already knew that Frederick Judd had owned at least three businesses: a restaurant, a nightclub and a hairdressers. These had been closed down when he and his cohorts were arrested and subsequently jailed, but they were likely now to be under new ownership, especially as the properties they were in were almost certainly rented.

Asking questions in a hairdressers – Google informed us that there were getting on for a dozen of them – being impractical for several reasons, we decided to forego those. There were around two dozen restaurants of all kinds so as we did not have a week to spare we decided to find the nightclub. Patrick has a notion that that is where you start when looking for low-life anyway. What we wanted more than anything was, of course, gossip.

The nightclubs, four of which were listed, would only be open from about six o'clock onwards. It was now well into the afternoon but we still had several hours to wait. Patrick is not good at waiting and rang his new contact, the DI at the police station, to discover which club it had been. Her name, I now gathered, was Janice, and he was obviously cosying up to her like a real scoundrel to get as much information as possible.

'It was called The Dead Zone,' he duly reported. 'It closed down for good and the property is now a recently opened Chinese restaurant.' He pointed. 'That one over there, The Paradise Garden.'

'Just as well you asked,' I said.

He looked at his watch. 'A beer. I need to think.'

We ended up at a nearby hotel, a new one, in order that I could have tea, but I was not expecting any cerebral miracles from my particular choice of beverage as we seemed to have hit the buffers.

'In my view,' Patrick murmured after a while when he was

down to the last inch of his pint, 'we ought to take a room so we can stay the night here and, later on, have a Chinese meal.'

'At The Paradise Garden? What will they know about Judd and Co.?' I asked.

'Nothing, perhaps, but it means I can have another beer.'

Why not? I suggested he booked in and fetched the car *first*, adding that I had seen something about an underground car park for residents. Patrick went off and, as fast as you could say Fuller's 'London Pride', he returned, carrying our overnight bags, which we always keep ready packed in the Range Rover. Dumping them on the floor, he went over to the bar. I had already ordered myself more tea.

'Test results from Bath,' he announced when he came back. 'Carrick rang me just now. There are no DNA records for O'Connor as he committed his crimes before their use became widespread in the UK. Then he scarpered abroad, but we still know that he was there, and in charge, when Sandra Stevens was shot because you saw him. As far as the other two are concerned there are no matches. So all negative then.'

'And they might have arranged to finish Judd off before Archie Peters had died,' I mused. 'You know, I'm sure Anne Peters knew Judd years ago. She might even have known O'Connor.'

'One big happy family? Actually there are far too many ifs and buts around for my peace of mind.'

Patrick's mobile rang and from what little I could hear it was James Carrick again. It was a short call.

'A body's been found in the River Avon,' Patrick revealed. 'White, male, with a bullet wound in the chest, so it could be the man I shot. The PM's tomorrow afternoon. D'you think you'd recognize him?'

I didn't, and said so.

'I ought to take a look at him. And the ballistics people will want to examine my Glock. As you know they can usually work out if a weapon's fired a certain bullet.' He smiled to himself. 'That's if they can find it in him as they make a hell of a mess – unless it went right through him at that close range, in which Scenes of Crime will have found it. Are you getting hungry yet? I'm famished.'

I have known this man for almost ever and love him to bits, but his cold-bloodedness is sometimes hard to stomach.

I reasoned that the recently wounded should be permitted to have squid, of which I have an absolute horror – when cooked, that is. When they wiffle around the oceans changing colour they're actually rather sweet; reduced to curly bits with suckers on a plate like a cross between a jellyfish and a spider I would rather not be around. Patrick – who loves it – understands this and normally, and kindly, avoids having it unless dining alone.

The place was very clean, opulent really, with subdued lighting, and like so many Chinese restaurants, ran like clockwork, a man in evening dress making sure that it did. He came over when we were eating and asked us if our meal was satisfactory.

Patrick told him that it was, adopting a slight Scottish accent and a somewhat superior manner. He had also combed his hair so that it flopped over his forehead, hiding the recent scar. 'We were actually looking for a nightclub in this immediate area,' he continued. 'But obviously our directions were wrong. The Dead Zone?'

The man, who was not Chinese, shook his head. 'No, sir, it was here but closed.'

'There are quite a few clubs in the area already,' Patrick observed in off-hand fashion. 'I suppose the tenant decided a restaurant would be more profitable. I'm only mentioning this,' he hastened to add, 'because I'm in business myself and thinking of moving to this district.'

'No, there's a new tenant,' the man replied. 'But the place had been closed for quite some time while a new one was found. I understand there was a police investigation involving the previous business – nothing to do with us, of course.'

'Is there a chance that I might be able to speak with whoever it is? Only I would value some opinions on this area from those in the position to know.'

'I'm afraid the lady is abroad on holiday.' He then excused himself, saying he had to get back to work and left us.

'The lady,' Patrick repeated thoughtfully. 'I wonder who she might be?'

* * *

There was a huge gathering at the hotel when we returned, a
company dinner dance by the look of it, the foyer packed with
people, some in evening dress, others not. It occurred to me that
we did not look out of place as I was wearing my black dress
with twinkly bits, and Patrick a dark suit and tie. I took his hand
and led him around the edge of the throng in the direction of the
music, he probably thinking we were heading for the lifts or,
more likely, the bar.

'We can't come in here,' he protested in a loud whisper when
we were almost on the dance floor, couples moving slowly to
quiet, smoochy music.

'You learned to dance again in order to reach full mobility,' I
said in his ear. 'Please dance with me.'

Still, he hesitated. 'The notice said it was some kind of engineering bash.'

'OK, you're the CEO of Balls and Balls for Hunky Rivets,' I
told him. 'Dance.'

We danced.

I caught sight of us in one of the large wall mirrors – an
attractive couple perhaps, he tall and dark, the woman also dark-
haired, her head on a level with his shoulder – and found myself
thinking that I would remember this always, a special moment
to look back on when I was old and perhaps alone. I can't bear
to think of being alone before I'm old, but I know I have no
choice in the matter.

ELEVEN

J oanna had been back to Wellow, asking more questions, this time pretending to be a journalist from a Wessex newspaper, telling people she was trying to trace Anne Peters, this being true, of course. By interviewing elderly men in the village pub, and buying them quite a lot of beer, she had discovered a few interesting details. One old man told her that Archie Peters had been a regular in the public bar at one time, before his health really started to fail. Yarning about the past, he had never mentioned a wife, only, comparatively recently, a housekeeper. No one had been really interested in anything he said as he had been a bore and 'a bad-tempered ol' bugger'. Gossip had it that the man had been wealthy but mean to the point of mental instability; anyone unwise enough to call round at the bungalow with a charity collecting box likely to have a shotgun poked in their face. The police had, apparently, visited him with 'advice' on more than one occasion, and he had finally lost his firearms licence. It was thought he had lived not all that far away before he came to Wellow, but no one seemed to know exactly where. No one knew anything about his housekeeper-cum-wife either.

'Oh, would Patrick give me a reference?' Joanna had asked at the end of her call to me while we were having breakfast the next morning.

I told her that of course he would.

'Did you believe that guy when he said the boss was abroad on holiday?' Patrick queried, lavishly spreading marmalade on a slice of toast.

'Not sure,' I replied. 'But I could stay here and try to catch sight of her while you go off to look at the corpse.'

'No, she really could be away and you'd hang around for no reason. Besides which, you're not staying in this place on your own.'

I had offered in order to try to make up for my 'freak-out'.

We left the local police to get on with their house-to-house enquiries and, while Patrick returned to HQ – having decided that the corpse would have to wait – as he still had to carry on with his ordinary duties, I went home. Several days passed and, having decided to turn the case into a plot, with all details changed of course, I started work on my next novel. I did a signing at a book shop in Bath and gave a talk to the local Women's Institute. People always ask me where I get my ideas from. I can hardly tell them. Being 'normal' like this always gives me a slightly surreal feeling, and I was amused when a couple of the ladies enquired why I had not brought my 'handsome' husband with me. I promised to, next time, wondering what Patrick would make of *that.*

The next morning, just before lunch, there was the news that a couple of police officers had been fired on and wounded, one seriously, while doing house-to-house enquiries in a district of Feltham. Passers-by and one motorist, whose car had been almost struck by a vehicle as it speeded away from the scene, reported that three men and a woman had run from the house, at least one man carrying a handgun. I was watching this story unfold on the TV news when my mobile rang.

'I'm going along there,' Patrick said, after asking if I had heard what had happened. 'Janice seems to want someone to be a bit supportive as her boss is on long-term sick leave and the super, who's not a lot of help at the best of times, is in hospital with suspected appendicitis as of last night. She has an idea I'll know who these people are. Descriptions so far aren't too good but one could fit O'Connor. I'll keep you right up to date.'

'D'you know the address?' I enquired before he could ring off.

'No, but I'm going with someone who does. Apparently it's in a road close to where Judd lived.'

'For heaven's sake, be careful!'

'I'll phone you again later.'

It followed then that if one looked out for flashing blue lights and police incident tape . . . I pulled myself up sharply. No, there was no point in my going all that way for no good reason. Just because I was writing a novel based on the case didn't mean I should always be present during the investigation.

Janice wants someone to be a bit supportive, eh?

And she's a *detective inspector*?

I indulged in mental teeth gnashing for a few moments then got on with something else.

'Later' finished up by being just before nine thirty that evening, by which time my nerves were not so much jangling as in tatters. But to keep bothering him for news, a distraction, when I was half expecting the house they were investigating to have yet more hidden explosives in it, was absolutely out of the question.

'According to neighbours the place was rented out,' Patrick began by saying. 'We got the bomb disposal unit to have a look round before we went in. Nothing in the way of explosives but Class A drugs and enough booze for a really good weekend party were just lying around. There was a dog tied up out the back that was a bag of bones, almost too weak to bark, and I called the RSPCA, who came and took it away. We touched nothing, of course, and Forensics are now working there. From what witnesses saw of these people, which wasn't much, one of the blokes was almost certainly O'Connor – he was described as a big bear of a man with long black hair and the beginnings of a beard – but the woman doesn't fit Anne Peters's description. Blonde, quite smartly dressed, perhaps in her late-forties. Everything all right at your end?'

'Fine,' I replied.

'I'm on my way to that Chinese restaurant now, mostly to get something to eat and also to keep my eyes and ears open.'

'Where are you staying?'

'Tonight? At Janice's. She takes in lodgers, only members of the force, that is, but one's just left so there's a room spare.'

I remained silent, eventually driving the man in my life to say, 'Look, she's like the back of a Routemaster bus and I don't fancy her. All right?'

Presented with a vivid image of an overweight, red-faced woman, I supposed it was.

Then it appeared that the criminals we were trying to catch made a huge mistake. Patrick has a theory that they almost always do so eventually when the law is closing in on them. Therefore, when he was arrested later that night in Feltham for being drunk and disorderly, the doughty Janice, summoned from sleep on account of the miscreant's identity, immediately ordered that he be taken to hospital and tested for substances that might have been administered to him without his knowledge. Test results were inconclusive but the doctor who treated him concluded that as alcohol readings in his blood were very low he must have been

given substances unknown. The DI reasoned that the idea behind
such a move was that he would be removed from duty or it would
even ruin his career. He was treated appropriately by the medical
staff and then left to sleep it off for the rest of the night. Janice,
meanwhile, decided to hold her fire in order to make certain
people feel all warm and happy that they had got away with it,
and was planning to raid the restaurant the following evening.

Earlier that same morning, on hearing what had happened, I
had driven like a Valkyrie to London.

Patrick was at the nick, in the DI's office, drinking coffee. He
looked all right.

I said, 'I have an idea you went there with cop written all over
you deliberately to make things happen.'

'It pays off sometimes,' he said.

'Patrick, they could have killed you!' He wasn't as angry about
it as I had expected.

'It also pays to be underestimated by mobsters. I got a good
look at the woman in charge. Blonde, smartly dressed, mid-to
late-forties. Anne Peters.'

'*Seriously?*'

'You know I never joke about things like that. The hair might
have been a wig but I'm sure it was her. The rather angular way
she moved, dark eyes that didn't look right with the hair. Your
theory must be right on the nail – she was connected with Judd
in some way.'

'And she saw and recognized you. What did they put whatever
drug it was in?'

'Dunno.'

It occurred to me that, drugged up, he could have caused havoc
in the town centre, or might have started firing at things. Or
people. I said, 'It was just as well you told Janice where you
were going.'

'I mentioned it deliberately. In case.' He got to his feet. 'I'm
starving. Can you face the canteen?'

As it was, they served a very passable steak and mushroom pie.

We were sitting drinking tea – it was after three in the afternoon by this time – when a woman entered. She was tall, with
a rather stately bearing, middle-aged, had mid-brown hair piled

into an untidy bun on the top of her head and was wearing a very smart grey linen trouser suit with a matching blouse. A pair of spectacles hung on a pretty beaded chain around her neck. Always eager to file people away as potential characters for my novels – too eager, some people might say – I placed this lady as the super's wife or something similar. Her manner urgent, she came straight over to where we were sitting.

'This is Detective Inspector Janice North,' Patrick said, politely rising.

'And you're Ingrid Langley,' said the DI to me before Patrick could make the introduction. 'I read your books – when I have the time, that is.'

'Can I get you some tea?' Patrick enquired.

'I really can't stay.' She looked at her watch. 'OK, five minutes. Do you feel well enough?' she then asked in her slightly husky voice, gazing at him severely.

'I can probably walk ten yards and back again without keeling over,' he replied, smiling.

She beamed at him.

'I have you to thank for acting quickly,' I said as she seated herself. OK, these two had merely struck up a good friendship.

'Not a man to drink while on the job,' she observed reflectively.

'I'm worried that he might have hurt someone last night.'

'Oh, no. I have to tell you that I arranged to have him watched when he left the restaurant. You can't blink when there's a possible connection with mobsters like Frederick Judd. It soon became obvious that something untoward had happened and Patrick was carefully apprehended.'

I wondered what the hell they had said to him to get him to go quietly. 'Your wounded personnel – how are they?' I asked.

'Well, as you probably know, they're both in hospital, Constable Ellis with a shoulder wound and Constable Wright with a flesh wound in her upper arm. Hers isn't serious. As far as the house goes it would appear that it's rented, but not seemingly by the people who ran out and got away. We're still trying to sort that one out.'

Patrick returned with the tea, placed it before her and said, 'I'd like to come along tonight.'

She thanked him, put two heaped spoonfuls of sugar in it and stirred quickly, saying, 'I'm happy for you to do so. But I must insist that you're present as an observer only and I rely on an armed support team if needs be. If you wish to carry your handgun, as you're permitted to for self-defence purposes, that's fine, but I don't want you to take part in any armed aspect of the raid. For one thing, it's unlikely you're clear of those drugs they gave you. I hope that's agreeable to you.'

'Perfectly,' Patrick said. He then went on to tell her about his being convinced that the woman he had seen there was Anne Peters, obviously having given the DI full details of the case on which we were working. She made a note of it.

'And your boss?' I asked.

'In theatre right now, having his appendix removed,' I was briskly informed. 'Which means he'll be even more bloody useless than usual for a while. Now, if you'll excuse me . . .'

'A Routemaster?' I queried when she was safely out of earshot, taking her tea with her.

'I hear that the new ones are sleek and super-efficient,' Patrick said, straightfaced. 'And you were jealous.'

'You didn't mention me with regard to tonight either,' I said accusingly, nettled. 'I'm not an accessory like a handbag.'

He laughed at me then whispered, 'A damned fine handbag actually, madam.'

How do I love thee? Let me count the ways.

At just after eleven that night we found ourselves sitting in an unmarked van parked in a side street of Feltham in the company of sundry large policemen. They were wearing so much kit of various kinds that it was distinctly cosy. If they knew who we were, these two individuals attired in dark blue tracksuits and black trainers, they said nothing. They remained dumb anyway – nerves, perhaps.

'Leave the door ajar, please,' Patrick said sharply as they reacted to a couple of quiet taps on it and prepared to disembark. We've been shut inside a police van once in the past and Patrick was finally forced to shoot the lock off before we suffocated, which had the effect of writing off the entire door. The Met sent SOCA, as it was then, the bill for the vehicle's repair.

'Fresh air, thank God,' I whispered when we were alone – the interior had been filled with the aroma of lightly stewed blokes.

'What are you going to do?'

Patrick grinned at me. 'Observe, what else?'

We waited for a few minutes, not wishing to be right on their heels, then quietly got out, closing the door. Someone had remained in the driving cab, a precaution no doubt, in case the vehicle was stolen. We had not been invited to attend any briefings so were unsure exactly where we were, but my husband has an instinct for this kind of thing and set off in light drizzle towards a set of traffic lights on a road junction not far away. Before we reached it he turned aside, to the right, down an old lane, a horse-drawn wagon wide, which finished up in quite a large car park, a couple of dozen vehicles there, seemingly reserved for residents of the flats above the shops. Sections were marked off for the use of delivery vehicles. The area was quite well lit and Patrick made for where it was dimmer, perhaps on account of one of the orange lamps having failed. There was no sign of any police activity.

'I think . . .' Patrick muttered, setting off towards the main exit of the car park, 'That the building over there that we can see the rear of, the one which has the floodlit flag pole on its roof,' he pointed across the car park, 'is the council offices. It's situated around a hundred and fifty yards north of the restaurant on the opposite side of the road. Therefore we're nearer to it than that. I'm assuming there will be road blocks.'

Judging by the traffic being redirected and the proliferation of flashing blue lights in the misty distance, that was exactly what was happening. We crossed the High Street, having to wait a little while, and, anticipating that pedestrians would also be prevented from proceeding, cut down a side street almost directly opposite. This brought us out in a road parallel to the one we had just crossed where Patrick paused, listening. All I could hear was traffic.

'They must have gone in because they would have done that *first*,' Patrick said in an undertone, turning left. 'Keep close and watch out for any stray mobsters.'

We saw no one except for a couple of drunks and a woman hurrying along, perhaps going home from a job in a pub or club. Coming to a narrow gap between buildings, Patrick stopped again, sniffing the air.

'Chinese cooking,' he said with satisfaction. 'Rather good, too.'

He moved off but I remained where I was and, after a few steps, sensing that I was no longer with him, he turned. 'Coming?'

'Patrick, I've just had this crazy notion that there was nothing wrong with your meal last night.'

'No, there wasn't.'

'But didn't the Peters woman see and recognize you?'

'No. After I'd caught a glimpse of her on the way in I sat with my back to the bar.'

'You pretended you were drunk, doped, whatever?' I exclaimed in a kind of shrieked whisper.

'How else was I going to get Janice to raid the place?'

Bloody hell.

The little lane wove this way and that and housed the usual bins, rubbish and other detritus. We finally came to two police officers stationed by a pair of doors that had been forced, the cooking smells gusting from a large louvered vent nearby in the wall. Even in the dim illumination provided by a dirty light over the doors, it was impossible to tell whether this pair had been among those in the van due to all the gear they were loaded down with.

'You can't go any further,' one of them told us. 'Police investigation.'

'National Crime Agency,' Patrick informed him. 'I'm here as an official observer.'

'May I see your ID, sir?'

Patrick dug his wallet out of his pocket and waved the warrant under the man's nose. 'This lady's my assistant. What's going on?'

'There seems to be some kind of stalemate.'

'Has anyone left the premises through this back way since you arrived?'

'No, and we positioned ourselves here before the rest went in, here and through the front.'

'Are you armed?'

'No.'

'Be very careful if you detain anyone. They might be.'

And with that warning, Patrick went to the doors and gently pushed on the one that had suffered the most damage.

'You shouldn't go in!' one of the men said fiercely, but under his breath.

'I can hardly observe standing out here,' was the equally quiet response.

We went in. It was dark inside but I could just hear distant voices.

Thinking, I'm sure, that as we could see nothing, not even a glimmer of light, there must be at least one door between us and what was happening, Patrick switched on his tiny torch. This revealed large cardboard boxes, spare chairs and so forth untidily stacked everywhere: a store room. Taking great care not to dislodge anything, we made our way across the room, which appeared to be around fifteen feet square, towards a door on the far side. I noticed that Patrick had not drawn his Glock, something he would have done normally under such circumstances. My Smith and Wesson was in my hand, in my pocket.

'Hide!' Patrick suddenly hissed.

Moments later, the door burst open and light flooded in. From my prone position behind a stack of boxes I saw several regulation boots go by through a small gap at floor level. Judging by the noise they were making they went right out into the street.

'Anyone come this way?' a woman's voice, not Janice's, demanded to know.

'Only a couple from the NCA,' was the reply. 'We checked – they're on the line.'

'We haven't seen them.'

'Probably changed their minds and went out another way. No sign of the boss?'

'No.'

'How the hell did you manage to screw that one up? How can you lose track of a DI?'

'Apparently she was giving orders outside one minute and disappeared the next.'

The trio – I counted six boots – returned and left the storeroom. I waited for a few seconds and then, hearing movement from Patrick, emerged. They had left the door ajar.

'They've *lost* Janice?' I said incredulously.

'I have a very nasty feeling about this,' Patrick muttered. 'Time to stop hiding.'

We went through the doorway into a short corridor. To the left was the kitchen where around a dozen frightened Chinese, some in chef's whites, the rest obviously waiters, had been herded into a corner and were being watched over by a single police officer. He had his back to us and didn't notice our presence. Noting this, Patrick went back to the door, locked it and put the key in his pocket.

The corridor opened out into the restaurant. It was an assault to the eyes: scarlet, gold, dragons, tassels, gongs, fountains, the lot. There were plenty of people here, and several uniformed police grouped around six or seven sullen-looking individuals I immediately tagged as 'yobs'. On the other side of the room were a few couples who were probably customers, again in a corner, who looked as though they were mumbling their grievances about their ruined evening to one another. As we walked forward three men, I guessed CID officers, came down a wide staircase, followed by five members of an armed support group carrying semi-automatic machine guns.

'Who are you?' enquired the man who was walking slightly in front of the others, stopping in his tracks as he reached floor level.

'Gillard,' Patrick answered. 'NCA. Who are you?'

'DS Holberton. In the absence of the DI I'm in charge.'

'Where *is* DI North?'

'We don't know. She must have disappeared seconds after she gave the order to enter the building.'

'Have you searched upstairs?'

'There's a problem: I'm worried that she's being held up there.'

'How would anyone have got her upstairs without you seeing what was happening?'

'There might be other entrances.'

Visibly, Patrick clung on to his temper. 'What's up there?'

'More seating, three doors off, no sign of anyone.'

We went closer to enable the conversation to take place quietly. Patrick asked, 'Did you go into the rooms?'

'No.'

'You should have done.' Softly, Patrick continued, 'DS Holberton, have you had any experience of this kind of thing?'

'Er, no.'

'I have. Would you be offended if I offered a little advice?'

'I'll use it if I think it's useful.'

'Good man. First of all, go and talk to those henchmen over

there and see if anyone's willing to help the law in exchange for a sympathetic hearing at the nick.'

Holberton hesitated for a moment then went across. We shadowed him, but gave him room to move. It soon became obvious that one of the six men was endeavouring to conceal himself behind the man standing next to him.

'I know that man,' Patrick said to Holberton. 'I suggest you talk to him first.'

'Bring him out,' the DS ordered. 'As you know him you'd better talk to him, Gillard.'

This individual manifestly did not want to talk to anybody.

'Will, old son,' Patrick said chummily. 'Remember the last time we met and some pals of yours were trying to gun us down in a garage in East London?'

'No,' said Will Gibbs.

'In fact, we wrote down your surname. Gibbs, wasn't it?'

No reaction.

With a little bit of mime asking for permission to take Will aside, Patrick, without waiting for any kind of reaction, led the man away over to a window recess. I tagged along.

'Listen,' he was saying in an undertone as I caught up, 'the DI appears to have gone missing. If you tell me where she's likely to be I shall look upon you most favourably and put in good words on your behalf. Is she anywhere upstairs?'

The man licked his lips nervously. 'And if I don't talk?'

'I don't like being shot at. I shall find you, even if you're sent to prison for twenty years after this fiasco of yours, and wring your bloody neck.'

'Fiasco?' Gibbs said, puzzled. He had probably been brought to mind of a shot being put into the ground an inch or so from his toes.

'Fiasco. It means a total cock-up. We know who all those in charge are. Jinty O'Connor for a start – and I really do owe *him* – plus a woman who's been calling herself Anne Peters. They've left a trail of murders behind them – killings that yobs for hire like you will get the blame for. Where's the DI?'

Will was shredding his lips with stained teeth now.

'Is she upstairs?'

'No,' was the muttered reply.

Patrick swung round. 'Storm those rooms upstairs!'

Holberton and the armed contingent thundered off.

Patrick turned his attention back to Gibbs. 'Where then?'

'You will put in a word for me, won't you? I've had enough of this.'

'You have my word.'

'It was a plan they made at the last minute – someone saw the police coming. Watch for the one who gives orders, they said, grab them and use whoever it is as a hostage. God knows why they thought it would achieve anything – O'Connor's mad.'

'Where is she?'

'They'll be waiting in a car somewhere – until the fuss dies down.'

'What sort of car?'

'Peters's car. It's a silver Jag.'

'Is O'Connor with them?'

'I haven't clapped eyes on him in weeks.'

'So who's "they"?'

'Her and her boyfriend. Don't know his name. He doesn't speak to the likes of me.'

Patrick clapped the man on the shoulder. 'All sorted,' he said to me cheerily, making sure those around could hear, and then jerked his head in the direction we had entered.

When we were walking back along the lane at the rear and had past the two standing guard who were trying to look vigilant, Patrick said, 'My prime aim is to make sure the DI isn't harmed. But nothing is certain. First, though, we must locate this vehicle.' In the light from a street lamp in the nearby road, he turned. 'If we'd brought the cavalry there may have been a nasty stand-off with Janice getting shot out of sheer spite or by accident.'

I reckoned there were still far too many 'mights' and 'maybes'.

'Nothing's certain in war,' Patrick added, as if guessing my thoughts.

TWELVE

A group of young men, together with a few other people, were hanging around at the junction with the High Street, watching what was going on. Not much was. They gave every appearance of being law-abiding, and when Patrick appeared in their midst looked rather alarmed.

'Undercover cops,' he said very quietly to them. 'We're looking for a silver Jag. Seen one?'

They hadn't.

'May we borrow a couple of your baseball caps? I promise you'll get them back.'

Very reluctantly, two were handed over.

'We'll still look like cops in these blue outfits,' I mumbled as we were walking away.

'No, put it on back to front, like the lads did.'

'Where to?' I asked, removing it and ramming it backwards on my head – it was too big for me and smelt of greasy take-aways, but there was no time to make adjustments or be fussy.

'The car park we came through. The likelihood of the Jag being there depends on whether Peters was acting a bit thick when she came to the rectory, or if she really is.'

'The oracle says she has plenty of native cunning but isn't all that intelligent.'

'My feelings precisely.'

We hurried, my cap threatening to slip off, while I prayed that Will had been telling the truth.

A minute or so later, we turned into the main entrance to the car park and my partner immediately commenced to sing. It was a particularly filthy ditty sung, regrettably, slurring the words, to the tune of 'All Things Bright and Beautiful'. Patrick has a rather good tenor voice and, like that of all one-time and present choristers, it carries. Realizing that two drunks are better than one, I joined in with the right words, and, seemingly, a seriously inebriated pair staggered across the car park. We paused halfway across for a lascivious snog, taking the opportunity to have a look round while slowly revolving on the spot, on the point of falling over to anyone watching.

We both spotted the car, parked in the dimmer area where the lamp had failed.

Starting on verse two, we reeled a little nearer. Some twenty yards away Patrick fell down flat, laughing like a jackass, and although I was sort of prepared for something like that to happen I went down with him, mainly because he was holding on to me.

'Tyres!' he said in my ear.

My speciality. From my prone position I took out the front and rear tyres nearest to me then rolled away in case there was any returning fire.

A man got out of the driving seat, almost fell out actually due to the car's suddenly canted-over position. 'What the hell do you think you're doing?'

'Armed police! Lie down! Arms outstretched! You're under arrest!' Patrick yelled at him, getting up.

The driver moved to obey and then shouted back, 'I'll report you for this! You're raving mad!'

Patrick walked forward, holding his Glock two-handed, and suddenly there was no further argument.

A blonde-haired woman got out of the front passenger seat holding a handgun. 'We've got your Detective Inspector North in there!' she shrilled, pointing the gun towards the inside of the vehicle. 'Let us go and we'll chuck her out a short distance away.'

'You stupid cow, I said to bluff it out!' bawled her companion from his prone position.

Bending low, I had quietly moved around the rear of the vehicle until I was feet away from her. Eyes on Patrick, she did not notice me until I spoke.

'Last warning,' I said. 'Drop the weapon.'

When she did not immediately do so, I put a shot into the ground several feet away to her rear. This produced a loud shriek and the gun was flung at me. I ducked, then yanked open the rear door nearest to me.

'Out,' I said to the man seated within. 'Keep your hands in my sight or you'll lose them.' Truly, I shouldn't be talking like this. I was merely the consultant to an adviser of the NCA.

Bloody hell.

Darkly glaring at me he slowly, and a little unsteadily, got out of the car and both 'suspects' were garnered by Patrick and made to lie on the ground with the first man, the woman raving and swearing at us. I was not at all sure she was Anne Peters.

By this time the sound of the shots had attracted attention and there was a blare of approaching sirens, screaming tyres and flashing blue lights, the entire road show howling past the entrance to the car park.

'Ingrid, do go down there and wave when they come back,' Patrick said wearily. 'Are you all right, ma'am?' he went on to ask, addressing the interior of the vehicle.

'Just a bit bruised,' came the reply from Janice North.

As I walked away I heard Patrick add, 'I've detained your abductors. Would you like to arrest them?'

'Very much so.'

Class A and B drugs with an estimated street value of over half a million pounds were found in a hidden wall safe in one of the upstairs rooms of the restaurant, together with several thousand pounds in used notes and sterling, the blonde woman being commanded to open it. Another room, an office of sorts, yielded two handguns with ammunition and several knives. Three of the men detained, including Will Gibbs, were wanted to help with other enquiries, and the man sitting in the back of the car with the DI was an Italian wanted in his home country for murder. The driver of the vehicle had no previous convictions but was charged with being an accessory to the abduction. Whether he was the 'boyfriend' of the woman who was steadfastly denying that she was anyone by the name of Anne Peters would have to be established.

'Is that blonde hair a wig, or isn't it?' I was driven to ask later the following day when we learned of this. Earlier, having got some sleep at our usual hotel in West London, we had gone back to Feltham to make our statements, hung around at the nick in case we could question her but had been told, 'Sorry, no, not yet, she's still being interviewed about last night,' and were now leaving the building.

'Apparently not,' Patrick replied.

'Then she must have been wearing one under that ghastly hat when we saw her at the rectory.'

'You're still convinced it's her?'

'No.'

Men have no answer to this kind of female logic so Patrick merely smiled and murmured, 'I should have said this before – that was good shooting last night.'

'You didn't have to fire a shot.'

'My right hand was shaking but I would have done so if necessary. That's why I held it two-handed.'

'It will take a while to recover, you know.'

He did not answer.

'It's Friday,' I said. 'Let's go home.'

On Saturday morning, Patrick asked me to ride George, his horse, kept at livery nearby, saying he would go and view the body of the man that had been found in the River Avon and then get on with an emailed report to Michael Greenway. For me, this was a pleasure, of course – a blessing after recent events – and I took Katie with me on Fudge, who was now quite sound. Matthew is having lessons at the same establishment and doing well.

'Dad's arm looks terrible, it's all bruised,' Katie said at one point when we were riding abreast. 'Is that why he didn't want to take George out this morning, because it hurt?'

'Partly,' I answered.

'How did he do it?'

'Someone hit him,' I told her.

'Matthew and I think he ought to stop doing such dangerous things. Don't you?'

'He will,' I replied, deliberately not answering the question.

'When, though?' she persevered.

'I don't know,' was all I could say. Patrick and I had still not had our discussion about it.

When I got back, having dropped Katie off at a friend's house – yes, more ponies – Patrick was nowhere to be seen, but came in from the garden shortly afterwards.

'Janice North is very embarrassed,' he told me. 'She regards what happened as a massive failure on her part.'

'How on earth's that?' I asked, staggered.

'Yes, quite. I reminded her what the raid had yielded and said she doesn't have to mention our presence at all, but she's the sort of person who wants everything to be utterly correct in her report. Anyway, we can have a go at this woman who's saying she's not Anne Peters on Monday morning.'

'And the corpse in the river?'

'I couldn't say for sure as it happened so quickly and the body had been knocked about in the water, but he'd been wearing the same colour shirt as the guy I shot. There's no identification yet. They found the bullet and Ballistics have borrowed the Glock for a while to see if there's a possible match. Then we'll know for sure.'

A little later, he came to find me in my writing room to say, 'I've just had a call from Carrick to say that Sandra Stevens is recovering well. She wants to talk to us as she's remembered something. Coming?'

As might be expected, the woman was terribly pale, but smiled when she saw us. It was humbling when she thanked me profusely for the few flowers I had picked for her from the garden and arranged in a small glass pot. They looked nothing when placed alongside a magnificent bouquet of florists' flowers already on the bedside cabinet. It was a relief to know that she was being given armed protection.

'Thank you so much for coming,' she said in a weak voice. 'I'm afraid I don't have much information for you. But please, first tell me if those men have been arrested.'

Patrick said, 'No, I'm afraid they haven't. But we know exactly who the man in charge is and a warrant's out for his arrest. Two of them were shot and we're ninety-nine per cent sure that one's dead. The other hasn't turned up at any hospital in this area so it's likely he's in a bad way. They won't trouble you again.'

She looked puzzled. 'Shot by who?'

Patrick merely smiled.

'You! I didn't know you could do things like that.'

'We wouldn't be here otherwise.'

'No, of course not. It would have been dreadful if they'd got you too.' Sandra gave him a truly lovely smile back.

She really did fancy him then. It must be those grey eyes doing their ol' magic.

'DCI Carrick told me that you'd remembered something,' Patrick prompted.

'That's not *quite* true, but I didn't intend to mislead anyone.'

'Oh?'

She coloured a little, which actually made her look a lot better. 'I thought that if I didn't say something like that nobody would come.'

'Well, we're here now.'

'You were asking me about the night Hereward went back to Wellow because he'd left his mobile phone at someone's house.'

'That's right.'

'You must appreciate that I can't remember anything from the moment I was shot until I woke up here – I'm told it was a couple of days later. As far as real life's concerned, everything's a blank. But I've sort of had a dream, so what I'm telling you might be just that, a dream. I've had dreams in the past and some of them have been found to be, or come, true. But I'm worried that if I tell you something and you act on it and it's just a load of nonsense . . .' She drifted into silence.

'Let me worry about that,' Patrick told her. 'How I treat potential evidence is my responsibility.'

Her brow cleared. 'Oh, I see.' Having paused as if to choose her words carefully, she continued, 'It was horrible, really, as it was as if I was Hereward retracing his footsteps. But a ghostly Hereward, as though he was dead.'

'Take your time,' Patrick murmured when she stopped speaking, her eyes filling with tears.

I gave her a paper tissue from a box on the cabinet and after half a minute or so she recommenced talking.

'It was raining and the dream was so vivid that although there was no sense of my actually walking I could feel the drops hitting my head, soaking my hair. He had lovely hair, you know, a bit like yours, Mr Gillard. I, or he, came to a house. That was horrible too, like a witch's house inside a nasty little wood, with straggly trees with faces in them, like a Disney film. And this was where my dream became really surreal so don't take any notice of this next bit – I'm just telling you to show I'm giving you the whole story, as it were.' She gazed in the direction of a jug and glass tumbler on the cabinet. 'Please give me some water.'

This Patrick did and, shakily, she drank some.

'There was a cat there,' Sandra resumed. 'A big black one. It was beautiful – I adore cats. It spoke to me. It said its name was Henry and I mustn't go to the house.'

I think my hair stood on end.

'But I told it I had to as I'd left my phone behind and it ran off in a huff. I went up the path to the house, which seemed to be in darkness, and banged on the door. I knew the bell didn't work. A woman opened it, a different one from last time, and she looked very angry when she saw it was me. A man with a deep voice called out, "Who is it?" and she replied, "The undertaker again." I said I'd left my phone behind and she told me to wait and went away. Then she came back and practically threw it at me. I noticed a man standing in the darkness of the hallway just behind her, perhaps the one who had spoken. He was tall, broad-shouldered, had a mass of dark unkempt hair and looked as though he was growing a beard. I left as quickly as I could and all the way back to my car I felt as though he was prowling behind me, but every time I looked round no one was there.'

Sandra broke off and shuddered. 'That was it. The next thing I knew I woke up here.'

'A different woman from last time?' Patrick echoed. 'How was she different?'

'I've no idea. I just *knew*.'

'What about the bell? You knew that didn't work as well?'

'That's right.'

Patrick and I exchanged glances. The bell push at the Peterses' bungalow had actually been loose in the fitting, broken, and as there had been no knocker Patrick had had to bang on the door with his fist.

'I don't think I'm mad or psychic,' Sandra said in a small voice. 'It all must just be coincidences. Hereward must have told me about the different woman and the man with the beard and I'd forgotten about it. I seem to recollect fetching us some wine from the kitchen while he was talking. But it was in my subconscious. The rest's just silly.'

The business of Henry wasn't silly, it was mind-blowing. I said nothing.

Patrick turned to me. 'D'you still have that printed-off photofit and the mugshot with you?'

I did, and passed them over. We had learned earlier that there had been no fingerprints, not even partial ones, on the remains of the handgun I had shot from O'Connor's grasp. As I had thought, he had been wearing gloves.

Before Patrick gave them to Sandra one at a time in that same order, he said, 'Be assured that this man will be arrested very shortly. I don't want you to be afraid or upset.'

'But my subconscious interpretation of what Hereward told me might be quite different from the real thing,' she sensibly pointed out before looking at what was in her hands.

'Don't worry about that.'

'Oh, God,' she whispered, gazing at the photofit. 'It's him. Just about the same as in my dream, hallucination, whatever it was. But—' She shook her head, baffled, and then studied the other. 'This is a photo of him when he was quite a bit younger, without the beard, isn't it?'

Patrick told her that it was.

'Surely you won't able to use what I've just said in a court of law.'

No, unfortunately we would not.

The rest of the weekend saw us being an ordinary family. We took all five children out to a country park on Sunday afternoon – you need a Range Rover for this many, plus a buggy – somewhere the two boys could run a bit wild in an adventure playground. Matthew, I felt, was a bit self-conscious in the company of children mostly younger than himself, but I told him he was Justin's minder while Patrick and I looked after the two youngest, and that improved matters a lot. Justin needs minding. Hating anything to do with ropes and ladders and, naturally, not counted among the babies, Katie trailed along with us, polite but miserable as there were no ponies. She cheered up when Patrick took her out on the lake in a rowing boat but Vicky refused, point blank, to go anywhere near the water, or even to wave them off, so she and I sat on a seat with Mark, watching them.

Patrick and I had arranged to devote the evening for our discussion on his future so I gave it some thought in advance now. Would I be happy if my life was like this more often? Would Patrick? It went without saying that he would have to have some kind of job if he left the NCA, as although my writing earnings are healthy I could not support the whole family. And for how much longer would people want to read my books? If it was a less challenging job he would be bored. But we were both getting older.

I could come to no conclusions and had the feeling that while there was still breath in his body Patrick would want to go after the likes of Jinty O'Connor. Even if he retired from what he was now doing there would be no real let-up. We are still on the hit lists of several criminal and terrorist organizations so he would have no choice but be armed and attend training sessions. Unless they took his gun away from him, of course. This had not occurred to me before and it was a couple of minutes before the full implications sank in.

Yes, this man of mine could not countenance being defenceless and would buy a weapon and carry it illegally, even if, as he had jokingly threatened to, he started up a grass-cutting empire. To protect himself, his wife and his family. There would be a risk he would go to prison if found out. Certain policeman with whom he has had differences of opinion over the years would make it their business to find out. We would probably have to go and live abroad, perhaps in the States, where carrying firearms for personal protection is permitted.

I asked myself if Patrick would already have thought this and several other aspects of the problem through himself. I had an idea he had. Torn between my conclusions and the possibility that my worries were being a distraction to him I decided to suggest on the way home that we postpone all discussions until, one way or another, the O'Connor case was concluded.

When I did so Patrick hesitated and asked me if I was really sure. I was, and he agreed. I resolved to keep any fears I had to myself.

As was our habit, we called in to see Michael Greenway when we, or rather Patrick, arrived for work early on Monday morning.

I intended to stay in London just for the day and return home the next, and was quite looking forward to the interview with the woman who was insisting she wasn't Anne Peters.

'Richard Daws wants to see you,' Greenway said, his mind on something else. 'Look, as you know, Patrick, I'm not a complaining kind of bloke but d'you think this bloody room is big enough for me to work in without going off my rocker?'

Patrick eyed it up and then said, 'For anyone four foot nothing tall and fourteen inches wide it's absolutely perfect.'

'Thank you,' said the commander, grabbing his desk phone. 'I'll tell 'em exactly that.'

'I know you're expected at Feltham police station later this morning,' was Daws's opening remark, 'but I have a bit of news for you in connection with O'Connor.'

What didn't this man know?

We seated ourselves and had to wait for a few moments while he tidied and put to one side some documents on his desk. I had to admit that this wasn't a particularly large office either, but then noticed a couple of inner doors, suggesting that the room we were in might be the working area of a small apartment. Perhaps he lived here for part of the week and went back to Hartwood Castle the rest of the time.

'I understand there was no sign of him at the Chinese restaurant,' Daws said.

'No, sir,' Patrick replied. 'And one of the suspects said that he hadn't seen him for weeks.'

'You must appreciate that I've asked Greenway to forward your reports to me. I liked the way you got that DI out of a nasty spot. But I had to prevent your presence getting into the media as I don't want O'Connor to know the NCA is getting close to him.'

'I told him I knew who he was but wasn't that convinced at the time. It was Ingrid's photofit of him that clinched it. We also now have a completely unconfirmed report that he was at the Peterses' bungalow the night the funeral director returned because he'd left his mobile there.'

'Unconfirmed?' Daws queried with a frown.

'Yes, from Sandra Stevens. Hereward, her ex-husband, related

the episode to her shortly before he was killed – murdered –
some of the details of which she appeared to have forgotten
but dreamt or hallucinated about when she was unconscious in
hospital. It's not evidence.'

It was a real shame we couldn't ask Henry about it, I thought.

'No, not admissible,' said Daws. 'Well, we know that
O'Connor's been to Bath on a mission to murder that woman
although only one witness – you, Ingrid – identified him.
Following on from that I understand a body's been fished out of
the Avon with a bullet from your Glock 17 inside it. Yes, that
was confirmed first thing this morning,' he added when he saw
the look of slight surprise on Patrick's face. 'I got a look at the
photo of this man taken in the mortuary and I know who he is,
or rather was – Declan O'Leary, O'Connor's brother. He was the
explosives expert. As I'm sure you know, O'Leary is O'Connor's
real name.'

I did not glance in Patrick's direction but have an idea he
smiled.

'It's a positive identification,' Daws continued, 'because, as
you also know, before I went to MI5 I worked for a time with
Army Intelligence in Northern Ireland. He was connected with
a terrorist group and lived in southern Ireland. I've contacted the
police there as they might have a DNA sample in their records.'

'I take it there's no sign of the man Ingrid wounded in the
shoulder.'

'No. Another point I want to make is that as I'm sure you've
seen the news in the media that criminal gangs are spreading
into the provinces, something that we've known for a long time,
of course. It's fairly safe to assume from his activities in the
West Country that O'Connor's gang is one of them. But I do
have one problem. You've made no mention of any connection
that you know of that he has with this Peters woman that would
make this whole thing hang together.'

'Ingrid has a theory,' Patrick said.

Daws smiled at me, something he hardly ever does to anyone,
which shook me slightly. 'I like your theories,' he told me.

I took a deep breath. 'Frederick Judd might be the connection,'
I began. 'Based on the possibility that it was his body which was
cremated in Bath instead of that of Archie Peters, I have an idea

that O'Connor is working for Anne Peters, who – another theory of mine – was Judd's wife, or if not, was in a relationship with him. We know everyone left him, including his staff – fled, perhaps – when he went off his head with some kind of mental disorder. I have a picture in my mind of a woman bent on revenge who wanted to get back what she regarded as hers. Judd was reputed to be wealthy from the proceeds of crime. But she would need help – someone who had a reputation of getting rid of people, no questions asked. Someone like O'Connor.'

'Anything else?' Daws asked, looking thoughtful.

'We now know that Anne Peters has had experience as an actress. In my opinion, every time we've met her so far she's been acting. I've been thinking about this and pretty sure that the blonde-haired woman who shouted out to us that night in Feltham sounded very much like Anne Peters when she came to the rectory at Hinton Littlemore, and also when we talked to her at her home at a later date.'

'You might find out if you're correct soon,' Daws observed. He turned to Patrick. 'I still want this man alive. Is that understood?'

'Yes, sir,' Patrick said.

As we were leaving, Daws spoke very quietly to me. 'The pair of you were in fine voice.' Then, amazingly, he smiled again.

'Did you hear what he said?' I whispered to Patrick as we walked along a corridor towards the lifts.

'No.'

'He told me that we were in fine voice. Did you mention that bit about us pretending to be drunk in your report?'

'It's not the kind of thing you put in a report,' Patrick answered, mildly affronted.

'You know what it means then?' And without waiting for a reply, I said, 'He was *there*!'

THIRTEEN

If Janice North was still smarting over her escapade she was not advertising the fact and greeted us warmly after we'd almost literally bumped into her in a corridor at Feltham police station. Patrick and I had agreed that neither of us would mention it if she didn't.

The implications of what Daws had said to me were still fizzing through my mind. It was perfectly possible that he had been in the town that night as it would not be the first time he had directly involved himself with one of our assignments. Perhaps following our activities was a kind of hobby of his and, if so, I was not very happy about it. I could only hope that he had more altruistic reasons for what he was doing. But why had he dropped such a heavy hint? Why mention it to me at all?

'She's still spitting mad,' reported the DI. 'Refuses to answer questions, just stares down anyone who tries to interview her.'

'What about the other two?' Patrick asked.

'Well, as you're aware, the Italian's wanted in his home country for murder and we think he's connected with a local Mafia group. But he's terminally ill with advanced cancer, which he has been able to prove to us. He's been interviewed but is clearly very ill. It sounds callous of me to put it like this but I don't think he's going to be a lot of use. The driver of the car has no previous convictions and insists he's just a handyman at the restaurant. He knows the woman only as "the boss" and became indignant when it was suggested he was in a relationship with her.'

'Who's the registered owner of the car?' I asked.

'A leasing company. It's leased in the name of someone called Patrick O'Leary. I haven't had time to do any research on him.'

'Got her!' Patrick said with relish. 'It's O'Connor's real name.'

'I'll have her brought to interview room one.'

'Does she have a solicitor?'

'No, says she doesn't need one as she's just a restaurant manager and we've arrested the wrong person. Now, if you'll

excuse me, we're still dealing with the aftermath of last week
. . .' She hurried away.

Several observations crowded into my mind when we entered
the interview room and I examined the woman closely. First, the
blonde hair, cut into a bob, was definitely her own – it was
growing out dark at the roots; second, she was very expensively
dressed and third, the almost black eyes staring at me with
unconcealed malevolence were the same that had indicated my
presence was not wanted in Patrick's father's study at home.
Same hands, same bony wrists, same sloping shoulders. This *was*
the woman who had called herself Anne Peters.

'No more time-wasting,' Patrick began by saying, having
switched on the recording machine and formally opened the
interview. 'You know who we are and we know who you are.
You came to Hinton Littlemore rectory in an effort to cover
yourself following the criminal activities that surrounded Archie
Peters's funeral when Judd's body was substituted for his and
probably thought you were safe when I initially failed to find
out what had really happened. I'm sure you were desperately
hoping I wouldn't be able to discover anything. Whether you
really were Peters's wife or not doesn't interest me now. I don't
care a damn what your real name is either. As I said at the beginning of this interview, I work for the National Crime Agency.
All I'm interested in is arresting a man calling himself Jinty
O'Connor. Other police forces can take care of the rest.'

She sat back in her chair, crossed her arms and carried on
staring at me.

'I'm guessing that O'Connor had nothing to do with your
abduction of DI North last week,' Patrick went on. 'He wouldn't
have done anything so stupid. What were you hoping to achieve?'

She carried on ignoring him.

'There you are, presumably well off now you have Frederick
Judd's money – although Archie Peters's assets might prove
difficult to get hold of now – and are mistress of your own little
crime empire, using the restaurant as a front and with the
comforting thought that you have a mobster with a real reputation keeping you safe. Am I right?'

She said nothing but her expression said it all. He was right.

'On the other hand,' Patrick continued, 'things might not be so cosy after all. You hired O'Connor to help you get back at Judd – with whom at one time, we're pretty sure, you were close – and might have initially been under the impression that he was working for you. But O'Connor's not like that and here, I assure you, I'm on firmer ground. He'll want every penny you have and you'll probably end up as Judd did – burnt to ashes.'

This registered and she transferred her attention to Patrick, only to discover that he has a far better line in nasty stares. Flustered, she glanced away.

'The skull usually explodes, you know,' he went on chattily. 'Or the torso, or both. Pressure builds up because of gases inside and then . . . bang!'

'You're disgusting,' the woman said harshly. Speaking with a strong London accent, she went on: 'I've no idea who you are and have never heard of either of those men you're on about.'

'You have a car leased by O'Connor under his real name, O'Leary,' Patrick pointed out.

'Oh, really?' she responded in a bored manner.

'And were involved in the abduction of a police officer and also carried a handgun. You can't deny it. Those are very serious charges and you're apparently maintaining that the wrong person's been arrested.'

'But you're on about other stuff that I've not had anything to do with.'

'Has anyone here mentioned "other stuff" or just charged you with the crimes you committed the other night?'

She said nothing. We already knew the answer to the question: she had been charged only in connection with the Feltham crimes.

'You know perfectly well about the "other stuff",' Patrick went on remorselessly. 'And it's all very well connected.'

'You're trying to tie me in knots.'

Not difficult actually, duckie, was the thought that crossed my mind.

I said, 'The curate at Wellow heard you and Archie talking about when you used to be an actress. You're acting right now.'

'I don't know any curates. And I've never been an actress.'

'Never belonged to a drama group?'

'Oh, er, no.'

'You're lying,' Patrick told her calmly. And then said to me, 'We might be here for quite a while.'

'That's fine by me,' she mumbled.

But at least she was talking.

'Was Frederick Judd your husband?' Patrick said into the ensuing and rather long silence.

'Judd! No!'

'You've heard of him then.'

Confused, she answered, 'Oh, er – yes, in the restaurant.'

'Was he a customer?'

'No, he's dead. That's what I heard.'

'So how did you hear about him?'

'Just people talking.'

'From the man driving the Jag the other night?'

'No, he doesn't know anything – just does odd jobs.'

'And drives the car.'

'Sometimes.'

'Follows orders, that kind of thing.'

She shrugged.

'He was described to us as your boyfriend.'

'Someone must have been having a laugh,' she answered dismissively.

'Judd was, though – at one time before he went off his head and chucked you out. Although he might have installed someone a lot younger and more attractive before he completely lost it.'

'That's all a load of crap! How do you get this job when you're so bloody rude?' the woman shouted at him. 'Don't you have to show respect to witnesses?'

'But you're not a witness,' Patrick leaned over to whisper. 'You're a criminal, and have been, I think, for a very long time.'

'It wasn't my idea to kidnap the cop. It was Enrico's. He said it works in Italy when you're trying to get away from the law.'

In businesslike-fashion fashion, Patrick said, 'OK, let's go through what I'm sure of about you – count up the number of murders you're responsible for. There's probably Archie, although he was very ill. Slipped something in his food to finish him off, did you? Then there's Judd, who I think you lived with and wanted his money extremely badly. His body was cremated instead of Archie's. Poor old Archie's remains went up with the bungalow but we found his skull roughly where the kitchen used to be. There were two bullet holes in it that had happened after death and were done either by you or someone working for you, to try to make it look as though you'd been murdered when you'd really done a runner. Forensic science is a hell of a lot better than, clearly, you imagine. Slightly before that happened you arranged to have Hereward Stevens, the funeral director, murdered because he came back for his phone and saw O'Connor in your house. There was also the risk that Sandra, his ex-wife – who had been interviewed by the local paper and appeared in an article – had been told about this so it was fixed, by you, to have her killed as well. Only she didn't die and is under very impressive police protection in hospital. That's three murders and one attempted murder. Not bad, eh?'

And here, Patrick sat back and smirked at her. It was an infuriating smirk which even irritated me, sitting at an angle to the pair of them.

'Smug, pompous bastard!' the woman yelled. 'I know all about you, the holier-than-thou priest's son with a big posh house in Hinton Litttlemore and that stuck-up cow over there for a wife! You think you're the big man, don't you, parading around in your big posh car?'

She then buried her face in her hands, hating herself.

Patrick turned to me and laughed. 'You said she was thick, didn't you?'

'Too thick even to stick to the agreed plan regarding the DI,' I said.

This was not the first time he had used that particular ruse.

'So what's it to be?' Patrick continued. 'Are you going to give us the facts or end up being the only one charged with these murders?'

'You said you wanted O'Connor,' she replied, dropping her hands with a gesture of resignation.

'I do.'

'I'll do a deal – everything I know about him in exchange for—'

'I can't do deals,' Patrick butted in with. 'But the people here might listen to you more sympathetically if you fully cooperate.'

'Oh, God,' she mumbled.

'Tell me your name.'

After a pause: 'Marlene Judd.'

'But you said—'

'I was his sister!' she shrilled. 'And he turned his back on all of us! His whole family! His wife – only she's dead now, which was his fault as she was never the same after he beat her up one night – and his brothers, sisters, and even his poor old mum who had to go into a council home as she had no money. We had no money either as he never paid us for what we did for him. We just got promises, promises. He was *filthy* rich! I went to his house in Harrow, or rather mansion, and asked him if he'd pay for Mum's care, begged him to, and he just laughed in my face. Likely they called him Freddie the Bent and it weren't nothing to do with his accident. He got everything he deserved, the bastard!'

I was a little shocked to discover that I agreed with her.

Patrick said, 'You employed O'Connor to locate Judd after he moved from there and find out where his money was hidden – I'm assuming it wasn't in a bank – and—'

'Some of it was.'

'Oh?'

'Jinty did him a deal – that he'd let him go with some of it if he drew it all out.'

'And then killed him anyway.'

'Too right.'

'How much money are we talking about?'

'Altogether?'

'Yes.'

She sighed despairingly. 'I suppose I might as well tell you as I'll have lost it all now. Around two million.'

'All in cash?'

'No, stolen stuff partly that some fence had given him a rough estimate for. Jewellery, antiques, pictures. There were drugs too. They were hidden in the restaurant so you lot have probably found them now.'

'Where's the rest of it concealed?'

'I don't know where it is now. Hidden away. It was stashed away at Fred's place, under the floorboards. Jinty promised I'd get my share.'

Just a bullet or something a little more exotic actually, I thought.

Patrick said, 'But quite a while before all that happened you'd found yourself a rich old man a long way from London and adopted a new identity.'

'I was skint and needed to get away from Fred in case he went even madder and came after me, didn't I? The old man advertised for a housekeeper – skivvy more like as it turned out – and I soon realized that he was almost as crazy as Fred. And mean.'

'Did you kill him?' I asked.

Again that black stare. 'No, he had cancer everywhere. I knew it was only a matter of time when I took the job but it took a hell of a lot longer for him to die than I'd thought.'

'And you got rid of Fred's body by swapping it with Archie's.'

'That was Jinty's idea. He thought it was really funny even though it was a hell of a lot of bother.'

'A bit fortunate, wasn't it, Archie neatly dying just when you needed a way of disposing of a corpse?'

Marlene Judd set her face stubbornly.

'Tell the truth!' Patrick shouted.

She started. 'OK, OK – he fell over in the bathroom.'

'That's what you told the medics at the hospital, anyway.'

After a long silence, she said, 'Jinty did it.'

'Pushed him over.'

'Yes. He hit his head.'

Pausing for reflection for a few seconds, Patrick then said, 'Tell me about the coffins in the shed.'

'That was Jinty too. He wanted to store them there. I didn't ask any questions.'

'Archie's body was put in one them?'

'Where else could we have put it?'

'So where is O'Connor?'

'I shall want police protection.'

'You might get it if you're straight with me.'

'Oh, God,' she muttered again. 'How I hate you.'

'Where *is* he?'

'I haven't seen him for a bit. All I know is that he's planning some big job somewhere.'

'D'you know what it is?'

'No.'

'Where does he live?'

'All over.'

'You'll have to do a lot better than that.'

'He moves around to keep one step ahead of you lot.'

I knew that this could be true as it was precisely what mobsters do, staying with friends, family, employees and in hotels.

'Look,' Marlene Judd said, 'Jinty did all these things. He seemed the answer to my problems at the start but then it got a bit out of hand. He *likes* killing people – sometimes in weird ways too. It took me a while to realize it but he's actually *sick*.'

'Did he shoot Hereward Stevens personally?'

'No, that was someone else. I think killing someone like that didn't give him the right sort of buzz. As I said, sick.'

'Killing someone like that?' Patrick repeated.

'Oh, this hired guy shot out the tyres and windscreen of the car with one of those rapid firing guns. The car hit a tree, as he hoped it would, and burst into flames.'

'D'you know his name?'

'Collins. Everyone just calls him Randy as he's always after women. He's nuts about guns even more than he is women. I've never met him, mind. Jinty did all the organizing.'

But, I told myself, she had hired O'Connor to sort out her life. She had started off this chain of events, these murders. I couldn't believe that she hadn't heard through grapevines exactly what he was like and it suited her.

'So in reality, he's ratted everything up for you,' Patrick observed grimly. 'Not content with having his share of Judd's money he—'

'Sixty per cent – he insisted on it,' she interrupted.

'He carried on killing people just for kicks. I'm sure the funeral director never gave another thought to the man he caught sight of when he returned to the bungalow. He was angry that he'd missed a football match on TV. He mentioned having to go back for his mobile to his ex-wife but only because of that.'

'I see. Thought of like that . . .'

'You're in a far worse mess than you might have been,' Patrick helpfully finished for her.

'Yes, I suppose you're right.'

'Where is he, Marlene?'

After agonizing for at least a minute, she said, 'He might be hanging out with Randy. They're mates.'

'Where does he live?'

'He's got a flat over a shop in Bath. Waterways, I think the area's called.'

'What kind of shop?'

'Not sure, but it *might* be a betting shop.'

'You've never met this man, but do you have any idea what he looks like?'

'No, not really, but Jinty did once say that he'd had a chunk of his left ear bitten off by a police dog. He thought that was dead funny too.'

James Carrick was contacted and immediately organized raids – apparently there were two apartments – to take place very early the following morning at the only betting shop in Waterways, an area to the west of the city consisting of mostly local authority housing. The premises were situated in a small row of other businesses.

At approximately three a.m., the raids took place. A retired couple, in bed in the top flat, were offered profuse apologies with a promise to repair their front door. The other property was uninhabited but yielded a quantity of illegal firearms, plus ammunition. A more extensive search a little later found traces of drugs and bills and other correspondence addressed to Ray Collins.

There was no trace of him or O'Connor.

FOURTEEN

I t seemed pointless for Patrick to interview Marlene Judd again, especially as she was, in Janice North's words, 'talking practically non-stop now, raking through her memory for every last detail with which she can incriminate O'Connor'. The DI promised to forward any potentially useful information to us.

Late on Tuesday morning – I had abandoned returning to Hinton Littlemore for the time being – after we had been informed of all this and Patrick had dealt with a few other matters, we had a brainstorming session in his office.

'In case you're wondering,' he began by saying, 'I'm not going to throw the rule book out of the window and go after this man on my own, armed to the hilt with a knife between my teeth.'

'I'm extremely relieved to hear that,' I told him, the possibility of this having been a real fear.

'Coffee,' he decided, and got up to drive his new toy.

A few minutes later, Michael Greenway put his head around the door. 'That smells good.'

Patrick made him one.

'Well, you're nibbling away at this mobster,' Greenway observed, seating himself.

I called that damning with faint praise.

'It's been in my mind to ask you this, but have you thought about going undercover on your own, that kind of thing, to find him?' the commander went on in casual fashion.

'We were just discussing that,' Patrick answered. 'So, yes, I have thought about and no, I'm not.'

Greenway merely smiled.

'For one thing, if I do I shall probably end up by killing him and I've been expressly forbidden to do that.'

'Locate is the name of the game, surely.'

'And then call up support? Please get real. The time between locating and the opposition starting shooting can be seconds. Sorry, but you've had no experience of that kind of thing.'

'Daws wanted you hired because of your experience.'

'It's Daws who's forbidden me to kill him,' Patrick retorted.

'Only for publicity reasons, surely – an arrest is good copy for the newly formed NCA.'

I said, 'And if O'Connor dies in a hail of bullets that's not quite so nice because the great British public are so squeamish and spineless these days?'

The commander nodded sagely. 'Obviously, I can't speak for Daws but it might be something like that.'

'I'm not going to handle it like that,' Patrick said. 'Although I can't pretend that if, in the course of this investigation, I come face-to-face with O'Connor I won't defend myself, but I have no intention of deliberately setting up any kind of one-to-one confrontation.'

There was a little general conversation and then Greenway finished his coffee. 'OK, I'll leave you to get on with it then.'

When he had gone, Patrick looked at his watch. 'I'm too hungry to think. Lunch?'

We went to an Italian restaurant that we have used before where the menu includes 'light bites' which suits me fine. My husband nevertheless chose a pasta dish that came in a very large bowl and proceeded to demolish it.

'No questions?' he asked between mouthfuls.

'You said not all that long ago that you owed O'Connor a bullet.'

'I do.'

'So what was that bit of theatre about just now?'

'I found a bug in my office.'

For a moment I forgot to eat. '*What?*'

'I always check – it's a habit. He must think I've forgotten everything I know.'

'Who, Greenway?'

'No, think. Daws.'

'He's still checking up on you?'

'I can't even begin to guess his reasons.'

'Greenway trying to get you to go in undercover was a sting operation then.'

'Looks like it.'

'What are you going to do?'

'Nothing, and say nothing. I'll get rid of the bug, though –
he'll expect me to find it.'

'I don't like it that Daws doesn't appear to trust you.'

'Have I ever given him grounds to trust me to follow orders
to the letter?'

I shrugged and carried on with my lunch. Perhaps not. But
there was another reason Daws had wanted him: because he's
different.

'O'Connor,' I prompted when we were having coffee. I was
relieved that Patrick appeared to be more measured in his
approach to this mobster, for at one time . . .

Patrick drained his cup. 'Although Marlene described them as
mates, I don't reckon Ray Collins is part of O'Connor's outfit.
He's ex-army, has a list of previous convictions as long as your
arm and reckoned to be dangerous. But he's always been a loner,
just for hire to do one-offs. This means O'Connor could be left
with a load of thickoes now his brother's dead. He might have
to put on hold the big job Marlene Judd mentioned while—' He
stopped speaking as his mobile rang. 'Result!' he said succinctly
after the call. 'That was Carrick. Remember the man you shot
in the shoulder? Someone's turned up in A&E at the Royal United
Hospital in Bath with a seriously infected bullet wound. No
details yet as to exactly where but it has to be him.'

Following a 999 call the man had been found at an address just
off the Lower Bristol Road in Bath. He was delirious and when
admitted to hospital was found to be suffering from blood
poisoning. This was treated with strong antibiotics, the doctors
hoping that twenty-four hours later when he was a little stronger
he would be able to have an operation to remove the bullet. They
dared not wait any longer.

James Carrick asked DI Campbell, with suitable backup, to
investigate where the 'shooting victim' had been found but when
they arrived the house was locked up and seemingly deserted. A
neighbour revealed that the young woman who lived there had
taken her children and gone, possibly to her mother's, she had
added 'maliciously', as Campbell put it. The neighbour even
knew where the mother lived, three streets away. Campbell went
round there and was met with a pair of shrieking harridans who

hurled obscenities at him and tried to scratch his eyes out, and ended up by arresting the pair of them for obstructing a police officer in the course of his duty. Shortly afterwards, three filthy and obviously malnourished children at the property were taken into care by Social Services.

While it seemed unlikely that we would be able to interview the wounded man for several days, it was vital that we spoke to him as soon as he was deemed well enough. While we waited Patrick stayed in London to work on other matters and I took the train home. Much police work involves waiting but that did not mean I did nothing in connection with the case in the meantime.

I went to see Sandra Stevens, who was still in hospital although much stronger. I found her in a patients' lounge, reading, her watchful minder by the door. I had brought with me a photograph, taken at Feltham police station, of Marlene Judd. I also had a photofit of her with the short blonde hair replaced by the nearest I could find on the system to the tatty grey-brown locks we had seen at the rectory and also at her bungalow. After a little conversation I showed them to her, the latter first.

Sandra slowly shook her head. 'No, I don't think I've seen her before.'

I gave her the photograph.

'Oh. Is this to do with my dream then?'

'It might be,' I replied, deliberately vague.

'It *could* be the woman who opened the door of the house in the spooky little wood.'

'The different woman.'

'Yes. But hang on . . .'

I waited.

'It's the same woman, isn't it? Only in the photo she's wearing a blonde wig.'

'No, that's her own hair. As she appears in the other picture she's wearing a wig to make herself look older. She could have removed it by the time Hereward went back for his phone.'

'Gosh. I see. Is she a criminal?'

'You could say that. Thank you, you've been most helpful.'

'And Mr Gillard? Is his head better? It would be awful if he was scarred for life.'

'He heals well,' I told her. 'His mother's worried about that too but he made a joke of it and said he'd grow a fringe.'

'I had another dream, a silly one like the bit about that black cat, Henry. I dreamed you and he were married and had children.'

'How many children?' This was truly fascinating.

'*Five!*' She uttered a little shriek of laughter.

I took one of her hands. 'I really must tell you something.'

'What?' she asked a trifle nervously.

'That's not quite right, as although Henry's a real cat, he doesn't say a lot. And only three of the children are ours – we adopted the other two.'

After expressing utter amazement she looked quite sad as I wished her a quick recovery, said goodbye and left.

Nobody was underestimating O'Connor, which meant that the man with the gunshot wound, which was indeed in his right shoulder, who was still unidentified as he refused to give his name, was under police guard as well. Someone thought of asking the mother of the young woman, who were both also refusing to give their names, if she knew who he was. Both women had been charged notwithstanding and released on police bail, mainly because Sergeant Derek Woods, in charge of the custody suite, had flatly refused to house them for a moment longer. *Nobody* argued with Woods; he had been at Manvers Street, as James Carrick had once jokingly remarked, since the last Ice Age.

The elder woman had calmed down on arrival at home and gave whoever the someone was who had subsequently spoken to her – I never found out but guessed it was Lynn Outhwaite – her name and all the information that was needed. She admitted that the state of her grandchildren, whom she had not been permitted to see for quite a while on account of 'his' presence in her daughter's home, had shocked her terribly. The man, one Billy Efford, was not the children's father; in fact, she had no idea who was – 'several blokes probably', she had said on an afterthought. In her opinion, it had been her daughter who had called the ambulance as she herself had no knowledge of Efford having been injured in a shooting. Not that she was surprised, 'the lout'.

'All we need is a DNA match between Efford and one of the bloodstains on the carpet at Sandra Stevens's flat,' Patrick commented on hearing this when he came home for the weekend. 'I hope Carrick's asked for a fast-track result. But strangely, he has no previous convictions other than getting involved in fights after football matches.'

'James also told me Efford's had the bullet removed and might be fit enough to be interviewed on Monday, but we won't know until then,' I finished by saying.

'Good. I hope the lady who put it there isn't feeling guilty.'

'A bit.'

'He could have killed you in the next second.'

'I know.'

Patrick was engaged in his usual Friday evening just-come-through-the-door activity of absentmindedly spreading his belongings around the living room as he spoke. Cars keys in a china dish on a side table, briefcase and the one holding his laptop on different armchairs, leather jacket hitched on one corner of the back of the sofa. My suggestions on several occasions along the lines of that was what hallways were for, where there were coat hooks and other useful parking places, had had no effect. When he had a shower, in a couple of minutes' time, I'd usually relocate everything. He never appeared to notice.

'I interviewed Will Gibbs again,' he said as he went out of the door.

'And?' I enquired half an hour later when he reappeared and as though there had been no break in the conversation.

'Glass of wine?'

'Please.'

'He'd been brought back from Feltham nick for more questioning – and decided to carry on being helpful.' Patrick went off in the direction of the kitchen and, coming back with my wine, continued, 'He'd known for a little while that O'Connor was lying low on account of someone having shot a gun out of his grasp, doing unknown damage to his hand. Was he holding the gun on me with his right hand?'

I nodded.

'Gibbs doesn't reckon he has any plans to move his criminal activities down here, which will be a relief to James, but said he'd rented some kind of pad for six months in this area as a bolthole while they waited for poor old Archie to die, so they had a handy and fun way of getting rid of Judd's body when they killed him. As we now know, they hastened things along a bit. Gibbs reckons he's obsessed about how he disposes of, or deals with, the bodies of his murder victims. It has to be different every time – it's entertainment to him.'

I instantly had a vivid mental picture of O'Connor poring over a computer, or even pen and paper, writing 'scripts' and then being producer, director and leading actor in the 'action'. I said, 'But there were several coffins in that shed.'

Patrick shrugged. 'Just for storage purposes, perhaps – corpses, I mean.'

'I take it human remains weren't found in the ashes there.'

'No one's said anything about that, so no.'

He rummaged in the cupboard where we keep drinks – some people have cocktail cabinets, which personally I think really naff – found an opened bottle of single malt and poured himself a tot.

'Is O'Connor still likely to be in this rented pad?' I enquired.

'I asked Gibbs about that but he didn't know. The rental agreement could have expired by now.'

'Any hints as to what this big job might be that Marlene Judd mentioned?'

'He wasn't sure about that either but had an idea it involved her murder.'

'With the added bonus of another corpse to play with.'

'Sick, isn't it?'

'There's one thing I need to get straight in my mind,' I said on impulse. 'Although she had the jewellery that her brother had stolen, I think we've decided that there's no connection between Sarah Dutton and Judd's or O'Connor's criminal empires. Therefore, why did Will Gibbs and the two others grab Joanna when she was investigating her family in Leytonstone? Do they live there and were just hanging around outside the pub?'

'Good point.' Patrick grabbed his laptop, the only thing I had left where it was.

'Look, please don't bother to look up all the case notes now,' I hastened to add. 'It's your weekend break.'

'Yes, but it's something I've overlooked and need to know.'

'When we turned up at the derelict estate where we found Joanna, they said they didn't want anyone to interfere with what they regarded as their patch.'

'They *were* drunk.'

'Did the Met actually search that ghastly place?'

'For heaven's sake, woman, you're throwing all this stuff at me . . .'

'Sorry.' I battened down the oracle and subsided into a chair with my wine glass.

A couple of minutes later, Patrick said, 'Dougie Baker lived in Leytonstone, so they could have just been hanging around outside the pub. Will Gibbs lives on a council estate in West Ham, which is not far away; Joe Hurley, the one who was shot by what we're calling friendly fire and is still in hospital, is of no fixed address and refuses to answer all questions.' He looked up. 'It could have been a complete coincidence.'

'You're not supposed to have coincidences in crime stories and I don't like them in real life.'

He tossed down the remainder of his tot and then said, 'We must be careful here. Joanna had dressed smartly for a trip to London. She was carrying a designer bag that was big enough to hold documents plus a laptop although, as we know, she hadn't actually taken things like that with her. She looked like someone who was acting in some kind of official capacity. I really must have a word with her about working undercover as when a woman on her own, a stranger, goes to sink estates it can be dangerous. In this case it *was* dangerous and men, scum, like those three who apprehended her, would regard her as fair game.'

'Phone her,' I urged. 'Ask her how many houses she called at. Someone might have slipped out and tipped them off. And, don't forget, Sarah Dutton's brother's involved with gangs.'

Just then Justin burst into the room, followed by Vicky and then Katie, who was very carefully carrying Mark, Carrie hovering watchfully nearby. Matthew brought up the rear, brandishing what looked like a homework file, all five children heading in Patrick's direction. I left him sorting out the inevitable argument over priority for attention and went to phone Joanna and see to the dinner. When I returned, the two eldest children had gone into the annexe to have their evening meal with John and Elspeth, the usual Friday routine. Carrie had taken Mark off to bed and Justin was proclaiming how hungry he was. Vicky, half asleep on Patrick's lap, had only recently been deemed old enough to stay up a little longer and have her dinner with whoever was at home, but I was having second thoughts as she tended to nod off in her dessert.

Just over an hour and a half later, having cleared away and when both youngsters were in bed – her father's quick reflexes having prevented Vicky from doing a header into her rice pudding – we both could finally relax in the sitting room. Not for the first time, I asked myself if mine was a bizarre lifestyle: one minute popping cute kids under their quilts – on this occasion Vicky – the next acting like something out of a *RoboCop* movie.

Patrick had been out in the garden sitting in the last of the evening sun while he smoked one of the small cigars of which he is particularly fond. 'Did you have time to phone Joanna?' he asked, flopping into a chair.

'I did. She went to three addresses, the last known one in records for Sarah Dutton's father, Harold Fletcher, and the houses on either side. She thought the man in the second house was evasive and suspicious, but because of the nature of the area put that down as normal. There were children in the house who she thought at the time ought to have been at school, but as there were quite a few others running wild on the estate it went through her mind that they were still on their school holidays.'

'A runner? Send a kid to tell the three invariably hanging around by the pub that a woman was nosing around asking questions?'

'It's possible.'

'You mentioned the brother, Guy Fletcher,' Patrick reflected. '*If* he ever worked for O'Connor, which I think is unlikely as he appears to be a burglar by trade, what would be the advantage of involving his sister and, possibly, Robin Williams? Blackmail?'

'It's not a crime to have an affair with your secretary,' I pointed out.

'OK, let's think of it from another angle. There *were* several coffins in the shed. Perhaps the idea was to gain some kind of hold over Williams in order to repeat the Archie scenario.'

'Yet Will Gibbs said O'Connor never repeated a method of disposing of corpses.'

'But if he'd hit on something really useful . . .'

'If Fletcher's still inside why don't you talk to him?'

There was a thought-filled silence, then Patrick said, 'We're going round in circles, aren't we? Big, big zeros. I should have been content to stay where I was – on the shop floor.'

'When have you ever been on the shop floor?' I countered crossly. 'O'Connor's hiding away, on the run. He's been flushed out from just about everywhere he's tried to hide since you took the case on.'

Still unhappy, Patrick got to his feet. 'I quite fancy a pint. Coming?'

'No, you go.'

'I'll see if anyone in the pub wants their grass cut.'

He went out, leaving me wondering if he had been serious.

I switched on my computer to access the NCA websites that are restricted to personnel only. I discovered, ironically, that Guy Fletcher, another who was listed as of no fixed address, had been released from prison the previous week. Surely by now he would have disappeared into the labyrinth that is London.

Unless he was staying with his sister and her husband in Larkhall, that is.

The following morning, as on the first occasion, Paul Dutton answered the door. Again, he looked peevish when he saw us and snapped, 'It's the weekend and not remotely convenient.'

'I just want to ask you a couple of questions,' Patrick said urbanely.

I wondered if he had been sorely tempted to express surprise that the man was still living here.

Dutton had opened his mouth to answer when a woman's voice called, 'Who is it, Paul?'

'The police – again.'

Sarah Dutton came into view. 'Why can't you leave us alone?'

'Have you heard from your brother?' Patrick enquired.

'Guy? No. He's in prison – as you well know.'

'He was released last week.'

'Was he?' she said stonily.

'Mrs Dutton, I'll ask you again. Have you seen or heard from your brother?'

'No, I haven't.'

'He's listed as being of no fixed address. Can you update me on that?'

'No, I've absolutely no idea where he might be. We've never been close.'

'OK, sorry to have bothered you.'

The front door slammed shut almost on our heels. But I remained where I was as Patrick had grabbed my elbow. Then he ducked beneath the adjacent window and went around the corner of the house, where there was a sideway. Feeling extremely conspicuous – there were people walking by, one of whom stared at me – I followed, having to brake hard as I almost ran into my partner, who was standing motionless. Like an animal, he was sniffing the air and then moved extremely quickly, going from my sight. Then I smelled it too.

Cigarette smoke.

'Police!' I heard Patrick shout. 'Stand still!'

I arrived just as a man bolted towards me, and he would probably have knocked me down if he hadn't been checked by a stranglehold on the collar of his sweatshirt. As it was, I side-stepped smartly as the pair's momentum meant they carried on for a short distance, the would-be fugitive ending up slammed face first against the house wall.

Holding him by the shoulders, Patrick turned him around so that he faced us and said, 'When a cop asks you to stand still he means what he says, and if you even think of trying to get the better of me I shall, first, be forced to act in self-defence, which you won't like at all, and, second, arrest you. Is that understood?'

The man, medium height, sallow complexion, pale blue eyes, thin, sandy-coloured hair, nodded sullenly and Patrick released his grip.

'You're Guy Fletcher?'

Another nod.

'We can talk here or down at the nick.'

'I've done my time,' Fletcher muttered. 'I don't want to go to no more nicks.'

'OK, but this isn't about you. I want to talk to you about Fred Judd and Jinty O'Conner.'

'Judd's dead!'

'So he is. Were you around when that took place?'

'No! I didn't work for him! He was raving mad! And the word was he never paid no one.'

'Or around, on the side of those killing him?'

'No!'

'You worked for O'Connor?'

'No! Never!'

'Freelance burglar then?'

'Most of the time.'

'And the rest?'

Fletcher merely shook his head. Then, having been on the receiving end of one of Patrick's stares, he stammered. 'Well, I – I was inside quite a lot of the time, wasn't I?'

'D'you know where O'Connor is now?'

'No, how could I?'

'Because you've been inside.'

'I don't know where he is. I don't get involved with people like that. I didn't do time with people like that.' It seemed as though he might burst into tears. 'Look, this time I've been trying to turn myself around, right? Been learning to decorate people's houses, wallpapering, painting, that kind of stuff. I – I'm actually quite good at it . . . going to get a job.'

The outer door of a small conservatory to one side of where we were standing opened and Fletcher's sister emerged. 'Why don't you go and bully someone your own size?' she yelled at Patrick.

There was no constructive answer to that and we left. Patrick does not have to justify his actions to common criminals.

We were no further.

FIFTEEN

'I can only suggest that you outthink this mobster,' I said that evening after dinner.

'So he presents himself to me on a plate with an apple in his mouth?' Patrick said sarcastically, pouring himself a drink. He seemed to be drinking rather a lot of whisky.

'What would you have done in MI5 days?'

'I didn't have to deal with mobsters in MI5 days.'

'You know what I mean. Methods.'

'I had any number of people I could call on to stake out possible places where he might be, twenty-four hours a day for as long as it took. I don't have that now.'

'"Involving whichever police forces I think necessary,"' I quoted.

'But you have to have some idea where to start. I've absolutely no idea. That's what we've been trying to find out: where to start. Dead ends all the way.'

'This is the final offering from the oracle before you take me for a glass of wine over at the pub, where I suggest you only have one more drink.'

He just looked at me, negative, miserable.

'I've already mentioned the place this weekend – the hell-on-earth estate where we found Joanna.' I rose to my feet. 'I'm ready to go out.'

He made no move so I set off on my own, crossing the road to walk on the smooth grass of the village green. It was a fine evening, the sun having set, the sky a deep azure with a hint of crimson flushed with pink on the western horizon. Swallows dipped and dived, hunting for the last flies of the day to feed their broods of young.

Not wishing to enter the Ring o' Bells on my own and start tongues wagging – 'They've had a row, you can tell' – I sat on one of the seats on the green. Hardly anyone was around and it was very peaceful, just a little birdsong and the distant sound of a certain amount of roistering going on in the pub. A lot of cars were parked in the narrow lane around the green, which always annoys the residents of the cottages that front on to it, denoting that the car park at the rear of the inn was full. Perhaps a darts or skittles match was taking place.

My mind wandered. Patrick is so good at darts that he now refrains from competing with the locals as they always play for money and he invariably wins, which embarrasses him. When there is an inter-village competition, however, or even a match against a team from Bath, the captain of the Ring o' Bells team comes knocking on the rectory door.

We have known one another since we were at school in Plymouth, but not being particularly interested in boys, I only really noticed Patrick when he was sent to help me with my physics homework. Our fathers were close friends at a time when the Gillards lived in that area and all I knew about their eldest son was that he sang in a church choir and went fishing in the River Tamar with a boy called George.

Having said a grudging hello, Patrick had seated himself at the kitchen table and glowered at me, no doubt plans for his morning having been ruined. I had stared back, knowing that if I dropped my gaze and giggled, I was finished. For here, right in front of me, was the man I wanted for ever and ever.

Good manners had surfaced and he had explained the physics, but I had hardly heard a word, mesmerized by those wonderful grey eyes. Finally, he had worked it all out for me but made a couple of small, deliberate mistakes so the teacher would not think I had had assistance. This I had not found out until much later.

We had walked the dogs, picnicked on Dartmoor and I had discovered his main attraction was his ability to make me laugh. We laughed a lot and I suppose fell in love a little but both of us had been very strictly brought up and were naive, to say the least, regarding sex. Then, one hot sunny afternoon somewhere on the moor we laughed until we cried, hugging one another with the sheer joy of being alive. I had felt the way his sinewy body had rippled beneath his thin shirt and that was that.

There had been quite a few such picnics during that uncharacteristically hot, dry summer, and it had been a miracle that I hadn't got pregnant. For some reason we'd still thought of ourselves as children, and had an idea that kids couldn't make babies. Then

Patrick had had a crisis of conscience and asked me to marry him, and I'd been forced to reveal that I was only fifteen. He had gone so pale I'd thought he was about to faint. But he had repeated the offer and I had accepted, on the condition that it would have to happen when I was old enough.

We married when we were in our early twenties. He was a junior army officer by then; there was a whole world to explore and he didn't want to be tied down. We were still children, frankly, and there were bitter arguments after my resentment at his absences had surfaced. Oddly under the circumstances, he had wanted children, while I hadn't. Then one night, there had been a final awful row and I had thrown his classical guitar down the stairs, smashing it – I still burn with shame about that, even though I offered to buy him a new one when we met up again – and then thrown him out into the rain for good measure. It was my cottage, bought with money my father had left me and early royalties. We were divorced.

In an accident with a hand grenade during service with Special Forces, Patrick was very seriously, injured. When he was recovering, Colonel Daws, as we then knew him, had offered him a job with MI5. One of the conditions was that he find himself a working partner as, initially, socializing would be involved, and the view was that a lone, slightly saturnine man would be too conspicuous. Remembering that we had always got on famously in public, Patrick had approached me, limping, still in severe pain and convinced that of all the women on the planet I would not want to go to bed with him, his injuries having left him with a crushing lack of self-confidence.

Having probably grown up by then, miserable – yes, subconsciously missing him – and finding the pitiful state he was now in utterly unbearable, how could I have refused? The old magic had worked again and we had soon sorted out the sex bit.

And now, glancing at my watch on Hinton Littlemore's village green, far more time had elapsed than I would have thought possible.

No, to hell with this, I decided – a lone glass of wine it would have to be.

The public bar was busy, someone's birthday party by the look of the pink balloons everywhere – oh yes, it must be the shrieking, semi-inebriated blonde on the point of bursting out everywhere from her too-tight pink satin dress – so I went into the lounge, which was relatively quiet, several tables unoccupied, more people in the restaurant beyond through an archway. I bought my drink and sat at a table for two in a corner, feeling a mixture of annoyance and anxiety.

I forced myself to relax.

Writers, always hungry for material, tend to surreptitiously scrutinize those around them. The young couple, not saying much to each other, both in a world of their own: a relationship falling apart? The elderly man, a regular, on his own; were all his friends dead? The retired foursome, the men in earnest conversation yarning about the old days in the Royal Navy, the women staring into space, bored out of their skulls – were they wishing they were at home watching soaps? The man sitting quite close to me on my right, part of his left ear missing . . .

I took a largish sip of my wine, surprised to find that my hand was quite steady, and glanced again in his direction. He was probably in his forties, dark-haired, his skin tanned, and was wearing a pricey leather jacket one would have thought too heavy for a summer evening. A whisky was in front of him, and he appeared to be playing a game of some kind on his smart phone, a smile occasionally twitching at his lips. Then, as if sensing my interest, he looked directly at me and smiled – or rather leered.

I made a play of looking at my watch, frowned and rose to my feet quickly as though I had suddenly remembered I ought to be somewhere else. And just then, Patrick appeared in the doorway. I took in all the details in a detached, automatic kind of way: black jeans, the plain white T-shirt with the Adidas logo, nowhere to hide the Glock. Unarmed.

Was the man on my right Ray Collins? He had noticed the new arrival enter. If so, surely he wouldn't start shooting in the pub.

'Shall we sit outside?' Patrick called from the doorway.

Deliberately placing myself on a line between them, I approached the doorway.

'You've forgotten your drink.'

Heart pounding, I made myself go back for it, to act normally.

'Sprog emergency,' Patrick reported when we were standing just on the edge of the green opposite the building's main entrance. 'Katie tumbled down the last half-dozen stairs coming to say goodnight – she's OK.'

'There's a man in there I—'

'I know. I thought you might like some peace and quiet when I saw you sitting on the green so I walked along the lane behind you and went into the public bar to get a beer. You can see right through into the lounge along the counter. It's Collins. I recognized him from a fairly recent mugshot. I've called Carrick and he's coming, definitely no bells and whistles but with a firearms unit on standby. We'll arrest him when he gets here.'

'There can be only one reason why he's here – to kill you.'

'I shall enjoy asking him.'

'Patrick, he might leave before Carrick gets here.'

'Then *I* shall arrest him – but I rang Carrick a good ten minutes ago.'

'You're unarmed!'

'There's no way I'm starting some kind of firefight here.'

Several agonizing seconds ticked by.

'I think you should go to a safe distance,' Patrick said gently.

I gazed at him for a few more moments and then walked away. Turning to look again when I had gone about twenty yards, there was no sign of him.

Fear was like cold lead in my stomach.

But why was the man coolly sitting there, for anyone to see him, in the Ring o' Bells?

As requested, I carried on walking and then had a truly shocking thought. Would this be how it would all end? Like this, on a summer's evening? Would the story that had started with us sitting face-to-face at a kitchen table come to a full stop here? The thought that he would be gunned down virtually in sight of his children was obscene.

But surely, something told me, O'Connor would not be content merely to take out a contract with Ray Collins for Patrick's death. He would want something more 'satisfying', a method of getting rid of him that would give him a thrill. But the real thrill, it appeared, was provided by the way he got rid of the body afterwards, which suggested that Collins might merely be in the pub to act as bait.

By this time I had reached the edge of the green, virtually opposite the rectory drive, and turned to look back again. Any number of people could be concealing themselves in the parked cars. Quickly, almost running, I crossed the road, went down the drive, gained entry to the house through the conservatory and checked that the front door was locked, bolting it for good measure. No one was going to walk casually into my house with malice aforethought. Going back through the conservatory with a view to locking it behind me, and having collected the Smith and Wesson and shoved it in the pocket of my slacks, I met John coming out of their door.

'Trouble?' queried this one-time naval reserve officer.

'There might be,' I answered. 'There's a wanted man in the pub and Patrick and James Carrick are going to arrest him. I'm worried that he might have friends with him.'

'Break out the shotgun?'

'You could keep watch from the front bedroom window.'

'I will.' And without another word, he went back into the annexe.

Another crack shot – at clay pigeon shooting.

I went back outside and walked slowly down the drive. And then quickened my pace, putting my hand on top of the weapon. Pausing on the edge of the green, again I could see only a peaceful English scene, dusk now approaching – 'dimity', the country people call it. A few more folk than before were around, some sitting on the grass, while a foursome of boys were playing cricket. The party in the pub was still reverberating.

As I got closer, I could see that only two tables outside the pub were occupied, one on each side of the door. I recognized none of the people sitting at them. I went in. Everything seemed to be perfectly normal, even in the lounge bar where three men were sitting at the same table I had.

Patrick glanced up and then patted the chair next to him. I seated myself.

'Your wine,' he said, indicating a glass on the table in front of me. Then he said to me, 'You know who this man is. James and I are going to have a short discussion with him.'

I gave the DI, who looked exceedingly grim, what must have been a very small smile.

'And this woman who I saw here just now is the one Jinty mentioned to me – your wife?' said Collins.

'My wife,' Patrick agreed. 'I take it O'Connor has paid you to remove me from the land of the living.'

'That's what he wants, yes,' Collins drawled.

He spoke precisely, with a slight accent, mid-European perhaps, but I guessed this was as a result of having lived abroad for a while to escape British law courts. Either that or it could be an affectation. This seemed more likely as he was supposed to be always chasing women. What did they see in him? He was as cold as death itself.

He was giving me his full attention, together with what he might have thought was another of his fascinating smiles.

'I don't like snakes,' I said.

He uttered an empty laugh, but I had seen the flash of anger in his dark eyes. They were dark like those of Marlene Judd, come to think of it. Was it a characteristic of murderers?

'So you come here in broad daylight and sit in the pub hoping I'll just wander by?' Patrick continued.

'You did,' Collins pointed out.

'No one but a fool would kill someone in such a public place in front of around fifteen witnesses.'

Whether the man took this as a compliment or not was impossible to tell, but he nodded gravely.

'You're hoping to do a deal?' Patrick prompted.

'I might be.'

'I haven't the time to play riddles,' Carrick had harshly, his Scottish accent always more pronounced when he's angry. 'And I can assure you that Wiltshire Police won't be prepared to do any deals as you're wanted for the murder of Hereward Stevens, the funeral director. One of us is going to arrest you right now.'

'But you won't,' said Collins. 'Because you want O'Connor. I can give him to you.'

Carrick jerked a forefinger in Patrick's direction. '*He* wants O'Connor, not me. I'm doing no deals with you.'

I left the glass of wine where it was. I might need it.

Collins shrugged. 'In that case, I shall leave and then, very shortly, fulfill my obligation to Jinty. A contract's a contract – and it's a lot of money,' Collins finished by saying, gazing intently at Patrick.

'And then what? O'Connor will then roll up having prepared a little plan to dispose of my body? That's where he gets his real kicks from, isn't it?'

'I think he's got the idea he's going to boil the flesh from your bones, feed the meat to his dogs and post what remains to this woman of yours.'

I almost vomited.

Patrick leaned forward and spoke quietly. 'He killed a friend of mine who was unarmed. He knew he was unarmed. I'm of a mind to arrest you, and then the pair of us will take you to a very quiet place where we'll paste all hell out of you until you tell us where this bloody mobster's hiding out.'

To Carrick's great credit, he didn't say a word.

'You're not allowed to do things like that,' Collins declared, as proved only recently, the time-honoured comment.

'I'm quite prepared to lose my job over it.'

'What is your deal?' I asked Collins. We were getting nowhere and they would be snarling at one another all night at this rate.

He considered me and visibly decided that I might have a crumb of intelligence. Then he said, 'O'Connor's dangerous. He says something one minute and changes his mind the next. And he's also treacherous. He might even contact you tomorrow, Gillard, and offer you a large sum of money to take me out. It would amuse him – you must have discovered by now that he has an unusual sense of humour – if we spent the next twelve months stalking one another like a couple of morons in a movie. I don't operate like that. Frankly, he's beginning to bore me. I like a simple life and it would suit me admirably if he was behind bars or on a mortuary table. You can have him in exchange for an amnesty.'

Furious, Patrick said, 'You must know perfectly well that no one here has the authority to agree to that.'

'You said you'd put your job on the line.'

'But I won't,' Carrick interposed.

'All I ask is that you look the other way when I leave for the airport.'

'No,' both men said in unison.

'I could have shot you last night when you entered your own front door,' Collins said to Patrick through his teeth.

'No, you couldn't,' he was told, but without elaboration.

'Then we have no deal and you don't get O'Connor. Arrest me and I shall go to prison. You won't get O'Connor. You won't be able to prevent him from carrying out his next job which I understand is to start taking out senior cops in the Met and leaving their bodies in public places – outside infant schools, that kind of thing. Just for fun, you understand.' He broke off with a humourless grin.

Carrick prepared to rise. 'The man's making fools of us. I'm going to call for some backup.'

'Tell *me* where he is,' I said to Collins. 'I'm a sort of a go-between.'

He smiled broadly, displaying what my dentist would call heavily restored teeth. 'But you don't like snakes.'

'It depends on the kind of things they hiss at me.' I found the will to give him a smile.

'Will you spend the night with me if I do?'

I already had my hand over the Smith and Wesson and it slid from my pocket like a dream. 'No, I shall merely put a bullet in you if you don't. Right now. In here. Then we shall both go to prison – if you survive – but my husband will have a better chance of staying alive with you out of the way.'

He caught sight of the weapon and actually gaped at me.

Then bolted.

For several reasons I was right behind him. Out on the green, running, I yelled, 'Armed police! Stop or I'll fire!'

He stopped, snatched under his jacket, spun around and there was a gun in his hand.

I jumped aside, fired and he performed the greater part of a cartwheel into the ground.

Patrick was suddenly right by me as Carrick speeded past us. Carefully, he removed the gun from my grasp, using his handkerchief, holding it by the barrel.

'This is all going to be done properly,' he said very quietly in response to a look from me. 'By the time witnesses have been interviewed in connection with this we'll have drink-fuelled tales that I, or even Carrick, shot him in a fit of rage. And no, I don't for one second want you to take any blame as no crime has been committed.' He pecked my cheek. 'That was fantastic shooting.'

I returned to the pub, drank the glass of wine in one, then went home and stood down John with his shotgun. He showed no surprise when I had to explain my involvement, merely patting my arm.

SIXTEEN

The next day, Sunday, the church was unusually full for the morning service. I stayed away, not wishing to be the target of around a hundred and fifty pairs of eyes, but Patrick went and did a rough count of the worshippers. His father made a statement after the sermon, making it clear that both his son and daughter-in-law worked for the police and that the previous evening a man wanted for murder had been arrested. The circumstances of the arrest had been witnessed by Detective Chief Inspector James Carrick of Bath CID but, as was laid down in the rules, the incident would be reported to the Independent Police Complaints Commission.

I anticipated having to put up with a lot of whispering behind hands and stares from now on as I went about the village. The children were another matter – the eldest ones, that is – and after discussing it with John and Elspeth we decided to explain the true state of affairs to Matthew and Katie that afternoon and deal with any other problems as they arose. The result of this was that I suddenly became elevated in their opinion to a mixture of Lara Croft and Scott and Bailey. This, I have to confess, would more than make up for any nonsense I got from the locals.

Patrick abandoned interviewing Billy Efford, for the time being at least. One reason for this was that he was still very poorly as a result of his wound having initially been neglected; another that we now had a much bigger fish in the pond. Ray Collins had suffered a serious flesh wound to his leg and both his tibia and fibula were fractured. Three days later, during which Patrick worked from home, and my Smith and Wesson was returned to me, Collins was pronounced fit to be interviewed. On the Thursday morning, having shown our IDs to his armed guard, we found him propped up in bed in a side ward.

'Oh, it's you again,' he muttered angrily.

It soon became obvious that he was not really angry with us.

'O'Connor!' he practically spat. 'The bastard!'

'That is the general view of him,' Patrick observed when we had found two chairs and seated ourselves.

'He told me that when they went to silence the woman in Bath and you were already there – you shot his brother and a man called Billy someone or other and then he broke your arm. They'd already taken care of the woman. This woman *here*' – he jerked a contemptuous thumb in my direction –'hid herself behind a sofa. On the way back, he bleated, he shut his hand in the car door. I don't believe that now. Your arm isn't broken. I think he set me up and it's the only reason I'm talking to you now.'

Patrick said, 'The real story is that I shot his brother who, as he fell, fired a shot that smashed an overhead light fitting. A piece of glass hit my forehead and I couldn't see for blood, whereupon O'Connor brought his handgun down on my arm, causing me to drop the Glock. This woman *here* shot Billy Efford and then the weapon from O'Connor's hand. They then ran for it.'

His arm was still deeply bruised and, worse, shaky.

'I'll kill him,' Collins muttered.

'You're due for a long jail term so no, you won't. Think about it for a moment. He has a win-win situation as far as you're concerned. You came to the village convinced that you were up against a man whose shooting arm was out of action and a woman who hid behind sofas. No problem, you do the job, ridding him of me. But, he reckoned, you might get caught and arrested, thus ridding him of both of us and he doesn't have to pay you. Or I might kill you anyway and he still doesn't have to pay you. You've been arrested and achieved absolutely nothing. And you told *me* he was treacherous.'

Collins closed his eyes and put his head back on the pillows.

'All the intelligence about the village came courtesy of Marlene Judd, I suppose,' Patrick continued.

'"That stupid bitch", O'Connor calls her. I don't know; I've never met her. But it would figure. He said she's the sort of person who hates everyone.' He yawned. 'I think she's next on the list. Then he won't have to give her any of Freddy the Bent's money.'

'Do you actually know where that is?'

'It's where O'Connor is. He told her he was putting it in a very safe place. I can't imagine why she trusted him.'

It's called desperation, I thought.

'And you reckon she's next on the list?' I said. The man obviously had no idea she had been taken into custody.

'He said so himself. I think he's going to chuck her off a bridge somewhere in a sack weighted with bricks.' He chuckled.

'Before he starts on the Met cops?'

He stared at me. 'Did I mention that the other day?'

'You did.'

'No idea. But probably.'

'D'you have details of that?'

'No. Do I have to talk to you for much longer?'

I ignored the question. 'In the pub you also mentioned a deal you hoped to do with us. Were you offering to lead the police to O'Connor in exchange for your freedom or would you just have indicated where he could be found?'

A crafty look came over the man's face. 'Is there a deal to be done now?'

'No, and you know what happened last time,' I retorted.

'You lied to me. You said you were a sort of go-between.'

'I have sometimes acted as a go-between. That doesn't mean I'm not going to do something about it if you threaten to kill my husband.'

'What if I turn Queen's evidence?'

'I haven't the authority to make that decision,' Patrick said abruptly. 'Answer the question. Was what in your mind when you suggested a deal?'

'I would have led you to where he is,' Collins replied after a short pause.

'Into a trap.'

Another yawn. 'He does seem to have a bit of a thing about you.'

'You realize we would both have probably died in a hail of bullets.'

'It's beginning to sink in,' the man mumbled.

'Where is he?' Patrick whispered.

'You still might die. You will, actually. I've just decided that I don't care.'

He was falling asleep.

'Did you learn about weapons in the army?'

Collins woke up a bit. 'Yes.'

'Same here.'

'That's what the Judd woman said apparently. Only that you were an officer.'

'Tell me where O'Connor is and I'll do my best to put in a good word for you.'

Eyes wide, Collins said, 'You would?'

Patrick nodded. 'I looked up your records – you were a sniper, among other things. What went wrong?'

'Nothing. A job's a job. I'm good at it. I'm not a monster. I don't go round hurting people for fun or abusing little kids. Look, is that it? I'm really tired.'

'Where is he?'

Slurring his words, Collins went on: 'He doesn't wash very often either. Or clean his teeth. He stinks. God, I hate him.'

'Where is he?'

After a long silence when I would have given up, Collins mumbled, 'He moves around quite a bit but his favourite place is in . . . some kind of rat hole in east London . . . a block of flats due to be knocked down . . . they've made some kind of secret bunker so it won't be easy . . . like Hitler did . . . yes, that's a good one, just like Hitler.'

'Have you been there?'

'No . . . No one's allowed to go there but his closest oppos . . . We always met in a . . .'

His voice drifted away; he was asleep.

Almost absentmindedly, Patrick checked that Collins still had a pulse and hadn't died on us. Then we left. Outside in a corridor, he said, 'It's bound to be that horrible hole where we found Joanna. You were right.'

'I simply can't believe that you'll say there are mitigating circumstances.'

'He was invalided out with severe post-traumatic stress disorder after a tour of duty in Afghanistan where some of his chums were blown up by a landmine. Tell me he isn't a bit strange in the head after his remark of "a job's a job" and I won't do it.' When I remained silent, he added: 'Blood's thicker than water, Ingrid.'

He meant the army, his life blood at one time. No, come to think of it, it still is.

'If we send in half the Met with armed personnel and dogs and he's not there word will get round and he'll never go back,' Patrick said on the way home. 'A "secret bunker", Collins said. That could be anything from a hideaway in the basement of a utility outhouse – there was something like that, if you remember – to a den in the roof. Or they might have done work on one of the abandoned flats and turned it into some kind of fortress.'

'I think you should now leave it to the Met,' I said, turning the Range Rover into Hinton Littlemore's narrow High Street.

'Umm.' Said thoughtfully. It meant no.

'It's time to let go,' I urged quietly. 'You've done your bit. And you've been promoted – there's no need for you to risk yourself any more.'

This was heresy, of course. There were many reasons going through this man's mind as to why it was important for him to bring O'Connor to justice personally.

I listed the ones I knew about aloud. 'But there's the need to arrest the murderer of your chum David Bowman, your reputation to think of, to prove that your service injuries have had no lasting effect on your efficiency, the thought that senior army officers, past and present, must never be bested by common criminals, that inner torment that you've never been able to live up to your father's expectations, the guilt that you feel about your brother's death because he was shot by someone who initially had thought he was you – and your professional pride.'

'I'm not proud,' Patrick said roughly.

'OK, it's whatever it's called that makes you want to hand this man over to Daws. I know you really admire him and he was responsible for you getting this job as well as the one with MI5, but he's completely ruthless.'

Patrick made no reply and when I had parked the vehicle around the side of the rectory – he never uses the front door as then he's in full view of anyone armed with a sniper's rifle – I turned off the ignition and gazed at him.

'I'm not proud,' Patrick said again, staring straight ahead through the windscreen.

'Daws is the one who's going to get the knighthood when he retires,' I persisted. 'And you might just be a flower-covered grave in the churchyard next door.' I had promised myself I would not get upset but even the best-intentioned promises can be impossible to keep. 'The kids will grow up knowing that they had an heroic father and will be able to visit your grave next door and tell you how wonderful they think you were. For *what*?' I slammed both hands down on the steering wheel, inadvertently sounding the horn. 'So some filthy bastard of a criminal serves a prison sentence when there are a thousand and one filthy bastards who are criminals out there still to be caught?'

Knowing that I was about to cry uncontrollably, I flung myself out of the car and ran indoors, all the way up to our room.

By the time I emerged around a quarter of an hour later, he had gone.

I found a quickly penned note propped up on the mantelpiece in the living room. He would leave the car in Bath railway station car park with a four-hour ticket. (I had heard it start up some five minutes earlier.) He went on to promise that this was the last time he would go off on his own. Then he must have changed his mind a bit because in the next sentence, he scribbled – ye gods, had he been upset as well? – that he gave me his word he would keep his promise and not work alone and arrange backup. He loved me, he finished with. No signature, just some scrawled kisses.

'You stupid, stupid man,' I sobbed.

Matthew came into the room. 'Where's Dad?'

Not wishing to make any kind of fuss or do anything that would cause John and Elspeth to worry, I quietly left the house and, after a ten-minute wait in the High Street, caught the bus into Bath. Luckily there are at least three sets of keys for the Range Rover as I have a horror of either losing them or dropping them down a drain in the road. There was plenty of time left on the ticket so I called in at Manvers Street police station. James Carrick was talking to someone behind the glassed-in reception desk.

'Just keeping you up to date,' I told him. 'We spoke to Ray Collins earlier.'

He smiled a greeting. 'Come upstairs and have coffee. Patrick said he'd bought a state-of-the-art coffee machine so, not to be outdone, I got one too.'

'I'm sure you're busy.'

'Never too busy to talk to the National Crime Agency,' he joked.

In his office he busily pressed buttons on the gleaming machine, a bigger one than Patrick's. Glancing quickly at me, he said softly, 'I ken you've been crying.'

'Patrick's gone off to find O'Connor,' I told him, trying to keep my voice even.

The DCI turned in surprise. 'On his own?'

'He left a note saying he wouldn't go alone but—' I shrugged.

'The man seems to have a need to do things like that – to prove himself.'

'I blame Richard Daws. He's constantly tested him and monitored his activities over the years. We're fairly sure from something he said to me that he was at Feltham the night the Chinese restaurant was raided and Marlene Judd was arrested.'

'That's rather extraordinary.'

'Patrick didn't seem too bothered actually.'

'Patrick told me O'Connor killed a friend of his. I've known him long enough now to have an idea that means only one thing.' Hastily, he added: 'Not that I mean he'd kill him in cold blood.'

'Reality check,' I said. 'He would. Daws knows it too and said he wants him alive. Which is a hell of a lot more difficult than blasting the bastard from the face of the Earth.'

Carrick gave me a worried look and handed over a cup of coffee. 'Biscuit?'

'No, thanks.'

'I hope you're not thinking of setting off after him alone.'

'I can't set off at all. I must think of the children.'

'You have in the past.'

'Yes, but in the past I had Terry Meadows or a man called Steve who worked for MI5 for a while, or even a Scottish DCI not a million miles from here.'

Carrick laughed and seated himself at his desk. Then he said, 'And the episode at the farm in Sussex?'

I love the way he always pronounces it 'farum'.

'Yes, that was a lone effort.' I gave him a straight look. 'Are you trying to persuade me to follow Patrick?'

'No.'

I sipped my coffee. 'He's got to retire. Or change his job.'

'You're wondrously good at it, hen.'

What?

'What did Collins have to say?' Carrick went on to ask.

'It was interesting. In short, he reckons O'Connor, having given him the wrong story about what happened when he shot Sandra Stevens, set him up. He was expecting Patrick to have a broken arm and me to be just . . . well . . . a housewife.'

'Get your hitmen arrested or killed and then you don't have to pay them. O'Connor must be very certain the police aren't going to catch up with him. Disgruntled hitmen tend to talk.'

'Collins mentioned a secret hideaway, a bunker, whatever, that O'Connor's got. Patrick has an idea that it's somewhere in the condemned blocks of flats near Leytonstone where we found Joanna.'

'Didn't the Met search the place?'

'Probably not. At the time there was no obvious connection mobster-wise between Joanna being locked in a garage there by yobs and the rest of the housing estate. Patrick's worried that if the Met turn up in force and O'Connor isn't there then word will get round and he'll never return.'

'So Patrick'll go there first.'

'No idea. Not one clue.'

'What else did he say in the note – if you don't mind my asking?'

'Not at all. Only that he'd left the car at the railway station with a four-hour ticket. I'll collect it when I leave here.'

There was a short silence, and then Carrick said, 'Look, Ingrid, if you hear nothing and feel you have to go and look for him, I'm your man.'

I couldn't speak for a moment and then managed to thank him, finish my coffee and leave without getting upset again.

Almost a week went by. I did not expect Patrick to phone me as he always leaves his own mobile at home and takes a 'work' one which has no personal phone numbers in the memory. It could be exceedingly dangerous for everyone concerned if the phone fell into the wrong hands and someone started trying to investigate previous calls.

This business of a 'radio silence' had happened quite often in the past and I have learned to cope. There were people living with and around me who, wittingly or not, relied on me to cope. The children were used to Patrick working away from home and only queried where he was the following weekend. John and Elspeth are obviously aware of a lot that goes on and don't ask questions, although I know Elspeth worries terribly about her one remaining son when he is away for any length of time. In view of his family responsibilities, she sees no reason why he should continue to hazard himself, and I now agreed with her.

Coping meant throwing myself into domestic matters, turning out for local jumble sales, doing those jobs that don't come within the remit of the home help like taking down curtains and either washing them or taking them to the dry cleaners. I baked cakes for tea and for Elspeth's various fundraising events, freezing some as I had made so many. Matthew and Katie are old enough now to realize the reason for my fevered activities and tried to amuse me, this culminating in an 'entertainment' that they put on for all the adults on the Saturday evening, a kind of spoof of *A Midsummer Night's Dream*, a children's version of which Katie was doing at school. Justin played the part of one Alf Bottom, completely oblivious of the fact that he was perfect for the part. Even Mark was in it, as an elf. It was so good, so funny, that John made them promise to put it on over Christmas in the village hall, and the youthful impresarios went away to rewrite it more ambitiously with a larger cast. But I really would have to tell them that they must delete the delightful and bitingly accurate caricatures of some of the village residents before it was seen by a wider audience.

On the following Monday morning I was still in a lighter mood as a result of this and opened the door to the postman in pleasant anticipation, as I had seen through the window that he was bearing a parcel and I was expecting some books I had ordered. But it soon became obvious that it was not what I thought it was as the label addressing it to me was untidily hand-printed, not the kind of thing used by a company.

I know all about dodgy parcels from MI5 days. Once, I had even been sent a bunch of flowers, very beautiful ones that had originated at a florist, that had explosives concealed in them. There was nothing about this parcel that told me what was in it or where it was from, the Post Office label being difficult to read. Carefully, I weighed it in my hands. It was medium heavy, a little too heavy for the square box that a tear in the outer paper revealed as it was starting to collapse. It was a little damp.

Gingerly, I sniffed at the dampness on a lower corner. The smell was indescribable but a little like cooking. Like a stew or a stockpot perhaps, but stale as though it had started to go off. Had someone sent me some kind of food parcel? A haggis? A batch of black pudding? Several pounds of sausages? Surely not.

I took it into the kitchen as that seemed a more suitable place to investigate further, and dumped it into the Belfast sink. Whatever it was, it was leaking. Very lightly, still thinking about those flowers, I began to tear away the brown paper wrapping and then, my cat's whiskers now registering a freak-out level right off the scale, remembered that I was supposed to be a sort of police officer and fetched a pair of nitrile gloves from my study.

The lid of the box, which looked the kind of thing office stationery might have once been packed in, was only fixed on with masking tape and, once the light support of the paper had been removed, it started to peel away as the damp cardboard of the box sagged beneath it. I pulled off most of the tape and extremely carefully prised up one side of the lid. The smell of stale cooked whatever wafted upwards and I almost retched. Resisting an impulse to put the whole thing straight in the dustbin, I took the lid right off.

Nestled under a layer of screwed-up newspaper on more newspaper was a human head and, just before I fainted for only the third time in my life, I saw every last detail.

It had been boiled.

All the teeth had been knocked out, the remains of some of them just shattered stumps. Before he was killed?

What was left of the skin and flesh hung off the skull in grey, greasy folded strips.

And the sunken, boiled eyes were staring up at me.

SEVENTEEN

choked, stinging fumes up my nose.

'It's me, Ingrid,' Elspeth's voice said. 'Don't worry, I've covered it up. What a ghastly thing to send anyone.'

I discovered that I was lying on the kitchen floor covered by a coat, my teeth chattering, every limb shaking uncontrollably. Elspeth was kneeling by my side.

'He said he'd boil the flesh off his bones, feed the meat to the dogs and post the rest to me,' I discovered I was gabbling.

Elspeth stretched up and put the little bottle of smelling salts on the worktop. 'Who, dear? No, lie there for a bit longer. You've had a nasty shock.'

'A criminal Patrick's gone after,' I muttered. 'Sorry, I shouldn't have said anything.'

'And you think . . .' Aghast, she got up and went over to the sink. I struggled to my feet – it was my turn to be supportive.

Visibly bracing herself, Elspeth removed the kitchen towel she had flung over the box and its contents.

'In the shock of seeing you lying on the floor I didn't realize this was real,' she said, gazing at it. She turned to me in desperation. 'You know, I thought it was one of those stupid Halloween things children get up in.' She snatched out a lacy handkerchief and held it over her nose. 'Oh, dear God, it's real all right. It smells horrible.'

'I have to ask you this,' I said, an arm around her, my teeth clattering together so much I could hardly speak. 'D'you think this is Patrick's?'

With a huge effort, she forced herself to carry on looking at it. Then said, 'I really can't say. I think it's a man's because of the width of the jaw but nearly all the teeth are gone or broken so—' She burst into tears.

I tossed the towel back over the box, took Elspeth into the living room, sat her down, gave her a little brandy and grabbed the phone.

'James?' I queried when there was a click as Carrick's phone was lifted, but no one said anything.

'Sorry, I'm just off to an important meeting at HQ,' he came on the line to say. 'You can get me later.'

'It's Ingrid,' I gasped.

'Sorry, I thought it was an internal call. What's wrong?'

I told him and he swore in Gaelic before promising that he'd be right over.

'No,' Elspeth said determinedly, having finished the brandy. 'It isn't Patrick. No son of mine is going to finish up like *that*. Besides, it doesn't look a bit like him.'

If only I could delude myself too. Patrick was dead. He had probably died horribly.

The DCI arrived. He was swiftly followed by a van with a couple of members of a forensic team who took photographs of the parcel and its contents in situ and then, having checked that my fingerprints were on record and that no one else in the household had touched it, carefully secured it in a large evidence bag and left. One of them immediately returned and apologized for not requesting something that might have Patrick's DNA on it, plus a photograph of him. I gave them his comb from the bedroom and one of a couple of recent photographs he had had taken in order to renew his passport. By this time I was hitting the brandy and Elspeth had gone to tell John, who had just come in from taking a funeral service, what had happened.

'I've asked for fastest possible DNA results,' Carrick said, dropping into a chair opposite me and taking one of my hands. 'And for what it's worth, I had a look and don't think it's Patrick.'

'You're really kind,' I said, trying to smile.

'You must try to be positive and wait for the test results to arrive.'

'I will,' I lied on both counts.

'I'm really sorry but I have to go to this damned meeting. Would you like me to ask Lynn to come over for a while to keep you company?'

'No, I'll be all right, thank you.'

He leaned over, kissed my cheek, looked embarrassed and went away.

For some reason I was suddenly no longer shaky but ice cold inside. I poured the rest of the brandy in my glass – rather a lot – back into the bottle, locked the living-room door and removed the Smith and Wesson and some ammunition for it from the wall safe. There is money kept in there too – an emergency fund. My movements precise and deliberate – it was as though I was two people, one watching the other do this – I took out five hundred pounds in sterling, put it in my pocket and then, wrapping the weapon and ammunition in the nearest thing that came to hand, a cardigan belonging to Katie, I left the room. Pausing only to collect the important things from my handbag and my mobile phone from the study, I went out to the Range Rover. It is fully equipped for instant deployment with bags packed with spare clothing, toiletries and other necessities – seeing with anguish that Patrick's had gone, something I had not noticed – and we always make sure that the fuel tank is kept more than half full.

Going back to the house, I knocked and went into the annexe. John and Elspeth were in the living room, he with his arms around her.

'Sorry,' I whispered. 'I – I'm going away for a few days.'

'My dear . . .' John began, and then didn't know what to say.

'You're too shocked to drive,' Elspeth said, ever practical.

'I'll be all right,' I told her, and fled before I changed my mind.

I had reached the end of the drive when my mobile rang. I pulled up, in a real mess, crying. I shouldn't be driving.

'It's Joanna,' she said. 'James has just rung me with the awful news. But it might not be Patrick.'

'It is,' I gulped. 'Ray Collins told us that was what O'Connor was planning to do.'

'James has an idea that you might go and blow the brains out of that mobster, and if so says I'm to talk you out of it.'

'I'm already on my way,' I said. 'Going down the drive right now.'

'Then I'm coming with you.'

'You *can't*. You have Iona to think of.'

Roughly, she replied, 'The nanny's a much better mother to her than I am.'

'Joanna, you mustn't. I seem to remember that you have an

interview in connection with rejoining the police soon. Tomorrow, isn't it?'

'Bugger careers. Friends are far more important. And Patrick did once save James's life.'

On reflection, more than once. I said, 'Sorry, the answer's still no.'

'I'm coming right over. James can collect my car later. The walk'll do him good.'

I parked outside the church just around the corner and out of sight from the house, switched off the engine and tried to stop crying.

'James is really sorry he had to leave you,' Joanna said, climbing into the passenger seat only ten minutes later and throwing a small rucksack into the back. 'The meeting was about how they're going to close the nick and sell the site for redevelopment. He reckons he'll either be working out of a cupboard in Keynsham or have a room in the council offices over the road.'

'You're kidding,' I exclaimed, aware that she was trying to divert me from my misery.

'No, it's true.'

'But that's crazy. Bath's a city. It needs a proper police presence with all those thousands of visitors every year.'

'Early days yet, apparently.' She gave me a broad smile. 'It isn't Patrick.'

Yes, I was afraid it was. Collins had said it would be.

I had to put it from my mind, of course, or would drive the 4×4 into the nearest ditch.

It was late afternoon when I parked the car in an empty space at Feltham police station. Joanna had insisted that we stop for lunch as she herself was 'starving', and also insisted that the driver should have something to eat. I was beginning to realize how valuable her company was going to be.

DI Janice North was in the building but giving every sign of being about to go out – that is, she was wearing a light jacket over her work clothes and had her handbag under her arm. I introduced Joanna and asked her if she could spare us a few minutes. She took us back to her office.

'I know this isn't on your patch,' I began, 'but I need to know if any kind of in-depth search has been made fairly recently of a local authority housing estate due for redevelopment in Leyton, near Leytonstone. Sorry, but I have no contacts with the police there and this is a very low-key enquiry on my part.'

'Patrick had all the details, though, didn't he?'

I related the latest developments and the woman went pale.

'Oh, we've all heard of "Jinty" O'Connor, or Patrick O'Leary – his real name,' Janice said, her voice a little faint. She cleared her throat. 'Oh, my goodness, how ghastly. I'll find out for you.' Switching her computer back on, she looked at me over the tops of her half-moon reading glasses and added: 'You needn't explain any further. What the NCA does regarding dealing with most wanteds is their business, not mine.'

I liked her discretion and choice of words. As far as I was concerned, 'dealing with' was a nice way of putting it.

'OK, one DI John Masterson,' Janice murmured a couple of minutes later, having got the information off the screen. She picked up her phone. 'Let's hope he's still there.'

A faint but deep grinding noise on the other end of the line indicated that the DI was.

'John!' Janice cried. 'Hi. It's DI North from Feltham. Are you well?'

The grinding noise appeared to suggest that the DI was absolutely fine.

'I have a bit of a lead, a rumour really, as to the whereabouts of a mobster I want to get my hands on. Just a local boy, you understand. Have you had cause to turn over a housing estate due to be demolished in Leyton recently? . . . Yes, Shitsville, I do know what you mean . . . No? . . . Oh, several years ago . . . Right . . . Thanks.'

'They raided the place to get rid of squatters, as you might have heard, several years ago,' she told us. 'He reckons it would take an army and if there's anyone there he'd rather the bulldozers sorted them out.'

'You know him, then,' Joanna commented.

'Oh, no. But he was in a filthy mood when he picked up the phone. That's so unprofessional. So, Ingrid, I'm afraid you probably can't expect any help from him unless you get your boss involved.'

I suddenly realized that I hadn't said a word about what had happened to the commander. I would, but not yet.

I thanked her and we left.

'Shall we find somewhere to stay the night or are you intent on combing this hellhole in the dark?' Joanna enquired.

'We might as well stay at a hotel here,' I answered. 'I know it's not nearby but we need to be at the town hall in Leytonstone first thing in the morning.'

Admirably, she asked no further questions.

To my utter disgust, the planning office at the town hall did not open to the public until ten a.m. I was first through the door, Joanna in my wake, and this was absolutely the right time to use my warrant card.

'How can I help?' asked a balding man, having glanced at it without comment. He was slightly out of breath as though he had only just arrived. The lifts were out of order so he would have had to climb the stairs, as we had done.

I said, 'I would like to borrow a map or plan of the derelict estate at Leyton that's due to be demolished for redevelopment.'

'You mean of how it will look? The proposals? That's still with the planning committee.'

'No, how it looks now.'

'I can give you photographs.'

I hung on to my temper – almost. 'I know what it looks like. I need detailed floor plans.'

'You'll need the archive department for those.'

'Where can I find that?'

'That's me, too,' he sniggered.

Truly, truly, I could have boxed his ears.

'We've loads of 'em,' the idiot went on. 'From when they were first built. You're lucky, actually, as we were going to shred most of them this week and just keep a couple for records. One moment.' He disappeared through an open doorway and then put his head back around it. 'How many would you like?'

'Two, please.'

An age went by, probably a couple of minutes, during which I could hear him either talking to himself or to someone else, and then he reappeared. 'Denise in there,' he jerked his head, 'says this is the second request we've had for these within the past few days. One of your colleagues, perhaps?'

The door was marked PRIVATE but I almost barged the man out of the way to get through it. 'What did he look like?' I demanded to know, addressing an immensely overweight woman overflowing a chair behind a desk.

She looked most surprised and snapped, 'The public aren't allowed in here.'

'I'm not the public,' I snapped back. 'Answer the question.'

'Well . . . er – yes, I remember now. It was a man. He was quite tall with black hair going a bit grey. Slim. That's all I can remember about him.'

'When was this?'

'I'll have to look in the records.'

This turned out to be a battered exercise book of the kind children used to have at school. She flipped through it.

'Last Friday morning at ten forty-six,' she announced.

'Was he on his own?'

'Yes.'

Back in the outer office I was handed the plans, a rubber band around them.

'Unprofessional behaviour,' I muttered when we were outside in the fresh air. 'Patrick was here a week ago doing exactly the same thing.' Then, even more unprofessionally, I wept, standing there in the street.

Joanna steered me into a nearby café and sat me down. While she ordered at the counter I endeavoured to pull myself together but did not make a very good job of it. Then my mobile rang. It was Elspeth.

'Is Joanna with you, Ingrid?' she asked.

'Yes, she is.'

'Good. That's all right then. I know she left a message on James's mobile yesterday and he's collected her car but you know me, I do worry. I don't suppose you've heard from those forensic people.'

'No, but we'll probably get any news from James,' I told her.

'Please promise me that you'll look after yourself,' she finished by saying.

I promised.

I knew exactly what the findings would be.

'That cop in a filthy mood was right,' Joanna said a little later when we had cleared the café table of clutter and opened out one set of plans. 'It's as bad as it looks and we will need an army.' She glanced up at me. 'What would Patrick have done? What *did* he do? Come on, woman, if you keep bursting into tears like this we'll never get anywhere.'

'But he's *dead*,' I sobbed.

'How many times have you thought he's dead and he wasn't?'

I blew my nose. 'Several, actually.'

'What was the worst one?'

It was churlish not to give it some thought as Joanna was really trying to be helpful. After a few moments, I said, 'Right in the beginning when we'd just got married again and were on an assignment for MI5. We were in Scotland and Patrick was supposed to be arriving at a country house on a motorbike. A sniper shot the man on the motorbike within sight of the house and it crashed into a wall and burst into flames. I ran down the hillside and there he was, dead, blackened, smouldering. God.' I put my hands over my face for a moment at the memory, then continued, 'The woman who owned the big estate, Pippa, picked me up in her car and we sat in it, overlooking the road he had just come along, just sitting there, numb. People were running around and an ambulance was arriving. Then Pippa snatched up her binoculars and shouted, "That's my Hamish! God help anyone if that pony breaks its knees on the road!" I looked and saw that a man was coming along riding a Highland pony, a garron that are used to carry down the dead deer after a shoot. The pony knew he was coming home and was galloping. If the situation hadn't been so terrible it would have been one of the most wonderful things I had seen in my life, the way the pony's ears were pricked, his mane was flying and his big hooves were throwing the gravel on the road in all directions. He was enjoying himself playing the warhorse.'

'And it was Patrick.'

I nodded. 'Someone else had ridden the bike up. Patrick had

been out in the hills as he had an idea some kind of attack was
going to be made and borrowed the pony.'

'Look, please forgive me for saying this, but if you can't
recognize your own husband when he's been burnt you're hardly
likely to know him when he's been boiled.'

I stared at her in absolute horror. And then laughed until I
shed a few more tears.

We studied the plans until one of the restaurant staff asked us
if we would be staying for lunch. So we left, but with no real
ideas. It was perfectly obvious that we needed an army and there
would probably be people on watch which made turning up at
all downright difficult. If O'Connor was even there.

Back in the car - the NCA vehicle pass that meant it could
be parked just about anywhere was proving to be extremely useful
– I said, 'I think Patrick would go undercover. Pretend to be a
surveyor or something like that and carry a clipboard. Or perhaps
dress down, like a drop-out. He'd probably go and live rough in
that underpass.'

'One against how many, though?' Joanna said dubiously. 'No,
sorry, this is us we're talking about.'

'There's old stuff bought in charity shops in a kit bag in the
back,' I told her. 'We can be old slags in no time at all, keep
watch and call the police if we see anyone suspicious. Especially
if we see O'Connor.'

'You appear to have abandoned filling this man full of lead.'

'I'll probably have to settle for getting him arrested.'

'You realize we'll probably be gang raped if anyone's there.'

'Not a chance; I have the Smith and Wesson and you can carry
Patrick's second-best knife. They're both in the cubby box here.'
I patted the top of it between the front seats.

'Ingrid, I've never carried a knife in my life!'

'You can joint a chicken with something like a Sabatier, can't
you?'

Wide-eyed, she nodded.

I drove to somewhere quiet, not easy to find, and finally had
to settle for a defunct filling station where, having removed all
our make-up, the pair of us raided the kitbag. I ended up with a
pair of jeans, split but not where it really mattered, and a man's
large sweater, then bundled my hair inside a curly blonde wig I

simply hadn't been able to resist at a village jumble sale. Joanna settled on another pair of jeans, too big for her, so she had to roll up the legs and wear a belt to keep them up. I saw with a pang that she had hauled out Patrick's favourite 'lucky' one to use in such circumstances that has a brass skull buckle and red glass eyes, but made no comment. The outfit was topped with a holey jumper and she then pulled her lovely Titian hair back into an untidy ponytail, tying it with a short length of string. We muddied ourselves up a bit with water and heaven knew what else from a dirty puddle.

Where to leave a sixty-thousand-pound-plus car without it being stolen? It would be quite a long walk, but I finally settled for Leytonstone police station, saying nothing, and just left it in their car park. The NCA pass said everything necessary and if they didn't like it they could pick up the phone and complain to HQ.

When the pair of us were hiking along the road in the direction of Leyton – I had put a few of my things in Joanna's rucksack and we would take it in turns to carry it – I suddenly woke up to exactly what I was doing. Reckless? Childish? Stupid? All of those.

'What's the matter?' Joanna asked when I stopped dead.

'Grief and shock have addled my brain,' I muttered. 'We have no plan; haven't the first idea what we're going to do. I'm risking your life. It's madness.'

'What would Patrick do right now?'

I felt a surge of irritation. She was now being . . . irritating. Reminding me. Giving her a look, I said, 'He would go there and have a quiet recce, I suppose.'

'Shall we do that then?'

I carried on walking without making a reply.

A shortish taxi ride can prove to be quite a long trek and it wasn't as though we were walking through attractive countryside. The traffic was quite heavy, the air thick with diesel fumes, and trains rumbled close by but out of sight behind buildings. A chilly breeze had sprung up and it looked like rain. This place was the utter pits, I thought.

'At least no one's taking any notice of us,' Joanna remarked at one point.

'That's because everyone round here's a bit off the wall,' I retorted.

'The trains, the bloody trains. I sometimes have nightmares about being locked in that garage. I convinced myself I was going to die in there.'

I was being horribly selfish: Joanna did not want to be here either.

We came to the first of the redevelopment sites where Patrick and I had looked for her. It looked exactly the same. We carried on past it and about ten minutes later arrived at our destination. This looked exactly the same too, from the outside – what was going on within was anyone's guess. As we got closer it became obvious that most of the rubbish had been cleared away, including the broken-down fencing. There was no sign of anyone, not a movement except for a few pigeons and crows.

'Perhaps it'll all be knocked down soon,' Joanna said hopefully.

'Which would get rid of O'Connor and his mob but they'd go somewhere else,' I said, mostly to myself.

'The underpass, then?'

It would have to be the underpass.

EIGHTEEN

The first thing we noticed were the dead and dying rats, the latter semi-paralysed, dragging themselves around in small circles, around and around, or lying twitching. They were everywhere on the road approaching the underpass. The crows were pecking at them, both the living and the dead.

'They've been poisoned,' I whispered, tearing my gaze from one that had had its eyes pecked out. It was still just alive.

'The council did it, I expect,' Joanna said. 'You have to get rid of them; they're filthy, diseased things.'

'The birds will be poisoned as well if they eat them.'

'I don't see how it could be avoided.'

I had brought a good flashlamp with me so at least we would not find ourselves treading on them.

My mobile rang.

'I have a bit of news for you, but not from the lab,' James Carrick's voice said. 'How are you?'

'Surviving,' I answered.

'Is Joanna still with you?'

I replied in the affirmative, and then added: 'She's invaluable to me as a companion and offering really useful advice.'

'Oh, good. Please tell her I informed her interview people that she wasn't well so they're not expecting her. And Ingrid, I hope you're following safe procedures such as intending to involve the local police and aren't going anywhere near that condemned housing estate.'

'A little low-key surveillance, that's all.'

He sighed. 'Promise me you'll call out the Met if you even get a hint that O'Connor's there.'

'I will.'

'I've contacted a DI John Masterson at Leytonstone nick and he said he'd already had an enquiry about the place today. Was that you?'

'Yes, via DI Janice North in Feltham.'

He did not query this, but went on: 'I rang mainly because forensics found a note in the box. It was stuck to the inside of the lid, perhaps by the dampness. It's printed but looks like the same handwriting as is on the label. I'm afraid it just says that some of the rest is to follow. Postage is expensive and he'll expect you to refund it, the bastard says.'

I thanked him, knowing that I must keep calm.

'So stationing cops at local post offices, just in case, might be a good idea. Masterson says he'll arrange it. I had to explain the situation a bit more of course.'

Automatically I thanked him again and then asked when the DNA results might come through.

'Tomorrow, I hope. You won't believe it but there's a snag at the lab. Their electrics blew up.'

We switched off our phones. I knew that if anyone was here we would have been spotted by now, like two people walking across a desert. There was no cover – nothing would be gained by creeping along at the base of the buildings, the only place out of sight from anyone keeping watch was inside the underpass. Then, having travelled through that one would be in full view of another block, those at the rear of the ones here, not to mention the side windows of any number of flats.

Just inside the entrance to the underpass, I shrugged off the rucksack and found one of the sets of plans, which I had been forced to fold up in order to fit them in it. Gazing at one of them for at least the fourth time, I was no further in guessing where anyone would hide out. Just towers of apartments, at least a couple of hundred of them. Now, there would be no gas, electricity or water, and no furniture, unless the last of these had been brought in. At best it could only be used as a temporary place of concealment.

'So where—' I began. I made myself say it. 'Where did they do the boiling?'

'Good point,' Joanna said. 'Perhaps a gas bottle connected to an old stove in a lock-up garage? Water from someone's outside tap or a filling station?'

'Gas bottles,' I repeated, thinking.

'And a big pot.'

Everything went a bit fuzzy and I bent over so my head was near my knees.

Joanna put an arm around me. 'I'm sorry, sorry, sorry,' she whispered, a catch in her voice.

When I felt a bit better, I stood up straight again. 'I forgot to tell you. James has told the interview panel that you're ill.'

'We will be very ill if we stand here much longer breathing in all these dead rats.' And Joanna set off down the tunnel, into the murky interior.

Just call us Frodo and Sam, I thought inconsequentially, switching on the torch and setting off after her. I must have hallucinated a little then, or, more likely, my imagination had a bit of a breakdown due to shock, as I found myself thinking of the possibilities of Shelob lurking in the tunnel and Gollum creeping up behind us, while the bastions of the apartment blocks towered over us like Mordor.

We had to move carefully to avoid the rats, and came upon a couple of wrecked motorbikes I hadn't noticed the first time and sundry other rubbish. Obviously the council workers hadn't penetrated this far. One could hardly blame them – it still stank. We remained silent, all the better to hear the slightest sound other than the soft pad of our footsteps. I had a bad moment when the torch beam lit up what turned out to be torn strips of a plastic bin bag caught on a projection on the wall and gently waving in the slight current of air blowing through the tunnel. No, stupid, not the legs of a giant spider.

Then, ahead, our light flashed over metal, a barricade of super-market trollies. It was not very high, two, perhaps three, piled one on another, and there were narrow spaces left at the sides.

'This wasn't here last time,' I remarked as we squeezed through the gap.

'It proves that someone's in residence who doesn't want visitors,' Joanna said.

The little breeze in our faces brought with it another smell, a familiar smell, a smell that immediately made me turn to the wall of the tunnel and vomit. Joanna ran over to me and held me tightly while I helplessly threw up.

'Ingrid, you really shouldn't be here!' she exclaimed when the worst was over but I was still retching.

'It's the same smell,' I gasped.

She sniffed the air. 'Just a sort of stale cooking smell.' Our eyes met. 'Oh, God,' she said. 'You stay here while I go and look.'

There was the distinct sound of the buzzing of flies.

I couldn't let her go alone and, ahead of me as I slowly brought up the rear, I saw her stop towards the end of the underpass. It was lighter here and as I approached I saw that her face was ashen as she turned towards me. I switched off the torch.

'Human remains,' she managed to get out before turning away, but added, 'cooked,' in a choked voice.

My ears making strange singing noises, I went over to where an odd jumble lay at the side of the road surrounded by a cloud of flies. It was very difficult to make sense of it without touching anything and everything seemed to have been sprinkled with a whitish powder. Finally, after mostly ineffectually waving away the flies, I was able to make out that the corpse, the flesh falling away from the bones, had been chopped into sections: two arms severed at the shoulders and divided at the elbows, a torso split into four, a leg cut into two at the knee. I couldn't see the other one. There was no head. The entrails, which I tried not to look at, had just been dumped a short distance away. My one fleeting glance in that direction had told me that they had not been subjected to any heat, but I shied away from thinking of them as 'raw'. Animals and birds had pecked, pulled and torn at everything. Fingers and toes were missing.

'These are the remains of Patrick,' I murmured, using one hand on the tunnel wall to support myself and feeling faint again.

Joanna turned, her voice shattering the black pit that seemed to beckon me. 'How on earth can you tell?'

'There's only one lower leg and foot.'

She came over and put her arms around me. 'Look, it's such a muddle. The other one might be . . . well . . . underneath.'

The body was the source of the poison.

Footsteps approached somewhere out in the fresh air. We ran, on tiptoe, back into the gloom and flung ourselves down on the road. Almost immediately, two men were silhouetted against the light, one carrying what looked like a plastic bin bag. Either my eyes were playing up or they were both swaying on their feet. The other man, taller and skinny, came up the tunnel to the corpse and appeared to regard it thoughtfully for about half a minute. Then he stooped and, muttering, no doubt swearing under his breath at the flies, selected what looked like – from where I was lying anyway – two sections, perhaps a lower arm and leg. I shuddered as he shook them violently to rid them of loose flesh and then dropped them into the bag held open by the other man.

'Rat bait – you have to hand it to Jinty,' one or other of them, probably the taller man, said, slurring his words and with a loud laugh. 'I hope you're enjoying this, ratties,' he shouted down the tunnel, his voice echoing eerily.

After they had tottered from sight, we stayed where we were for half a minute or so and then cautiously got to our feet. Whispering, I told Joanna what her husband had said about the note in the box, something else I had forgotten to mention.

'It's so horrible I can't think of anything to say,' she said.

'We should go and look for gas bottles,' I said, the words coming out automatically. Hell, it was a goal – something to aim for that would fill a tiny corner of my brain that was otherwise empty of ideas. He was dead, end of story, and had finished up as rat poison.

Joanna said, 'I reckon if we call out the local police and they arrive like something out of a cop show anyone here will have time to do a runner before they've even done their risk assessment.'

'My thoughts exactly,' I told her. 'But I thought you wanted back in.'

'I do. But there's nothing like a last fling. For Patrick.'

I gave her a quick hug.

'What if we spot blokes like that pair of cyborgs and they see us?' she then said.

'I'll probably have to shoot them.'

Having made quite sure that the men were not anywhere in sight, we set off, walking quickly and quietly along the road. We already knew the roadway led to the rear where the rows of lock-up garages were. We were just two women, walking, perhaps lost, not craning our necks in order to try to see if they were being watched, definitely not looking for mobsters.

'I'm an utter fool,' I muttered as we approached the area where the large rubbish bins had been. 'I've looked at those plans several times and didn't hoist it in.'

'What?' Joanna responded, quickly wiping away a few tears. 'Sorry,' she gulped. 'I loved him a bit too, you see. Sorry.'

There was nothing I could say to this and fought back some ready tears of my own. Then I said, huskily, 'There's one place in this whole complex where I'm sure you must be able to see every main entrance of the other buildings, either close by or at an angle some distance away. It's marked on the plan as an office so might have been used as that when the place was first built and deliberately sited there. There's a chance a caretaker or some kind of handyman lived there afterwards.'

'Where is it?' She was trying to look interested but wasn't right now.

'It's a ground floor flat in the first block as you come in.'

Joanna took a deep breath. 'You reckon O'Connor might be there because of that advantage? The man's probably too thick to work it out.'

'In which case we could break in and keep watch.'

'Ingrid, do we have to go back through that bloody underpass?'

'Sorry.'

We sprinted and for some bizarre reason I felt a sudden lightness of mood. My cat's whiskers perhaps, telling me that I was doing the right thing.

'I hope someone's looking after us,' Joanna said all at once as we ran, the torch beam bobbing along on front of us.

'Bound to be,' I panted.

'D'you sort of believe that . . . ?' Her voice trailed away.

'I'm beginning to think . . . that there has to be something in it.'

We reached the end and came to a standstill, gazing around warily, getting our breath back. Nothing moved but the dying rats, and after a minute or so of careful observation we headed for the block of flats I had pinpointed in my mind's eye. Leaving the main access road, we took a wide path off to the right, had to go through and around all kinds of rubbish the council, or whoever, had missed, and eventually arrived at the entrance. I had noted on the way that the curtains, rags actually, at the

windows of the apartment in question were closed on this nearest
side. The main door to the block was not locked and we pushed
through it and went in. Within, the lobby was a stinking lavatory,
awash with urine, human excrement at the sides and in the corners.
Used syringes were everywhere.

'Let's go!' Joanna said, swiftly in reverse.

I took the Smith and Wesson from my pocket and in a mood
where I would have cheerfully filled with holes any armed mobster
who answered the door, battered on it with my fist. Weirdly, what
should have been merely a series of indiscriminate raps manifested itself into one of the coded knocks that Patrick and I had
used when we worked for MI5 and have done since. Habit
perhaps.

Ready to fire, I leapt back as the door was opened. The business end of a Glock 17 appeared.

Then: 'Is that you, Ingrid?'

I couldn't speak. I discovered that I could barely stand and
leaned on the wall. Even that didn't help much.

He must have seen Joanna first and looked around the door
frame, a week or so's growth of beard, eyes hollow from lack
of sleep, layers of dirt and all.

I snatched the wig off when he just stared at me. Then he
said, 'I didn't see you coming – must have nodded off.'

Joanna came forward and, not for the first time that day, put
her arms around me. 'Ingrid was sent what she thought was
your head in a parcel,' she told him tersely and with quite
amazing composure. 'Boiled. We just found the rest in the
underpass.'

They took me inside and I think I was laughing hysterically.
I can't really remember much except being firmly shushed and
given a quick hug. Joanna hugged him too. He seemed a bit
baffled by the emotional state of us.

'O'Connor's not there,' Patrick said. 'But he'll be back, and when
he arrives I shall call up the cops. I haven't before as he left
almost immediately. During the time he's away the others drink
or take drugs and I get the impression they're in hiding. They're
all plastered now, including the two who were wandering around
with a bin bag a little while ago.'

'We saw them,' I said. 'They put a couple more body parts in the bag.'

It had emerged that Patrick had been living on the barest essentials, mostly on army survival rations which he had acquired from somewhere or the other, and water which was only available from the hot tap in the kitchen so must be the dregs from a tank. He was putting purification tablets in it to be on the safe side but it still tasted horrible. I knew because it was all there was to drink and I had a tin mug of it in my hand.

I still could not believe that he was alive, right in front of me, having a quick look through a gap in the curtains.

'I wandered over one night when I knew O'Connor's wasn't there,' Patrick continued. 'They're on the second floor and the door was open, perhaps because they can't be bothered to keep getting up to let people in and feel very safe where they are up there – and to let the stink out. Hardly a bunker. They have just a couple of camping lamps for when it gets dark.' He smiled reflectively. 'I walked around inside. It was like a shipwreck with unconscious bodies and the remains of takeaways everywhere. I counted and there were thirteen of them without O'Connor. Unlucky number for some. Oh, and someone's injured – there were bloodstained bandages in the bathroom and empty packets of over-the-counter painkillers. It might be O'Connor himself after you shot the gun out of his hand, Ingrid. Which is good news, of course.'

'You promised me you wouldn't work alone,' I said.

'But I'm not now.' This with a big smile. 'No, seriously, I tried to contact Terry Meadows but, as often happens these days, he's in the States.'

I said, 'I really would like to put your parents' minds at rest.'

'There's no signal here for some reason so when O'Connor comes someone's going to have to go away until they can get one. Try your phone.'

I did. No signal.

'You don't have to wait,' Patrick said, 'I can escort you to the main road when it's dark.'

'I'll wait,' Joanna replied firmly. 'You'll need someone to man, or rather woman, the curtain.'

'Thank you.' He chuckled. 'You're wearing my jeans and belt.'

'I'll wait too,' I said.

I don't think either of us wanted to let him out of our sight.

'O'Connor'll be back tonight,' Patrick said, having another quick look through the gap in the curtain. 'He brings the food so they must have transport somewhere. My main worry is that he'll abandon his henchmen and not return at all, but that carries the risk for him that they'll be arrested and sing like canaries to get even.'

'Have some rest first,' I suggested. 'We'll woman the curtain.'

'Sure?'

'Perfectly sure.'

He lay down on the sofa and was instantly asleep.

'What are these survival rations then?' Joanna whispered to me. 'I'm absolutely famished.'

There wasn't much left but we found several high energy bars, a few hard brown biscuits with little tubs of pâté to put on them, tea, coffee and one meal in a pouch that was cooked and could either be heated or eaten cold. We left the last of these for Patrick and had a couple of high energy bars each, then tried stirring instant coffee into the cold water from the tap. The result was even more horrible than the water on its own but we drank it anyway and then took it in turns to keep watch while the other lay on the floor on Patrick's anorak.

Four very long hours went by and it was now late afternoon. Patrick was still asleep and Joanna appeared to be dozing, curled up on the anorak. Outside, nothing moved except crows and pigeons, and I was thankful that I couldn't see the dying rats from my position by the window. This had been opened just a crack to enable us to hear what was going on outside as well. Trains incessantly rumbled out of sight. I suddenly remembered that I had a couple of bars of Kendal Mint Cake in my pocket and ate half of one.

Someone laughed and I heard voices, children perhaps. Whoever it was wasn't close by, perhaps somewhere down on the entry road. Patrick was instantly awake and came over.

'Kids come here after school,' he said quietly. 'Big kids, that is. They try to break in, bring stuff to start fires but usually get scared off by the rats. Someone shouted at them yesterday, one of O'Connor's mob, and they ran off, so this might be a different lot. I don't think they need concern us.'

I wasn't surprised – the smell the lobby's stink had permeated everywhere in the flat. It was the kind of stench that you felt would be in your lungs for ever.

'Where d'you reckon O'Connor goes?'

'At a guess, to collect money from various protection rackets he has and to milk the drug dealers who operate with his permission and pay a heavy fee. Marlene mentioned a big job he was planning, if you remember.'

'Killing top Met cops and leaving their bodies outside primary schools, wasn't it? And murdering Marlene for good measure.'

'Well, the latter's on hold as she's in a remand centre. As for the other, I did prime Mike Greenway. You get some rest now. Did you eat all the rations?'

'Of course not. Can't we flush the loo?'

'Only if you fill the cistern with a battered saucepan I found among some junk in the kitchen. But I've no idea how much water's left so I suggest you don't – in case I'm here for longer.' He nudged me in the ribs. 'It's still better than what's outside the door.'

Only just.

Before it got quite dark, late-ish, as it was mid-September – no lights allowed – we finished up nearly all of what remained of the rations. Joanna and I insisted Patrick had the last meal as we reckoned that, having only just arrived, we were much better nourished. I gave him my last Kendal Mint Cake for 'dessert'. Then he took over the watch at the window while Joanna and I sat on the sofa. It appeared to be on the point of collapse.

We waited.

'I wonder whose corpse it is in the underpass?' Patrick said to me at one point. 'And why send the head to you?'

'We might never know,' I replied, preferring not to have to resurrect that nightmare moment at all.

After another age had gone by it became as dark as light pollution allows in big cities. I felt myself nodding off, and by my side Joanna's breathing told me that she was soundly asleep. I wanted to ask Patrick if his arm was still troubling him but thought better of it. He didn't need to be reminded right now. Then, silhouetted against the window, I saw his body stiffen and he said something under his breath.

'Yes?' I said.

'I think so. Two of them, on the road, and as well as bags they're carrying a torch this time. They haven't done that before.'

'So they don't trip over the dead rats in the underpass, I expect.'

'You don't have to go through the underpass. There's a footpath but they don't seem to use it.'

This was really good to know.

'I suggest we go for it. But first I must verify that it's O'Connor and not someone else. You two stay here.'

'We're not letting you out of our sight.'

'You can see me enter the block from here.' He sounded surprised.

'We'll come part of the way. And then one of us can phone.'

'Oh, all right.'

Gently, I shook Joanna.

NINETEEN

Going out into the open at least meant we could have fresh air. Unconsciously, perhaps, we all took several deep breaths, and then Joanna and I followed Patrick as he turned left and took a narrower path that ran a short distance away from the front of the building we had just left. The reflected glow of the lights of London on the low-cloud night sky meant we could see fairly clearly. Our path skirted the wreckage of the children's playground and then curved around to the left, which fortunately meant we were now not in view of our target. Meanwhile, whoever had just arrived was going through the underpass.

Roughly halfway there, Patrick stopped. The ground rose a little and there were a couple of low retaining walls at right angles where our path joined another. There was yet more rubbish in the small dip created but it would provide a little cover.

'You two wait here,' Patrick whispered, drawing the pair of us towards him. 'And be careful. Another two yards to your right and you'll be in view of some of the windows of the mobsters' flat and also the main entrance. Bend low and conceal yourselves behind the wall. I'll go inside and listen. I'll come back here but if I don't return in five minutes, phone. You'll have to go some-where out in the open to do it. As I said, be careful.'

He gave us both a peck on the cheek and walked away.

A minute or so later, when we were crouched down behind the wall, Joanna had a quick peep and said in my ear, 'I can't see him. Can you?' Silently, we had had to shift a few soggy cardboard boxes, redolent of tomcats, out of our way.

'No.'

We waited, frequently taking quick looks over the top of the wall.

'D'you reckon those two have come out of the underpass yet?' Joanna then asked. 'I haven't seen them either.'

'God knows,' I muttered.

Surely five minutes had gone by, I thought after what seemed half the night had elapsed. I couldn't even see the time by my watch in the gloom. I counted up to a hundred and still nothing moved. The distant traffic roared on, ambulance and police sirens blared, at least two car alarms were going off somewhere, trains carried on rumbling.

Then, two figures approached the entrance, the same two: bags, torch. Was it my imagination, or was one of them big and broad, the head indistinct as though bearded? He shambled inside while the other, who was carrying the bags, followed. About a minute later, a cheer came from within, a deep, booming voice I recognized, then shouting them into silence.

'O'Connor!' Joanna hissed. 'It's him! Phone!'

I told her I would come straight back and went, bent low, to where I could no longer be seen due to the corner of another building blocking the view and stood up, cramped. The nearest and safest open space was back down on the access road. I ran, pausing every twenty yards or so to try my phone but did not get a signal until I was outside near the main road, a long way that took far too much time.

I thought 999 a bit low key and potentially slow so I rang the NCA emergency number I have memorized, where one speaks directly to someone working within the organization. All I had to do was quote my personal password and give the location. One no longer has to provide a postcode but I was able to pinpoint the block as it had what appeared to be a mobile phone mast on the top. I warned that the underpass was blocked to vehicles, adding that there was a route for those on foot by the children's play area.

I ran back to Joanna and once there had a longer look over the wall. Nothing whatsoever appeared to be happening.

'They're stuffing themselves,' she said dismissively.

'Patrick told us that they had two camping lamps,' I said. 'But I can't see any light which means there must be curtains. If the food's arrived no one might be keeping watch.'

'You're going over there?'

'I'm supposed to be his backup,' I fretted.

'Then let's back him up. We might meet him coming back.'

We did not and soon there was no choice but to cross the open space between the blocks. This appeared to have been originally intended as a car park but local youths had turned it into a football pitch with makeshift goals. Broken glass was everywhere, our feet crunching on it as we moved quickly and lightly. Perhaps it had been strewn there by O'Connor's gang, or others, to prevent any play taking place.

Arriving, we flattened ourselves against an outside wall, listening. I could hear low voices and, looking up, saw that a small window was open. It was impossible to hear what was being said, but I could hear sirens again and prayed that they were not coming here as I had emphasized that as silent an approach as possible was imperative. They faded into the distance.

'Do I have to repeat myself?' O'Connor's voice suddenly yelled. 'If I say we're moving out, we're moving out. D'you think I can keep filling you lot up with booze and nosh out of my own pocket for no return? You can start working for your living. Anyone who wants out, go right now, but don't expect to come back and not get a bullet.'

We were around a corner from the entrance but, if anyone exited and came this way, they would see us. I looked about me: there was absolutely no cover and above us came the sounds of movement. Grabbing Joanna's arm, I pulled her into slightly deeper shadow a short distance farther away and we froze, listening. Either one person was coming down the stairs, muttering to themselves, or there were two of them.

'As I said a while back, I've thought for weeks that it was a bloody waste of my time,' a man said when they must have been almost out in the open air. 'And now he's buggered up his hand by shutting it in—'

Silence but for the merest hint of swift effort followed by a few soft thuds. Then, moments later, someone appeared, his back to us, dragging another. This one was dumped down to be quickly joined by a second; the pair then rolled as close to the wall as possible. The one responsible for all this came towards us.

'Can you hear anyone else coming down?' Patrick whispered.

'No,' I replied, my heart pounding in my ears.

'I hope you phoned.'

I told him I had.

'Some were talking of mutiny just before he got here.'

Overhead, O'Connor shouted something – I thought I heard the word 'van' – but indistinctly, as though he had gone into another room. Tramping feet then started to-ing and fro-ing, as perhaps the men gathered their stuff together, but it all sounded very erratic, and there was a bang followed by swearing as someone either fell over or walked into something solid.

The three of us stood there and, as we watched, three unmarked cars and one police area car left the main road and parked blocking the access road of the estate. Around a dozen darkly-clad figures got out and approached, fanning out, four heading for the underpass, the rest going from sight as they sought cover. Three must have moved very quickly as they were fairly soon just a short distance from us, approaching the entrance. But they didn't see us until Patrick waved and I found myself gripping his other arm for a moment as their weapons were instantly ranged in our direction.

Palms outwards in a gesture of peace, Patrick quietly said, 'NCA. They're coming out.'

The burly individual in front of the trio marched right up to him, having gestured to the other two to get out of sight. 'ID?' he mouthed.

I produced mine. 'You don't carry IDs when you're working undercover,' I informed him in a whisper.

'He's with you?' This with a thumb jerked in Patrick's direction.

Overstrung nerves were sorely tempting me to clout him somewhere where he wasn't protected by his dark blue Ninja turtle outfit. Instead, I told him Patrick was indeed with me.

'Stay out of the way and you won't get hurt.' He turned away to organize some of the rest of his group, who were just arriving.

'There's two here.' I indicated the two prone figures almost at our feet.

'Oh . . . right.'

A police Range Rover with flashing blue lights but no sirens then came into view, bumped over various kerbs to circumnavigate the road block, performed a niftier off-roading over other obstacles and speeded in the direction of the underpass.

'Did you mention the blockade in the tunnel?' Patrick said to me out of the corner of his mouth.

'Yes,' I said.

'Must be at least a super who's decided to turn up. Shall we go and watch the fire escape?'

Joanna and I shadowed him towards the rear of the building, if indeed such hideous structures have backs and fronts. We heard the semi-subterranean crash when we'd gone about twenty yards and my working partner swore under his breath and then stifled a laugh. He was probably – it was too dark to see – still smiling when he turned to us after having had a quick look around the corner of the building.

'I've previously checked and the door's actually locked,' he reported. 'So if they come this way they'll have to shoot their way out. We'll stay here and await developments.'

We couldn't see it but heard the Range Rover, no doubt a little dented now having battered through the shopping trollies, arrive in a scream of brakes – we discovered afterwards that it had nearly hit a row of concrete bollards. Whoever was inside, in charge, had brought a megaphone with him and now used it.

'Armed police!' roared a bullfrog-like voice I seemed to recognize. 'Come out! You're all under arrest and completely surrounded!'

'They ain't,' Patrick said in my ear.

'Masterson,' I said.

'Super?'

'DI.'

'Bloody hell.'

Out the front there was the sound of breaking glass and a shot was fired. Seconds later what could only be the Range Rover roared away in reverse and another shot banged off metal. Someone was firing from an upstairs window.

'Developments,' Patrick said, and was gone, moving quickly in the lee of the building, his destination out of sight from where we were. I glanced round at Joanna and she gave me a little push by way of answer. We ran.

'Stand back!' Patrick shouted when he saw us, and fired two shots at the lock on an outer door we saw when we arrived. He kicked in the door and went inside. But not up the stairs, I discovered when I switched on my torch – he was standing to one side in the lower stairwell, which turned out to be the only place we had come across so far in this godforsaken hole that wasn't full of rubbish, or worse.

Upstairs there was incoherent shouting, upheaval and then repeated bangs as though they were trying to kick through a door. Was it one of those that allowed access to this fire escape?

The stairs were open plan, made of rough concrete, and there was a primitive metal handrail on both sides. Shoving Joanna and me into the stairwell recess like a couple of parcels, Patrick rummaged for a few moments in one of his anorak pockets, found whatever it was he needed and, making me understand that he wanted me to shine the torch on what he was doing, went up four or five stairs. Working quickly, he hooked one end of something – I couldn't quite make out what – to one of the handrail's uprights, about a foot up off the steps, and then stretched it across to the other side. There it was passed around one of the handrail's mounts in the wall, brought back again, pulled tight then wrapped round and round the upright before being anchored by a rough knot. The result was not level but would suffice.

Snare wire turned into a trip wire.

'Get rid of the light!' Patrick hissed.

Above us the door gave way and smashed violently back against a wall, broken glass tinkling down. There was more shouting and I made out, 'Bugger O'Connor! If he wants to kill all the cops let him!'

'Jinty's been good to us!' another man bawled back.

'Then go and lick his arse!'

'There'll be cops out the back as well, you moron! Didn't you hear those shots? We're surrounded!'

The reply was a string of obscenities.

We drew back into the depths of the stairwell as they descended, one, by the sound of it, tripping on a landing and being thoroughly cursed as someone else fell over him. The whole circus came thumping down the stairs and the inevitable happened. In the dimness I saw the first two cartwheel and slam into the doorway, and this carried on in most satisfactory fashion until there were around eight of them in one large pile. The wreckage started at the bottom of the stairs and almost entirely blocked the doorway, most of the men jammed in the gap, unable to move.

Patrick went forward and spoke quietly, but then had to raise his voice a little as they were all panting for breath. 'Armed police,' he told them. 'Several of us from the National Crime Agency, in fact. We're the ones who shoot first and ask questions afterwards. One of you move and you're finished.'

He came back to me and spoke in an undertone. 'Keep the torch on them. If one does move, fire a shot through the doorway. Don't accidentally kill Masterson, though – that would be rather awkward.' Then, carefully stepping over the trip wire, he went up the stairs.

Joanna and I exchanged deeply worried glances. These mobsters didn't look as though they intended to stay put, whatever Patrick had said. One on the top was already trying to push himself upright. Joanna kicked his backside, hard, while I leaned out over the top of the lot of them, had a quick look to see if anyone was around and fired a shot skywards. It smashed a window somewhere.

This did have the effect of bringing up reinforcements – three of them.

'National Crime Agency,' I declared, in case it was a different three as they panted up. 'Several more suspects for you. My husband has gone to find the rest upstairs.'

Up in the darkness there were three shots in quick succession and a man screamed.

Just remembering the trip wire in time, I ran up the stairs while undertaking a little arithmetic. Thirteen, Patrick had said. Two outside, unconscious, seven or eight in the heap – hard to tell exactly – which left two or three plus O'Connor, unless Patrick hadn't counted him in.

There was no way I was going to play Murder in the Dark so I kept the torch switched on. This mindset did prove to be the right one when I came upon a man – drunk? wounded? – draped over the handrail on the second flight of stairs. I settled on the former – he reeked of spirits – just before he moved and tried to grab me as I went by. I resisted the temptation to tip him over, carried on then heard a scuffle behind me. I saw that he had got hold of Joanna, who I hadn't realized was with me. She had no such qualms, thumped him midships and upended him over the rail.

More cautiously, we reached the second floor. The torch beam immediately picked out a horror figure reeling towards us, a man with blood pouring from his mouth. Eyes glazed – he looked literally dead on his feet – he plunged headlong down the stairs. Ahead, there was a dim light through a smashed-in door to the immediate left of us. Without saying a word, we stood one on each side of the door and I switched off the torch.

Shouting outside now, silence here. Like a grave.

'You're under arrest for the murder of David Bowman,' I heard Patrick say.

'Who the hell's *that*?' O'Connor's voice snarled.

'He was a friend of mine. Plymouth. I'm sure you remember gunning down an obviously unarmed constable in the Devon and Cornwall Police.'

'Oh, him. He got in the way, that's all.'

'Drop the gun.'

O'Connor laughed. 'You've got one, I've got one. I can easily kill you even with my left hand. Who's going to shoot first?'

'You won't escape. There are any number of cops outside. And, by the way, I'm the one you thought you'd cooked.'

In the next second there was another shot and, not stopping to think, I plunged through the doorway, into a short passageway, through another door and into a room beyond and fired, wildly as it happened, at the bear-like outline standing swaying in front of the window. He went over like a felled tree.

Patrick was on the floor, struggling to get up.

'Are you hurt?' I cried.

'No, I flung myself down just before he fired and clouted my head on the wall,' he replied, succeeding in standing. 'God, you really do see stars. Is he dead?'

'I don't know,' I whinnied after having had just one fright too many.

In the dim light from a rapidly fading camping lamp, Joanna had gone over to look at the prone man who suddenly, and alarmingly, flailed his limbs, also trying to get up. 'How d'you work this thing?' she shouted at Patrick, her voice a little squeaky with fright.

'What is it?'

'Your other knife.'

'There's a tiny button at the top of the hilt which you can hit with your thumb as you're right-handed.'

Therefore, O'Connor had an Italian throwing knife sprung right in his face, a little too close as it happened, as she had no idea how long the blade was and it nicked the end of his nose. He subsided with a shout of panic and by that time Patrick was there.

The man was unhurt. He had fallen over, drunk, but my shot could only have missed him by an inch or so.

We had to wait for a few minutes as medics were carefully removing the man on the stairs – the main staircase was blocked with police – as at this stage it was thought he was still alive. Then, between us we got O'Connor down the stairs and into the open. Patrick formally arrested him and he was taken into custody and virtually lugged away. We took our time, needing a few moments to get our breath back and, as far as I was concerned, composure. As we rounded the last corner I saw that a lot more police vehicles, together with a couple of ambulances, were arriving, presumably having got through the gap in the barricade made by the Range Rover. This had been driven forward again and was parked in the bright illumination proved by the vehicles' headlights. Radios chattered and paramedics pushed through to tend to the injured. Cops were everywhere.

'Better go and say hello to Masterson,' Patrick muttered. 'Thank him for his invaluable support.'

'They *are* carting them all away for us,' Joanna pointed out. 'Oh, do have your knife back. I'm not keen on knives at all.' She handed it over.

'The British tend to be scared of knives,' Patrick said absently. 'God, I need a shower, several showers, in fact, a beer, steak and chips, kidneys, liver, mushrooms, some of Mum's apple crumble . . .'

Masterson was nowhere to be seen and, as we approached it, two other men alighted from the Range Rover.

'That was a neat piece of work,' said Michael Greenway.

'And you got him alive,' Richard Daws commented with one of his rare thin smiles. 'Good.'

The gaze of both of them came to rest on Joanna and Patrick made the introductions.

'That's that, then,' she said sadly, having shaken their hands.

'James told the interview board that I was ill and couldn't attend today, but now I've met you gentlemen I'd better come clean.'

'Your interview?' Greenway queried.

'I'm trying to get back in the Avon and Somerset Police. I was James's sergeant at one time, you see.'

Greenway and Daws exchanged glances and then the commander said, 'So you came along as backup for Ingrid.'

'She thought Patrick was dead. O'Connor sent her a boiled head in a parcel.'

'So I understand. Your husband contacted me about that.'

Daws turned to get back in the car, saying, 'Well done, everyone. I shall expect you, Patrick, at a debriefing of this case first thing tomorrow morning. It's been of particular interest to me. Are you coming with me, Mike?'

'No, sir, I'll find my own way, thank you.'

The car door slammed and the vehicle moved away.

Jingling the loose change in his pocket, Greenway looked up at the sky for a moment and then said, 'Mrs Carrick—'

'Sorry, but it's Miss Mackenzie,' Joanna interrupted. 'I'm keeping my maiden name for professional reasons in the same way Ingrid does – as a protection against criminals who might carry out retribution because they make a connection between us and our husbands' work.'

'So you're ambitious.'

'Very.'

'I think you'll find there'll be no problem with your interview being rescheduled. I certainly won't say a word and, as far as we're all concerned, Daws doesn't inhabit the same planet. Now, can I arrange a lift for you all to a hotel for the night?'

'Just to Leytonstone police station where I left the car, please,' I told him.

'Should I have called them sir?' Joanna anxiously asked Patrick on the way first to collect her rucksack. It didn't appear that he was letting us out of his sight now.

'Not *yet*,' he answered.

As I walked I recollected the scene in that room. O'Connor had fired more than one shot at Patrick, and mostly because he was drunk and had the weapon in his left hand, missed. When I had first seen him in the split second as I had entered the room,

Patrick had had his Glock trained on the man but had not fired. What price obeying orders?

After Patrick had phoned his parents I took the three of us to our favourite hotel in the West End, quite a long way across London, but we all, I think, needed to get right away, both physically and mentally.

After his shower and shave, Patrick found that he had a large splinter in his left hand, possibly as a result of diving down on to the floor when O'Connor took a shot at him. This soldier of mine can shrug off being shot at but not the removal of splinters so he came in my direction reluctantly. Seating himself on the bed, he gazed everywhere else while I found a sewing needle in my bag, then took his hand.

'Will it hurt?'

'Yes.'

'Good.'

Having thought him to be joking and replied in kind, I gave him a quizzical look.

'Because of me you were put in serious danger – again,' he said. 'That's it. No more. And you want out, don't you?'

'I hope you're not going to resign without giving it more thought.'

'I ought to – for your and the family's sake.'

'Let's talk about it tomorrow.' I added, a little warily, 'Your right hand seems OK now.'

'Yes. Dad said a few words over it. Ow!'

'I haven't done anything yet!'

TWENTY

'There was only one fatality,' Daws said, gazing at a report in front of him. Although there was an up-to-the-minute computer on his desk he still asks for initial findings on paper so he can make notes in the margins, and, anyway, hates reading off a screen. 'The man who you say O'Connor shot in the back as he tried to escape from that room in the derelict flats.'

'I don't shoot people in the back,' Patrick said quietly.

'You misunderstand; I was merely referring to your own report which I've not had the chance to have more than a quick look at.'

This had been emailed to him the previous evening, but I had brought a hard copy with me and placed it on his desk as we had entered. I glanced at Patrick sideways, willing him to relax: having to attend a debriefing with Daws was a new departure. It was not taking place the following day as he had originally instructed but forty-eight hours later, as he had forgotten he already had commitments. I was not even sure if I was supposed to be here but reckoned myself part of the package.

'Masterson says they're all playing being the victims of violence and coercion,' Daws went on. 'The two who it would appear were tasked with finding you, Patrick, are keeping quiet, but one of the others has grassed on them. They were told what you looked like, that you probably had a broken arm, where you lived and who you worked for, the information given to O'Connor some time previously by that Judd woman. They discovered that you weren't at home – apparently they hung around the village for a while then left when they were thrown out of the pub for loutish behaviour. So they abandoned going to London, gave up looking for you and grabbed someone who fitted your description. We still don't know who he was or where they boiled the corpse. Quite disgusting, if you ask me – both perpetrators are drug addicts. I've never come across anything like it.'

The memory of the contents of that parcel will remain with me for the rest of my life.

'As you now know a large quantity of stolen property was discovered in the flat they were using, together with weapons, ammunition, drugs and currency, a good percentage of which is counterfeit,' Daws continued. 'We can only assume that some, or even all of it, was what they found in Frederick Judd's house in Feltham when they ripped up the floorboards.

'It would appear from what these people are saying that O'Connor was high on drink and/or drugs for most of the time and obsessed with dead bodies. He killed for money and to provide himself with corpses to dispose of as the fancy took him. I'm beginning to wish I hadn't ordered you to bring him in alive – he'll have probably forgotten everything, or will pretend he has by the time he's sobered up and off drugs and, his other offences apart, the defence'll have a grand time.'

'I arrested him for a murder he committed in Plymouth years ago,' Patrick informed him.

'Really? That's good news. Witnesses?'

'Several.'

'In my opinion, the work on this very complicated case that you and others have done will have the effect of completely destroying a large but increasingly fragmenting criminal organization. This man, and Frederick Judd, who it would appear O'Connor murdered and took over his gang, were responsible for a large proportion of the crime committed in that area. A good number of his henchmen have been arrested. That's good work. Thank you. Both of you.'

Into the silence that followed, Daws went on: 'This isn't really a debriefing. I want you to know that I'm retiring, probably next year – although I shall be available to give advice if anyone asks for it – and I've put Mike Greenway's name forward to take over from me. This, you must realize, I'm telling you in the strictest confidence although, obviously, he's aware of what's going on. He'll need support from people with preferably services backgrounds – we know how the police shilly-shally over some matters, don't we? – in other words, advisers. There will be a number of posts as things are being restructured and a couple will be filled in-house. Are you interested in being considered?'

Patrick looked at me.

'I think you'll find the work will be considerably less hazardous,' Daws added.

'You seem to know everything about us,' I commented.

'Enough to know that you mustn't be squandered going after violent low-lifes and that it worries you personally. Yes, don't look surprised; I have been quietly observing you. You have five children to think of, something that unfortunately has never come my way. But there's a wayward, almost anarchic sense of humour that you both have that enhances your relationship. I admire that and I don't want to be responsible for sending you to your deaths by ordering you to arrest insane trash like O'Connor. The new job will be different.'

'And Ingrid?' Patrick enquired.

'I did say there would be two posts to be filled in-house.'

'Well?' Patrick said when we had decided to have an early lunch at a nearby Italian restaurant. It had been a very early breakfast.

'We mustn't be squandered,' I said, pulling a face. 'He doesn't want to be responsible for sending us to our deaths. Perhaps I just don't like his choice of words. And, meanwhile, you have to carry on as before.'

'I have absolutely no intention of carrying on as before. Besides, if he wants us to stay alive long enough to fill those job vacancies it's in his interest not to, as he put it, send me after insane trash like O'Connor.' Here, Patrick laughed.

'Wait and see then?'

'Why not?'

Two months later, when we were having a long weekend in France, an armed intruder broke into Hartwood Castle and shot both Richard Daws and his bodyguard. Neither survived.

Lightning Source UK Ltd.
Milton Keynes UK
UKOW02f0703071015

259980UK00001B/4/P